USA TODAY BESTSELLING AUTHOR

KARA KENDRICK

un•stoppable

SEAGLASS BEACH SERIES

CONTENTS

Cover Photo: **SP Photography/Stacy Powell**
Model: Mason Castello
Cover design: **MadHat Studios**

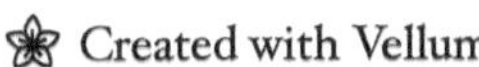 Created with Vellum

Read UNEXPECTED - the Prequel for FREE!
https://karakendrick.com/unexpected/

BLURB

He's not my type. So why is this grumpy baseball star living rent-free in my head?

Griffin Carter.

Tall, dark, and d*ckish—and not in a good way.

Ever since the surly injured pro baseball player rolled into town for a rehab vacation, he's been an absolute downer.

Rude. Condescending. And, unfortunately, sexy as hell.

After his aunt falls and breaks her wrist, he's stuck running Seaglass Scoops, the ice-cream parlor adjacent to my family inn. After scooping one too many cones together, Griffin's gruff exterior begins to melt, and I catch a glimpse of the real him.

I should stick to the plan and not get involved. But after one taste of him, I'm not sure I can resist temptation. I know I'm setting myself up for heartbreak—he's leaving as soon as he gets the all clear from the team doctor.

Besides, everyone knows baseball is his true love—but

maybe I can convince him life after baseball can be just as sweet.

1

POPPY

True-confession time: I've always wanted to be an ice-cream flavorologist. I know it sounds made-up, but it's a real thing—the dream job of developing new ice-cream flavors. So fun, right?

Which is why I'm living my best life with Jess Carter, who runs Seaglass Scoops right next door to the Seaglass Inn. She lets me help with the menu and be as wild and creative as I want to be, testing out all the unique flavor combos I can think of. Blueberry lavender ice cream? Sure. Buttered popcorn? Could be tasty. Pear and blue cheese? Let's give it a whirl. She'll try anything once, and I freaking love that about her.

"What do you think about a margarita sorbet?" I ask, scrolling through the notes app on my phone. I've been jotting down ideas when they come to me, day or night—I have more than one hundred of them stored at the moment.

"You have a recipe?" Jess glances up from her inventory

binder, where we've been keeping track of flavor hits and misses.

"Yep. Not that many ingredients—lime, triple sec, and tequila. Garnish with sea salt."

"Sounds good. Let's whip up a batch, see how it tastes. I'll add limes to the grocery list."

"Perfect. Oh, and I want to make the double-espresso chocolate recipe I found last week. That looked yummy."

"All right, adding that to the lineup. Poppy, honey, do you ever sleep?" She squints over at me, seemingly assessing my overall health and well-being.

"Mm-hmm. Seven hours every night, like clockwork. Why?"

"Between running the inn and helping out here, you can't have any free time."

"Free time's overrated. I love being here, helping you come up with new flavors."

"Don't you want to go out? Hang with your friends?"
Underlying subtext: Get a life.

"I do hang out. I meet Liv at the Tipsy Taco every Tuesday." I twirl a loose strand of hair around my finger, shuffling from foot to foot.

It's true—I have been spending a lot of time with Jess at Seaglass Scoops. Mainly because my best friend's now engaged to my twin brother, making me a clunky third wheel, despite their protests.

I'm happy for them, I am, but they're firmly in the honeymoon phase, and I'm a single pringle. Totally harshing their couple vibe.

"Plus, things are slow at the inn. Fall's a down time. I'll be busier again come the holidays. Oh—speaking of holidays. Seasonal flavors. I have a special folder for that. Hang on."

I pop a finger in the air as I flip through my notes, changing the subject. "Pumpkin everything. Also, apple spice, caramel apple crunch, oh—and here's a fig one I want to try."

Jess laughs, her face crinkling into a wide smile. "I love you, Poppy. But there's not enough time in the world to try all these recipes."

"Pshaw. Scoops is going to be here forever. Tons of time."

She shakes her head, gray hair falling across her brow. "I don't want you missing out on things because you're hiding away here, helping run the ice-cream parlor. What about dating? A cute young girl like you should be out there having a good time."

I wrinkle my nose in distaste. "Jess, Seaglass Beach is tiny, and I'm related to practically every man in town. Who, exactly, am I going to date?"

Her dark eyes twinkle under the bright fluorescent lights. "I happen to have a very handsome nephew staying in town for a while."

Somehow I manage to hold my eye roll in check. I don't want to hurt Jess's feelings, but her nephew is the last man on Earth I want to date.

Griffin Carter. Pro baseball star and the grumpiest person I've ever met. Sure, he's tall, dark, and handsome. Broad shoulders, just the right amount of scruff peppering his square jaw, rocks for biceps.

He's also a grade A asshole. Like, the worst. I don't even know if he has dimples, because I've never seen the man crack a smile, let alone laugh. His signature look is a scowl. He probably drinks sour milk for breakfast. Since he moved to town a couple of months ago—temporarily, thank goodness —every interaction we have seems to end up in an argument.

"He's single . . ." Jess dangles the idea out there one more time, just in case I wasn't picking up what she's laying down.

"Sorry, but no. Griffin pretty much hates me."

"Nonsense." Jess waves her hand through the sweet, chilly air, dismissing the notion. "He's in a bad place is all. Worried about his baseball career. Once that's sorted, he'll be back to his old self."

I seriously doubt Griffin's old self is any better than his current self, but I don't share my thoughts on account of Jess's feelings.

"Besides, I'm too busy to date. Between running the inn and helping out here, my calendar's jam packed. In the best way." I squeeze Jess's arm, reassuring her.

Jingle, jingle.

I glance over at the door as a rowdy group of teenagers spills into the shop, chattering loudly.

"Welcome to Seaglass Scoops!" Jess sings out, waving. The girls move toward the freezer, perusing the tubs of brightly colored ice cream.

"Ooh, salted caramel swirl sounds good. Can I try?" a curly-haired brunette asks, pointing at the creamy tan-and-white ice cream.

"Absolutely." I dip a tiny pink tasting spoon into the tub and hand it over to her.

She pops the spoon into her mouth. "Delish. Can I get a cone of that?"

"You bet. Sugar or waffle?" I gesture at the cone display perched atop the freezer.

"Hmm." She screws her mouth up, debating. "Waffle."

"Good choice." I grab a cone and scoop out a large, round ball of salted caramel, then another. "Here ya go." I hand the cone over to the girl, then help her friend, then another friend after that.

"Do y'all have a dog out there?" Jess cranes her neck, trying to see over the girl gang's heads.

"Yes, ma'am. Nathan got a puppy, and his mom asked us to walk him," the blonde teenager says.

"Oh, cute! What kind of puppy?" I scoop two round balls of vanilla ice cream into a cup and hand it to her.

Honestly, I can't believe anyone chooses vanilla when there are so many fun flavors to try, but to each their own.

"A goldendoodle. He's really adorable. Want to come see?" the blonde girl asks, plunking her credit card down on the marble countertop.

"I definitely would." Jess rings up the ice-cream orders. "Can he have a treat?"

"Sure."

Jess reaches into the glass jar next to the register and pulls out one of the heart-shaped dog biscuits she keeps for our furry visitors.

"Be right back, Poppy." She hustles from behind the counter, leaving me behind to listen to the chattering of the girl gang.

Apparently the brunette has a huge crush on Nathan, hence the accompaniment on the dog-walking errand. The blonde approves, but the other friend isn't so keen on the relationship. I lean in, fully engrossed in the middle-school drama.

Seriously, I have no life.

"He's into gaming, though. That's, like, really annoying. He's always playing with the boys," the dissenting girl protests.

"It's cool he has hobbies," the blonde points out.

The brunette bobs her head up and down. "Yeah. And he has lots of friends. That's a good sign, right?"

A shrill howl cuts through the girls' chatter, and I grip the counter, startled. Cold dread shoots down my spine as I stare out the window. I don't see Jess out there anywhere, and Nathan and his friend are hunched over, staring at the ground.

The friend pushes through the door, panic etched on his adolescent face. "Come quick! Ms. Carter hurt herself."

"Oh no!" I fly around the counter, my sneakers squeaking on the black-and-white-tile floor.

"Jess! What happened?" I crouch down on the sidewalk next to Jess. The kid who must be Nathan clutches a squirmy puppy to his chest, a long, red leash dangling down to the ground.

Jess's brows squish together, her eyes welling with tears, as she cradles her wrist. Her hand dangles at a geometri-cally funky angle—I'm no doctor, but that does not look good.

"The puppy got excited, running circles around me. I got wrapped up in the leash. Then he saw something across the street and started to sprint away. Took me straight down. I know I shouldn't have used my hands to break my fall, but it's reflex, you know? I think I might have broken my wrist." Her voice is reedy, threaded with pain.

"Oh no," I groan, stroking her shoulder. "I'll call 911. You need to go to the hospital."

"No, don't call. I can drive."

"What? You can't drive. Your wrist might be broken. I'll close down the shop and take you."

"No. You stay here and manage the shop. Call Griffin."

"Oh, I know!" I snap my fingers. "I'll call my brother. Parker's probably off work by now. He can take you." I slide my cell out of my apron pocket, my finger hovering over his icon.

"Don't bother Parker. Call Griffin."

I press my lips together, not thrilled at the idea of calling King Asshole.

"How about Roman? He's good in emergencies."

"Poppy! For the love—don't bother your brothers. Call Griffin." Jess's body trembles beneath my hand, and I know I should get her to the hospital quickly. Still, I can't force myself to make the call.

"I don't have his number," I say weakly.

"Use my cell. It's in my pocket." She tips her head down at her apron, and I hold in my protest, fishing her cell out while the teenagers huddle at a nearby table, petting the fluffball of a puppy.

"Can't make the call. Your phone's locked."

"The code's 1-2-1-2."

I punch in the numbers, and Jess's phone flashes to life —a cute pic of her hugging Griffin at one of his baseball games pops onto the screen. He's even smiling.

"He's pinned at the top. 'Greatest nephew ever.'"

Of course Jess would have him labeled that way. Probably the only person in America who likes the guy.

I dial his number, holding my breath, my heart pounding.

"Hello?" Griffin's deep voice rumbles down the line, and

my stomach flip-flops. Why, I have no freaking idea. I'm probably in shock.

"Uh, hey, Griffin. It's Poppy. You know, from the inn," I stammer, my usual confidence gone.

"Why do you have my aunt's phone?"

"There's been an incident."

"What do you mean? Is she okay?" To his credit, he sounds worried.

"Probably," I say, drawing out the word.

"What's that mean—she either is or isn't okay. What the hell?" he growls.

Such an asshole. And this is exactly why I hadn't wanted to call him.

"I don't know, Griffin. I mean, she's alive."

"Fuck. What happened? She's breathing, right? Did she have a heart attack?"

"No, not a heart attack. And yes, she's breathing. Calm down. She tripped. Over a dog. May have broken her wrist. I wanted to call 911, but she insisted I call you instead. So here we are."

"I'm on my way. Don't move."

He disconnects without so much as a goodbye, leaving me fuming on the sidewalk.

Jess peers up at me expectantly. "He's coming, right?"

"Yes. He said don't move."

"Ridiculous. Of course I'm moving." Jess tries to stand, pain dancing across her face as she struggles to get up.

"Let me help." I grip her elbow on the uninjured side, supporting almost all her bodyweight as she slowly rises.

Maneuvering Jess into a chair at one of the café tables set up outside Scoops, I peer over at the teens. "Hey, can you sit with her for a second?" I wave the brunette over. "I'm going to grab some ice."

The girl nods and I dash inside. I search for a bag, then dispense ice from the drink machine into the plastic bag and tie it shut. I grab a few paper towels and jet back out to the patio.

"I got some ice. Here." I try to hand the ice to Jess, then realize she can't hold it with her injury. Setting the bag on the table, I gently lay Jess's hand across the ice, and she winces and bites her lip.

Shit. This is bad. Very bad.

"You need anything else, Ms. Poppy?" the brunette asks.

"No, thank you for your help. Be careful with that dog. He's a wild one."

Nathan nods and the teens take off. I turn my attention back to Jess.

"Is anything else hurt?" I do a quick scan, taking inventory of the patient. Both palms scraped and bloody, but her face is fine, and she still has all her teeth. Some might even consider this a win.

"Did you hit your head at all?" I ask, dabbing at her left palm with a paper towel.

Jess shakes her head. "No. I caught myself with my hands. For better or for worse."

"How are your knees?"

"Sore." She lifts her right leg, then her left, kicking them out and grimacing. "But at least I'm wearing jeans. I'll be all right."

"Oh, Jess." I rub her back, trying to comfort her—and myself.

"Aunt Jess!" Griffin's gruff voice rumbles behind me, and

I jump, my entire body stiffening. Even his voice has me on edge.

"Are you okay?" He rushes to her side, his navy eyes filled with worry. "Did you hit your head?"

Jess shakes her head gingerly, pressing her lips together in a tight line. Her face is pale, her breathing shallow.

"Her arm should be elevated." Griffin shoots me a death stare, and I stand taller, puffing my chest out.

"She's icing," I say, spitting out the words.

"I know. You can ice and elevate at the same time. Ever heard of RICE?"

I swallow hard over the lump in my throat, annoyance gripping me. "Yeah, I have, Mr. Pro Athlete. But her arm hurts and the wrist is all dangly. So I had her rest it on the table."

"That's terrible for swelling." Griffin shakes his head in disgust, and a hot swirl of irritation rolls through my stomach.

This guy.

"I did the best I could. I'm not a freaking EMT. Plus, there was a puppy, and teenagers, and your aunt's in pain . . ." I list off all the complicating circumstances as Griffin scowls at me.

"Uh-huh."

Clearly he thinks I'm useless.

"Kids? Think someone could drive me to the hospital now? Or are y'all gonna stand around and debate best emergency practices all day?" Jess glances from me to Griffin, her jaw tight.

Griffin shoots me one last look of disgust, then helps his aunt to her feet. She clutches her wrist against her chest, and Griffin wraps his muscled arm around his aunt's tiny waist, supporting her. Together they slowly limp out to the parking lot, and Griffin eases his aunt into the leather seat of his black Range Rover.

"I'll mind the shop, Jess," I say, waving at her. "Don't worry about a thing."

"Thanks, Poppy," Jess whispers, closing her eyes against the pain.

Griffin says nothing as he pushes past me, the bare skin of our arms brushing. To my chagrin, a hot flash of something shoots through me.

Probably aggravation.

He climbs into the car and glowers at me through the windshield, shaking his head in disgust. The vehicle roars to life, and Griffin peels out of the parking lot, leaving behind a swirl of dust.

My heart sinks as worry sets in. I don't think Jess is going to be scooping ice cream anytime soon. And as much as I love the place, there's no way I can take on a second full-time job.

Which leaves one person.

King Asshole, Griffin Carter. The world's grumpiest human.

2

GRIFFIN

Out of respect for my aunt, I don't rip straight into Poppy. Even though I think she's a completely self-centered airhead. Irritating as fuck, actually.

After each interaction with her, I walk away annoyed.

And slightly turned on, which aggravates me further.

I hate this town.

Every single thing about it, but most especially her.

"How'd you trip over a dog exactly? Was it in the ice-cream shop? Doesn't that violate a health code—or twelve?" I glance over at my aunt, her eyes screwed tightly shut against the pain, her lips pale.

Stomping down hard on the accelerator, I'm grateful that at least this piss-ass Florida town doesn't have traffic like Atlanta.

"The puppy wasn't inside. I went out to give him a treat. The little rascal tangled his leash up in my legs and then took off after a squirrel. Ouch." She winces after I make a sharp right turn, her arm bumping against the door.

"Sorry," I say, patting her knee. "Trying to get you to the hospital quickly."

"It's not life or death, Griff. I'll be fine—take it easy." She blows out a long, slow breath, probably trying to disassociate from the pain.

Rationally, I get this isn't life or death—Aunt Jess'll be fine.

But still. Seeing her like this, shrunken down and shivering, affects me more than I care to admit. She's the closest family I've got, and she's always had my back, been there for me. I don't know what I'd do without her.

After swinging my SUV into the drive for the emergency room, I slam into park and race around to get the door for her.

"Griffin, honey, calm down." Aunt Jess pops her eyes open, her warm brown eyes catching mine. "I'll be okay."

"I know you will. I got you." I grip her elbow and her hip, lifting her gently out of the car. "Lean on me, that's right."

Together we hobble through the automatic glass doors, a cold blast of antiseptic-smelling air hitting my face as we cross into the mostly empty waiting room and head to the front desk.

"My aunt fell and probably broke her wrist," I explain to the intake receptionist, a woman who looks to be in her midfifties.

"Jess Carter? What in the . . . ? How'd you go and do that?" The receptionist shakes her head, typing away on the keyboard. "What's your birthday, sweetie? I'm gonna get a doc to take a look at that wrist straight away. Honey —" The receptionist turns her gaze on me. "I'm going to get your aunt back to a room. You go park your car, then hustle back to fill out the paperwork for her, okay?"

I nod. "Sure. Be right back, Aunt Jess." I hesitate a split second before heading outside.

I can't believe I'm back at a hospital. Hopefully I won't have some kind of trauma response.

I hate hospitals.

People die in hospitals.

My mom died in a hospital.

Exhaling a shuddery breath, I park and cut the engine, shoving my anxiety down.

I can do this.

Five minutes later, I'm back in the waiting room.

"She's this way. Room ten." The receptionist waves at me, pointing over her shoulder at the double doors to the right, and I push my way into a narrow, all-white hallway. I hustle down to room ten, but it's empty. I spy a clipboard holding a stack of paperwork, my aunt's name scrawled across the top. She must have been here.

Snagging the clipboard, I crash down into a plastic chair and fill in as much information as I can. Birth date, address, reason for visit.

I'd love to write *Poppy Montgomery* on that blank. Somehow, some way, I'm sure this is her fault; instead, I settle on *tripped by a dog and injured wrist.*

"Oh good, you found me." Aunt Jess's voice bounces off all the hard, shiny surfaces as a nurse wheels her into the room in a wheelchair.

"Thanks for the ride." Aunt Jess smiles up at the nurse, her words soft and slow. They must have given her a painkiller, because she seems a lot more comfortable now, her shoulders sloping, relaxed.

"You bet." The nurse pats Aunt Jess's shoulder, then whispers to me, "She got a shot of the good stuff so we could take x-rays. The doctor should be in shortly."

"Oh, the good stuff." Aunt Jess grins at no one in particular, giggling to herself.

"It'll wear off in an hour or two," the nurse says. "You'll probably go home with a prescription painkiller, at least enough for the next few days. Make sure to note your pharmacy."

"Right, got it." I flip through the sheath of papers and find the section. "Aunt Jess, which pharmacy do you use?"

"The one on the corner of Main Street. You know?"

I shake my head. "Nope, I don't."

"She's talking about Seaglass Sundries. Right, Jess?"

My aunt nods, lifting the index finger of her uninjured hand into the air. "Yes, that's the spot. I buy all my sunscreen and magazines there. Great selection."

"Super. I'll grab the details on my phone. Thanks." I search it up, jotting the name and number on the form.

"Griffin?"

I pause, glancing up from the paperwork. Aunt Jess stares at me, all serious.

"Yes?"

"They sell flowers there, you know."

"Uh . . . good to know." I have no idea where she's going with this.

"Just in case you wanted to pick some up."

"I'll get you flowers, Aunt Jess."

"Not for me, silly goose. For Poppy."

My gut twists and I choke out a strangled laugh, my face burning.

"What? I do not like Poppy. At all." I shake my head, frowning.

"Uh-huh. Sure you don't." Aunt Jess rolls her eyes and clucks at me, and I pray to god she won't remember this conversation tomorrow. "He definitely likes her." Aunt Jess tips her head back and stares up at the nurse, who's trying to hold back a giggle.

"Aunt Jess, stop. I do not."

"You should see how the two of them go back and forth with each other." Aunt Jess keeps on, despite my protest. "A stinger here, a quick jab there. Practically having sex right there in front of everyone."

Now my face is flaming, along with the back of my neck. *And here I thought this day couldn't get any worse.*

"How long did you say these drugs take to wear off?" I ask the nurse, her shoulders shaking with silent laughter.

"An hour or two." She swipes at the tears in her eyes, and I contemplate leaving my aunt alone for the exam. I've had enough humiliation for one day.

"Jess Carter? I'm Dr. Redmond."

Mercifully, the doctor steps into the room and the nurse scurries away, probably eager to share the stupid little rumor Aunt Jess just started.

The doctor does a quick exam, then pops the x-ray up on the light board. "Jess, it may not feel like it right now, but you got lucky. Distal radial fracture. We'll cast it in a few days, once the swelling goes down, and then you'll need to rest while it heals. But the good news is you don't need surgery."

"Oh. My." My aunt sighs, a loud exhale escaping into the quiet room.

"That's great news, Aunt Jess." I force cheer into my voice—extremely unnatural for me.

"What about the ice-cream shop?" Her voice tips up in panic as her eyes find mine, her gaze glassy.

"You're definitely not scooping ice cream anytime soon. In fact, I want you home, resting, as much as possible. The less you move that wrist, the better." Dr. Redmond points to the fracture on the x-ray. "You want this to heal because, believe me, surgery is a rough road."

"Exactly." I second the doctor's sage advice, being only a few months out from my own ACL surgery and still in recovery mode.

"I'm sure your nephew can help you figure out the shop," Dr. Redmond says, and I grimace.

"I mean, yeah, I could. I can. If you need me to." I trip all over my words, visions of Poppy's sunshiny face blinding me. Those bright blue eyes, the way she flips her honey-colored hair all the damn time.

"You'd do that, Griffin? Run the shop for a little bit?" Aunt Jess sounds so relieved, so happy, that I nod and press my lips together tightly.

Running Seaglass Scoops isn't on my agenda, but how can I say no?

"Sure."

"Griffy, you're the best."

The tips of my ears burn while Dr. Redmond fits Aunt Jess for a splint, then goes through the discharge procedure and writes a script for pain medication.

"Be sure to wear the brace 24-7 and ice aggressively over the next few days. Make an appointment at the desk for your cast. Take care." Dr. Redmond shoots us a wave and saunters out of the room.

I take a few minutes to complete the rest of the paperwork, filling in Aunt Jess's insurance information.

"Okay, all done here. Ready?" I glance over at my aunt, her head lolling forward, her chest rising and falling in sync with her soft snoring.

Oh boy. The painkiller knocked her out. I should probably drop her off, then go pick up her meds.

Wheeling Aunt Jess down the hall, I shove backward through the double doors and spin around to the front desk. The receptionist's cheeks turn bright pink as soon as she spots me, and my stomach twists into a tight knot.

You gotta be kidding me. The nurse already told her the story? Or maybe Aunt Jess said something else—something worse—when I was parking the car.

I need to get the hell out of here.

The ER specifically, but Seaglass Beach generally.

I clear my throat and shove the clipboard toward the receptionist. "Here's the paperwork. I need to schedule a cast appointment for my aunt in a few days."

The receptionist flips idly through the paperwork, then reads the doctor's order and pulls up a calendar.

"How about Wednesday at ten a.m.?"

I check my schedule; the only things I have going are gym sessions with a trainer and PT.

"Works for me." I type the date and time into my phone. "Can I leave Aunt Jess here for a sec and grab the car?"

She nods. "No problem."

Ten minutes later, I have Aunt Jess locked and loaded in the passenger seat—and she never even wakes up from her nap. I drive her home, listening to the beach's top country hits, Nate Smith crooning about lining drinks up and knocking them back, and that honestly seems like a good idea right now. Drumming on the steering wheel, I try to ignore the tension creeping into my shoulders, and I crack my neck to the side.

It's fine. Everything's fine.

How hard can running an ice-cream shop be? I'm a professional baseball player. I've totally got this. Anybody can pile a few scoops of vanilla ice cream onto a cone, maybe throw on some sprinkles.

Way easier than hitting home runs, and I did that on the regular.

Besides, I'm sure Aunt Jess will be back and better than ever in no time. And then I can go home to Atlanta and resume regularly scheduled programming.

This is a tiny blip in the plan, is all.

I'll just think of myself as the designated hitter in the ninth inning, ready to lead my team to victory.

Yep. That's the story and I'm sticking to it.

3

POPPY

Turns out running Seaglass Scoops is a blast. Way more fun than running the inn and sitting at the front desk all day. Maybe because it's novel—I don't know and I don't care.

What I *do* know is I'm living my best life. Music pumping, the sweet scent of cream, sugar, and vanilla tickling my nose, chatting with all the customers and helping them decide which flavor to try.

If Jess hadn't gotten hurt, I would declare today one of the best days ever.

A little before eight p.m., I shutter the shop and head over to the inn to check on things. The night clerk's already on duty, sitting at the front desk and reading a magazine. I wave to her, then head over to the kitchen. Everything's cleaned and shut down for the evening, but I scrounge around and manage to find a leftover tray of ziti and some salad.

Grabbing both, I trot out to my car and climb in, then turn the key in the ignition. The old Ford Bronco roars to life, and I ease out of the lot, turning onto A1A toward Jess's house. I haven't heard from either her or Griffin since this afternoon, and she hasn't returned my texts. She probably can't text with one hand, I'm guessing.

Ten minutes later, I pull into her driveway and park behind a shiny black Range Rover. Not Jess's car.

My heart does a weird flip-flop thing in my chest, and I take a deep breath, trying to calm down.

Relax. It'll all be fine. Just drop off the ziti, check on Jess, and jet out of here.

Easy-peasy.

Besides, he's not that bad.

With another deep breath, I grab the casserole and make my way up the tidy walkway to the front door. I ring the doorbell and shuffle from foot to foot, shifting my anxiety from one side of my body to the other. Nerves swirl in my stomach.

No answer, so I ring the bell again. I debate dropping the casserole on the porch swing and scooting out of here, but it's too warm for that. The food would spoil, a total waste of perfectly good pasta.

The door swings open, and my mouth goes dry as toast, heat surging through me.

Griffin stands in the doorway, all six foot two of him (I *might* have checked out his baseball stats), wearing nothing but a white towel wrapped around his waist. Tiny droplets of water bead on his tanned and sculpted pecs, marked with ink, and I try not to stare at his six-pack and the deep V-line at his hips.

"What do you want?" His gruff voice jolts me from my ab-induced stupor.

"I . . . uh . . . I brought your aunt some pasta—it's ziti."

I shove the cool metal tray at him, bumping against his wall of solid muscle. "Er . . . sorry."

His eyes flicker down to the silver tray, then slowly climb back to my face.

"She's sleeping. Been a rough day."

I lick my bottom lip, my cheeks burning. I hadn't considered she'd be asleep, but Griffin's right—she had a long day.

"Oh. Well, you can put it in the fridge, and she can eat it tomorrow. Or you can eat it tonight . . ." My voice trails off, and damn if a ripple of heat doesn't unfurl in my lower belly.

No. Uh-uh. Forget about it, Poppy. Griffin Carter's a total and complete asshole with a chip on his shoulder bigger than the entire Florida Panhandle.

He takes the pasta from me, our fingers brushing, and another stupid jolt of something I should not be feeling zings up my arms.

"Fine." Griffin stares at me, his gaze dark and dangerous, and I consciously have to work on standing still. Why does this man always make me feel like I'm being scolded?

"How's your aunt?" I ask, focusing on his face and pointedly ignoring the fact that he's practically naked.

"She's been better. Has a broken wrist. It'll get casted in a few days, but she can't work for at least six weeks."

"Oh. Sorry. That stinks. But she doesn't need surgery?"

"No."

"Well, that's good, right?"

"If you have to find a freaking silver lining here, that would be it, I guess. But I don't see too much good in the situation."

"Right . . ." I flip my hair over my shoulder, trying to come up with something else to say.

After what feels like an eternity, I ask, "So who's going to run Seaglass Scoops?"

He shoots me another withering look, and my toes curl in my sneakers. *Damn, what is it about this guy?* He clearly hates my guts, so why isn't my body picking up on the not-at-all-subtle message?

"Me, I guess," he says, his voice flat.

"Oh." I break the stare, shoving my hand in my pocket, my heart pounding wildly.

Another long, awkward pause, the faint pounding of the ocean waves in the distance filling the air between us. Or maybe that's the sound of the blood rushing in my ears, I don't know.

"I've been working with your aunt a lot. If you need any help, let me know."

"I won't." Griffin locks his eyes on mine, and I notice tiny cobalt flecks sprinkled in the deep blue of his irises.

Okay, then.

"Well, if you change your mind . . ."

"I won't." He swallows, his Adam's apple bobbing in his thick neck.

"All right. Tell your aunt I hope she feels better." I pivot and trot back to my car, trying hard not to break into a sprint.

Jess Carter may be the sweetest person on the planet, but her nephew most definitely is not. If it weren't for her, there's no way I'd ever even talk to the guy. It's no wonder he's still single, with a crappy attitude like that.

Gunning out of the driveway, I whisper a silent prayer

for Jess's speedy recovery, because I don't know how much Griffin Carter I can take.

Good thing he knows it all and won't be needing my help anyway.

4

―――――

GRIFFIN

SHUTTING THE DOOR ON POPPY, I SLAM THE ZITI INTO the fridge, then sag back against the counter.

What is it about her that drives me bananas? I don't know if it's her perpetual optimism, the natural lilt in her chipper voice, or the way she twirls her hair and stares deep into my eyes, like she's trying to see into my soul.

Maybe it's the combo of all the above.

Or maybe it's the fact that every time she's around I get a raging hard-on.

I shake my head violently, attempting to dislodge this ridiculous thought.

No. Nuh-uh. No fucking way.

Poppy and I are like oil and water—a terrible fucking combination. We'll never see eye to eye on anything, guaranteed.

No matter how attractive my dick finds her, I'm never going there.

Ever.

I adjust my towel, wrapping it tighter in an attempt to lessen the stiffy situation.

Forget about her perky tits. Those bright blue eyes that widen every time you talk. The way her skin flushes pink when you accidentally touch.

And definitely forget about how her naked body would look beneath you while you fucked the sunshine right out of her, leaving her breathless and begging for more.

No way in hell is that happening. Not in this lifetime or the next.

So forget it.

Do your time in this backwater town, heal the knee, and get the fuck out of here.

Baseball is my entire life—my passion—and I have no desire to mess that up for anyone, let alone a woman.

Especially a woman I find as utterly aggravating as Poppy Montgomery.

So why is every nerve in my body humming right now?

Crashing into the cool sheets of the twin guest bed, a quarter of my calves hanging off the end of the mattress, I fist my dick and give it a stern talking to.

Fine, she's cute. But we're not going there, buddy. So calm the fuck down.

My little chat doesn't do much. I huff out a breath at the popcorn ceiling, then stand and throw on a pair of gym shorts, working hard on ignoring the throbbing erection pressing against the gray cotton mesh.

But even my pregame meditation doesn't erase a certain pair of wide blue eyes from my mind.

FML.

I finally fall into a fitful sleep, visions of Poppy running through my dreams all night long.

5

GRIFFIN

"You sure you'll be okay here without me?" I ask Aunt Jess, shooting a worried look in her direction.

"Yes, Griffin! I'll be fine. I've lived alone for over a decade." She shakes her head and clucks at me, her gray hair bobbing around her slim shoulders.

"Yeah, but that wasn't with a broken wrist. I could always swing by the ice-cream shop and put up a notice that we'll be closed for a few days."

"No way! I have to pay the rent somehow, and we're just getting the shop off the ground. We can't close down now—we'll lose momentum."

I frown, my gut twisting at the thought of leaving her unattended.

"Fine, I'll go." I gather up her cell, a magazine, a glass of ice water, and her pain pill in one of those clear medicine cups, and deposit everything on the side table next to her recliner.

"Here's your next pill. Be sure to take it on time—you want to stay ahead of the pain. And call me if you need anything at all. I can pop home and then go back, no big deal."

"I'm fine, honey. Don't worry about me. I'm gonna sit here and watch daytime television until I nod off." She smiles up at me, her eyelids already heavy from the pain meds.

"Okay. Call me!" I hold my hand up to my ear, but her attention's turned to the remote as she clicks through the local stations.

Satisfied she'll be okay without me for a few hours, I grab my keys and head over to Seaglass Scoops.

It's another perfect day at the beach, the sun shining brightly in a clear-blue sky. If I were playing in a game tonight, I might actually be in a decent mood.

Instead, I have eight or so hours scooping ice cream for a bunch of tourists looming ahead of me.

Less than ideal.

I slide my Rover into a parking spot near Seaglass Scoops and ease myself out of the driver's seat, careful not to put my full body weight on my knee. The sooner this thing heals up, the better—for all involved, but I can't rush it and risk undoing all my hard work.

Unlocking the bubblegum-pink door to Seaglass Scoops, I hit the light switch, bright fluorescence blinding me as the light reflects off the black-and-white-tile floor. I flip the sign from CLOSED to OPEN and lumber back behind the counter, pulling up the stool and sinking down in front of the register. Aunt Jess gave me the key to the cash drawer, and I slide it open to verify I can make change on the off chance someone pays with cold, hard cash.

A pink Post-it sits on top of the neat stack of one-dollar bills. I rip it out of the drawer, squinting at the loopy handwriting.

> *Dear Jess,*
> *Hope you're feeling better. Everything went fine this afternoon, but customers missed you! The Key lime pie flavor is a hit—let's add it to the menu!*
> *xoxo,*
> *Poppy*

Scowling at the note, I squeeze my fist tightly and crush the paper into a tiny ball, chucking it into the trash bin. I'm not about to mess around with new ice-cream flavors while my aunt's laid up at home. Customers will have to be content with the standard vanilla, chocolate, and strawberry everyone knows and loves. If they want to get really creative, I'll add a swirl of caramel sauce and maybe a cherry if they ask extra nice.

After counting the cash, I shut the register and check my cell for texts or calls from Aunt Jess.

Nothing.

I take that as a good sign—she must be doing okay, because I'm sure she'll call if she needs me. Next I fiddle with the radio, finding the local country station and pumping it through the speakers. Then I sink back onto the stool and wait for a customer.

I don't have to wait long. A couple strolls in, hand in hand, wearing matching floral beach cover-ups and flip-flops. Both sport lobster-red sunburns, and the guy's fanning himself with his hand.

"It sure is a hot one!" He wanders along the length of

the ice-cream freezer, peering down at each tub, his heavy brow furrowing as he analyzes his options.

"Mind if I try your chocolate espresso bean?" He points at the dark brown ice cream speckled with chocolate-covered beans.

"Sure." I stand and dip a pink spoon into the tub, then hand it to him.

"Mmm, that's good." He smacks his lips, nodding.

"Is that what you want?" I ask, reaching for the silver ice-cream scoop.

The man holds up his index finger. "I don't know. I might not want a whole cone of it; it's pretty rich. Can I try the clementine sherbet?"

I nod, swallowing down my aggravation, and scoop the orange ice. "Here you go."

He takes the spoonful of sherbet and licks at it.

"Refreshing. I think you'll like that, honey." He taps her shoulder, and she smiles over at him.

"Yeah? I was thinking about the cream-cheese-and-bagel ice cream. I've never even heard of that!" The woman points to the far-left corner of the display, and I bite my tongue. *What kind of savage puts bagels in ice cream?* Sounds repulsive, but whatever—I'm not eating it.

"Can I try?" She leans forward to get a better look at the ice cream.

"Sure." I dip another tiny spoon into the white ice cream, trying to dislodge a chunk of bagel with the rounded plastic tip. The spoon breaks, and I mutter an expletive quietly under my breath, reach for another spoon to fish the first spoon out, and then toss the whole mess in the trash.

"Sorry about that. The bagel chunk got me. Hang on." I dig back in, heat creeping up my neck.

For fuck's sake, I'm a professional athlete. I sure as hell should be able to scoop a micro amount of ice cream onto a plastic spoon.

SNAP! The second spoon splinters, and I mutter another swear word, grab the actual metal ice-cream scoop, and plop a nice round ball into a cup.

"Here ya go. Taste away."

She takes the paper cup from me, and I fold my arms across my chest, leaning back on my heels and waiting for the two of them to make a damn decision.

"I only wanted a taste," she murmurs, licking at the spoon, the pink of her tongue levitating over the ice cream. "Not all this. I'm on a diet."

Oh boy.

"It's fine. That cup's on the house. You can pick another flavor if you want. Won't hurt my feelings."

The woman's gaze flits from the cup of bagel ice cream to the freezer, then back to the cup.

"Well, how is it?" the man asks, tipping his head to the side.

"Different." She draws the word out, gnawing at her lip. "You know, I think I'm just going to go with strawberry. In a cone."

I suck in a deep breath through my nose and run the metal scoop under the tap to rinse off the bagel ice cream.

"Waffle or cake?" I ask, pointing at her two options and trying hard not to sound testy.

"Waffle."

"Okay." I fix her cone while the man contemplates his order.

"Can I get two scoops? One vanilla, one espresso bean? I can handle one scoop of that."

"Sure. Cup or cone?"

"Cup."

Three minutes later, the sunburned tourists have their ice cream, and I successfully take their payment using the credit card swipe thingy. The woman actually shows me how to use it—apparently she runs an antique shop in Nashville and uses a machine just like it all the time.

"Thanks, I appreciate your help." I force a smile and she pats my arm.

"Anytime. I know how hard it is running your own business and having to learn all the things!"

"This is my aunt's shop, actually. But she fell and broke her wrist yesterday, so I'm the pinch hitter at the moment."

"Oh dear, I hope she's okay!" The woman wrinkles up her freckled nose.

"She'll be fine, thanks."

The door chimes and a Mommy-and-me group darts in, cutting my conversation with the tourists short.

"Sorry, gotta help them."

The tourists wave and head out, leaving me alone to face six eager toddlers and their accompanying mothers.

"Welcome to Seaglass Scoops!" I do my best to sound cheerful, but I'm not sure anyone can even hear me over the loud chatter of the kids.

"I want ice cream, Mommy!"

"Me too!"

"A cone! With sprinkles . . ."

The high-pitched voices all blend together, dull thuds of sticky hands banging on the freezer.

"Who's first?" My voice booms through the space, and

six sets of eyes stare up at me. Then a small hand flies into the air, followed by another, then another.

"Me!"

"Me!"

"No, me first!"

Shit. That backfired.

"Don't worry, kids. Everyone can have ice cream," I say, staring down at the tops of their small blond heads.

"Mommy, what are the flavors? I can't see!" One of the kids jumps up and down, trying to glimpse into the freezer, but he's not tall enough, nor does he have enough hang time to see anything.

"We've got vanilla, chocolate, strawberry, espresso— probably not a good choice for kids. Clementine sherbet— that's a fancy word for orange," I explain.

"I know that! We just had a hurricane named Clementine," one of the kids says, her eyes round as saucers.

"Right, exactly. There's also Key lime pie and bagels and cream cheese."

"Oh! I love bagels," the smallest kid says, grinning. "I want that."

"You sure?" I ask, glancing up at the moms for permission.

"Yes. And sprinkles." The kid's head bounces up and down in certainty, so I grab for the scoop.

"Cup or cone?"

"Cup." All the moms respond in unison, then break into laughter. Must be a mom joke or something.

I scoop the bagel ice cream, toss some rainbow sprinkles on, then hand the treat across the counter.

"Oh. I don't like blue sprinkles." The kid's face scrunches up in disgust, and I bite down hard on my lip.

"Sorry, bud. It's an assortment. If you want chocolate sprinkles, those are all brown." I point at the glass jar holding the chocolate sprinkles, and the kid tips his head, thinking.

"Maybe you can pick out the blue ones?" The kid hands the cup back to me.

"Henry, I'll do it for you." His mom takes the ice cream, leading Henry the Pain in the Ass away from the counter.

Crisis averted.

"All right, who's next?"

More wild hand waving and a shove to the back, but eventually it's Milly's turn.

"What are the flavors again?" Milly trains her dark eyes on me, and I recite the flavors once more to all the kids.

"Can I try chocolate?" she asks.

Really? The kid never had chocolate ice cream before?

I dip a pink spoon into the chocolate ice cream and hand it to Milly. Who promptly drops it on the ground.

"Milly!" her mom cries.

"It's fine. Here's a napkin." I hand a white paper napkin to her mother and scoop another tiny dollop of chocolate ice cream onto a clean pink spoon. Meanwhile, the kids on the end are getting restless, banging on the freezer, and one of the other kids is touching the merchandise display in the corner.

"I want the orange one!" another kid wails while Milly sucks on the spoon, trying to decide whether this chocolate ice cream measures up to whatever other chocolate ice cream she's had before.

I start scooping the sherbet and hand the cup across the counter, but Milly stomps her little sandal on the tile.

"It's my turn!" she screeches, then bursts into tears.

"Did you want chocolate?" I ask, trying not to scowl down at her.

"No. Too chocolaty."

"Oh-kay. How about vanilla?" I suggest, ignoring the freaking drumline happening at the end of the freezer.

"Boring," Milly proclaims, rolling her eyes.

"Strawberry? It's a pretty pink color." I point at the vibrant hue and the fat chunks of fresh strawberries.

"I hate pink. And that's kinda sexist."

Damn. Called out by a preschooler.

"Do you like citrus?" I ask, frowning at Milly. I was really starting to dislike this little girl as the percussion section heated up.

"Maybe. Can I try?"

I huff out a breath, diving back into the freezer lower than necessary, just to cool off.

Crash! A screechy wail sounds from the corner and my head flies up, banging on the top of the metal freezer.

"Ouch." I rub the back of my baseball hat, aggravation building in my gut. T-shirts and plastic tumblers lie in a heap on the ground, the mischievous boy responsible bawling next to the mess. A mom rushes over, shoveling the merch up off the ground and stacking it haphazardly back on the shelf.

"It's fine—don't worry about it. I'll fix it later," I call out across the shop, but she can't hear me over the little drummer boys.

The door chimes, and a hot flash of panic surges through me. I haven't even finished with these kiddos and now I have another customer?

"Hey, kids. Hey Milly, Steffi! How are y'all? Isn't the ice cream here great?"

I recognize that sunshiny voice even before I see the honey-blonde hair.

"Hey, Poppy! How are you?" One of the moms leans in and hugs Poppy, and the merch destroyer instantly stops wailing. All the kids rush up and give Poppy hugs, even the little drummer boys. I'm torn between being happy for the backup and being annoyed at how much better Poppy is at this than me, but I decide to go with happy for now. Or at least neutral.

"What's the matter, Milly-bug?" Poppy crouches down, holding Milly's little hand.

"The ice-cream man is sexist." She cuts her round eyes at me, glaring as hard as any grown adult.

The corners of Poppy's lips twitch, but she holds in her smirk.

"That guy? The tall one, scooping?"

Milly bobs her head up and down vigorously, like she's an eyewitness in court and I'm a perp on trial.

"Yes. He wants me to get pink ice cream just because I'm a girl."

I clear my throat loudly, waving the silver scoop in the air. "Untrue. I *offered up* strawberry ice cream because she's already rejected the chocolate for being too chocolaty and vanilla for being too boring. I didn't think it was a great idea to serve preschoolers espresso beans, and I don't know how she feels about citrus."

"What about the bagel-and-cream-cheese flavor? That one's yummy," Poppy says, locking her eyes on mine.

Sending a flash of heat roaring through me, straight to my dick.

Good grief. Not the fucking time.

I inch behind the freezer so no one can see what's going on below deck and meet Poppy's gaze.

"She wasn't into it," I say, my voice loud and strong.

"Really? People have loved that flavor. Tell you what, Milly. Give me one sec with Griffin and we'll make you something extra special, just for you."

The little girl's eyes light up, and she bounces up and down with excitement. "Yeah!"

Poppy squeezes her shoulder, then joins me behind the ice-cream freezer.

"I offered her every flavor we have." I shrug, shoving a hand in my pocket. "Good luck."

I hand the silver scoop to her and pop a squat on the stool, folding my arms across my chest.

"Watch and learn, grasshopper." She winks at me, and my cock twitches in my pants. I'm damn glad I'm sitting down, covered by the counter. Last thing I need is a rumor flying around Seaglass Beach about me and Little Miss Sunshine.

Poppy scoops vanilla, chocolate, and strawberry spheres into a bright pink plastic ice-cream boat, then shoots whipped cream over the entire thing. Next she drizzles chocolate sauce, following it up with rainbow sprinkles, and topping the entire concoction off with a cherry.

"For Miss Milly. The Seaglass Sundae. With extra sprinkles." Poppy slides it across the counter to Milly's mom, who shoots a beaming smile at Poppy.

"I love it, Poppy! Thank you!" Milly runs around the counter and squeezes Poppy's legs at the knees, and Poppy grins.

"You bet, Milly-bug. Enjoy. Now what about you, Xander?"

Five minutes later, Poppy has every kid and their mom happily eating ice cream. I ring up the transactions, and then the whole gang heads outside to enjoy the beautiful autumn afternoon.

Peace descends on the shop, and I stare over at Poppy, a giant lump of crow lodged deep in my throat.

A tiny smile tugs at her full, pink lips, and I swallow hard over that crow.

"Thought you weren't gonna need any help?" She stands with her hands on her hips, barely able to hold in a grin.

I roll my neck, stretching out my arms and cracking my knuckles. "I totally had that. The situation was under control."

"Uh-huh." Poppy smirks at me, those blue eyes flashing beneath the pendant lights, and an unexpected rush of desire washes over me.

Ignoring it—and her—I push past her and head over to the corner to fix the merchandise display.

"You need me to stay? Or do you have it all under control?" Her voice is close, her breath tickling the bare skin of my arm, and heat radiates between our bodies.

I don't dare turn around.

Instead, I grunt, "I've got it. But thanks."

The door chimes ring out, and she's gone, leaving me to figure out how to fold these damn T-shirts.

POPPY

"CAN YOU BELIEVE HE DIDN'T EVEN SAY THANK YOU?" I crunch into my taco, biting down so hard the shell cracks, meat tumbling out the bottom.

A trace of a smile flits across Liv's face as she takes a sip of her five-dollar Tipsy Taco Tuesday margarita.

"What?" I stare at her over my taco.

"Nothing." Her gaze drops to the salted rim of her glass, and I kick her foot under the table.

"What's that for?"

"I see you holding in a smile. Spill."

"You like him, Poppy. Admit it."

"I do not. In fact—just the opposite. I can't stand him. He's arrogant. Rude. Condescending." I tick all the things I hate about Griffin off on my fingers. Honestly, I could keep going if I had to.

"Uh-huh." Liv screws up her mouth, nodding.

"What? He is. Every time I see the man, he's a complete asshole. Take today, for instance. I popped into Scoops because I left my charger there last night and needed to grab it. When I get there, the shop's a disaster zone, Liv. Not even joking. Two kiddos crying, a mom chasing another kiddo through the shop, the entire merch display on the ground . . ."

"Really? That *is* bad."

"Right? And Griffin's standing there trying to reason with a four-year-old. Which we both know is complete madness. So I jump behind the counter and get everything squared away for him, and then he's a jerk about it."

"Was he? Really?" Liv narrows her eyes at me, and I shift in the booth.

Biting my bottom lip, I stare at the red plastic basket of tortilla chips. "Maybe not a complete jerk, but he didn't say thank you. And I saved his ass, Liv. Least he could do was thank me."

"Maybe he didn't want to be saved, Poppy." Liv snags a chip out of the basket and chews it slowly, thoughtfully.

"Nonsense. He definitely needed the assist. One hundred percent."

"He was probably embarrassed, Pops. You're really great at customer service. Griffin's a professional baseball player. I've got to think he's not used to working in the service industry."

She does have a point.

"Still. Common decency would've been to say thank you. I did him a solid, and all he did was turn his back on me and grunt like a Neanderthal."

Liv snickers as she reaches for another chip.

"What's so funny?" I ask, thrumming the tabletop.

"Nothing." She waves her hand in the air, dismissing my question.

"Something. What?"

"Pops—I hate to tell you this, but I'm pretty sure Griffin has a thing for you too. The two of y'all should just go ahead and get together. Save time all around. Besides, it's unclear how long he's going to be here. You should definitely jump on it while you can."

Margarita spews out of my mouth, along with a loud, maniacal laugh at this preposterous idea.

"Me and Griffin Carter? Never." I shake my head, wiping stray drops of margarita from my lips.

"Uh-huh." She picks up her phone, tapping on the screen. Seconds later, my cell vibrates next to me on the table and I reach for it.

> Liv: September 26. Poppy declares she will never get with Griffin Carter. Ever

"Why'd you text me that?" I scrunch my nose in confusion and reread the text one more time.

"I'm going to pull this text up on my phone after you get with him and remind you of your declaration."

Reaching across the table, I playfully shove her tanned shoulder. "Shut up!"

Liv giggles and I join her, relief flooding through me. At least our relationship feels back on track, even if she is engaged to my twin brother, Parker.

"You're ridiculous, Liv. Nothing's going to happen between me and Griffin Carter. Guaranteed."

After dinner, Liv heads home to be with my brother, leaving me standing alone in the dim parking lot. I don't feel like heading to an empty apartment and watching reality TV, so I hop in my trusty Bronco and motor slowly down Main Street, driving aimlessly.

Until I find myself idling outside Seaglass Scoops.

Why, I have no idea.

Well, maybe I have a *little* bit of an idea, as I stare through the window at a certain tall, dark, and surly pro baseball player. Griffin's wiping down the white counter-top, his tan biceps flexing with the effort. Damn, his T-shirt barely contains his rippling muscles . . .

Heat unfurls low in my belly as I watch him polish the quartz to a bright shine, then move from behind the counter to the front of the freezer. Glass cleaner in hand, he spritzes the display case, erasing the day's sticky fingerprints.

He may be a grumpy jerk, but the man has a fine ass, perfectly showcased in his jeans. And I've already seen his washboard abs. I didn't even know bodies built like that existed in real life.

The man is practically a Greek god, with an attitude to match.

Too bad he's Mr. Grumpypants or maybe I'd consider having a fling with him. Nothing serious, of course, but it could be kinda fun to make out with a pro baseball star.

Buzz, buzz.

The vibration of my cell jolts me from my drool session.

> King: Rome's birthday party. Friday night
> at 7, out at the ranch. You in?

That's my eldest brother—truly, a man of few words. I check my calendar, then text back:

Poppy: Absolutely. Want me to bring anything?

King: Get a cake

Of course I'm in charge of the cake. Surprised he didn't ask me to get the decorations, too, while I'm at it. The hazard of being the only girl in the family, ever since our parents died in a car crash three years ago. Thank goodness I'll have Liv in the near future.

Poppy: On it. You need decorations?

Figure I might as well preempt the ask.

King: He's turning thirty-five. Don't think he needs streamers at this point in his life

I chuckle into the dark. King's sense of humor is definitely unique.

Poppy: I'll see what I can scare up

King: Maybe a date?

Poppy: Harsh. And look who's talking, Single Stu

King: Peopling is overrated

> Poppy: You just haven't found the right
> girl yet

I stare at the screen, expecting an immediate response, but no text bubbles appear.

Tap, tap, tap.

"Ohmygawd!" I jump about three feet off the driver's seat, clutching my chest.

"What are you doing?" Griffin's muffled voice vibrates the glass, his gaze dark as I crank the window down.

"You scared the bejeezits out of me." I tug at the collar of my shirt, my heart hammering.

Solely from the scare, I'm sure of it.

"Why are you spying?" He furrows his brow, crossing his muscular arms over his chest.

"I'm not *spying*." I shake my head, fanning my heated cheeks.

"What are you doing then? Sitting in a dark parking lot with your lights off? Kinda sus and doesn't seem too safe."

I huff out a breath, my hair breezing up and back down on my forehead. "Relax, this is Seaglass Beach, not Atlanta. Crime's so low the police department hasn't hired anyone new in like five years. The worst thing that happens around here is kids playing ding-dong ditch."

Griffin scrubs a hand over his chiseled jaw, and I vaguely wonder what that dark scruff would feel like rubbing against my skin.

"Still—you never know. I wouldn't want my sister or girlfriend or whomever sitting in a dark parking lot alone."

My stomach swoops at the mention of the word *girlfriend*.

Stop it, Poppy. Three seconds ago you were thinking about what an ass this guy is. You are not *interested.*

"I'm fine, Griffin. Anyway, I'm not really sitting here. I just, uh . . . got a text. And I don't text and drive. So I pulled over and texted back. Safety first!"

"Uh-huh." Griffin lowers his chin, and I can tell he's not buying my story.

"For real. See?" I shove my phone out the window, waving it around in the cool night air.

"Okay, fine. Whatever." He holds his palms up in surrender. "Good to hear you're a responsible driver. Need to be because I doubt you can get any replacement parts on this car." He slaps his hand on the roof.

"Are you shading Smurfy?" I narrow my eyes at him.

"Excuse me? Did you actually name your car 'Smurfy'?" The right corner of his mouth twitches, and I'm pretty sure he's mocking me now.

"Yeah, I did. She's an antique, you know. Nineteen seventy-eight."

"Good gas mileage then," Griffin quips, smirking at me, and hot irritation and desire commingle in my stomach.

"Listen, not all of us want flashy status symbol cars."

He takes a step forward, the scent of his crisp cologne wafting into my open window. I smash down the urge to take a big sniff as his eyes flash at me.

"Are you shading my Rover?"

I tilt my head to the side, licking along my lower lip and catching it between my teeth. "Maybe."

One second then two go by, Griffin's eyes locked on mine, and I can barely breathe he's standing so close to me.

"Don't knock luxury until you've ridden it." He doesn't break his gaze, and my stomach flip-flops at his words, my cheeks flaming. "It has aniline leather seats, top of the line."

I swallow hard, my throat dry. "Yeah, well. I have leather seats too." I pat the seat, thwacking my hand on the non-aniline leather, hardened from years of sun, salt, and sand.

"Does this thing even have air-conditioning?" He leans in a little, peering at the dash.

"Gawd, yes! I live in Florida—of course I have AC. And a radio, thank you very much."

"Ooh, fancy. A radio."

"AM/FM only. I can't stream anything. But it's totally workable."

For the first time since I met him, Griffin chuckles, tiny laugh lines forming around his eyes.

And dammit, he's even cuter than before.

Not good.

Heat ripples through me, and I clench my thighs against the tingling between my legs.

"Let's go ahead and concede that Smurfy's the cooler ride," I say, twisting my ponytail.

Griffin stretches one arm up, resting his hand on Smurfy's roof, and leans in even closer, his white teeth flashing in the streetlight.

"Anytime you want a ride, you let me know." Smoldering heat simmers in those deep blue eyes, and my breath catches in my throat, my pulse racing.

He taps the roof twice, then turns and walks away. Pausing at the door of Scoops, he glances back over his broad shoulder at me.

"Have a good night. Drive safe."

Then he dips into the shop, leaving me alone and breathless in the parking lot.

Well, that's a twist.

I do believe Griffin Carter, King Asshole, just flirted with me.

And there's no way I'm telling Liv about it either. Can't let her know that she may be onto something here.

7

———

GRIFFIN

"Six, seven . . . one more, you got this . . ." Chris, my personal trainer, hovers over the bench press, his hands ready to spot me if I need it.

I grunt and push the heavy bar away from my body, pecs burning with the effort.

"Great job, man." Chris catches the bar, easing the metal back into the rack. "That's enough for today. Make sure you ice the knee later. We ran farther today than last week; want to make sure to keep the swelling down. But you're making good progress."

I grab a towel and wipe the sweat from my hands and face. "Thanks, man. I appreciate it. I'm hoping I'll get cleared to play by spring training."

Chris tosses me my water bottle and I catch it one-handed. "Keep it up and you've definitely got a shot. See you tomorrow?"

"You know it. Bright and early."

He shoots me a wave, and I head to the locker room to grab a quick shower.

"Griffin, what's up?" Parker, Poppy's twin brother, slaps my shoulder as I push through the door into the men's locker room.

"Not much, man. You good?"

He grins at me. "Better than good. Hey—heard about your aunt. She doing okay?"

"Yeah, she's all right. Getting her cast today, actually."

"Tough break, man. I'm real sorry to hear about that."

"Thanks. It's been kind of a rough year."

"Hey, listen. We're having a little thing for Rome's birthday on Friday night out at the ranch. Why don't you come? It's nothing fancy, just a few friends and family getting together, beers and burgers, that kinda thing."

"I don't know . . . ," I hedge, running a hand through my hair. These sorts of gatherings can be awkward at best, especially when you're from out of town. "I might need to take care of my aunt."

"She'll be fine for a few hours. C'mon—it'll be a good time. What's your number? I'll text you the address."

He thrusts his cell at me and, against my better judgment, I punch my number in. Thirty seconds later, I have a text with the address.

"See you Friday!" He waves and heads out, leaving me alone with my self-doubt.

Why'd I agree to attend a Montgomery shindig?

I hate people. I hate parties.

And I'm pretty sure Poppy will be there.

A few days ago I would have added I hate Poppy, but now that feeling's a lot more muted, and I'm not so sure.

And that aggravates me too.

After tossing my sweaty towel into the hamper, I grab a

fresh one from the stack on the shelf and storm off to the shower to wash my unease away.

"Griffin?" Aunt Jess's voice rings out as I push through the front door.

Tossing my keys on the small entry table, I hustle into the den. Aunt Jess waves me over from her upholstered recliner.

"The hospital called. They had to move my cast appointment from this morning to this afternoon. I hope that works for you."

"Sure. I'll run over to Scoops and hang up a note about a delayed opening today, no big deal." I shrug, secretly relieved to be off the ice-cream-selling hook for a few more hours.

"Oh, don't worry about that. I already called Poppy, and she said she can cover until you get back. Problem solved." She beams at me from her makeshift throne, her eyes shining.

"Doesn't Poppy need to be at the inn? Maybe we should look into hiring some high school kids or something." I run a hand through my damp hair, shifting from one foot to the other. I'm not used to uncertainty, and lately the only thing that's for certain is everything's up in the air.

Which makes this no time to be getting involved with any sort of feelings, even if it's purely attraction.

Nope.

I should avoid Poppy at all costs.

Not that I'm interested . . .

"Poppy said she has extra help at the inn today, so we're good. As soon as we're done at the hospital, you can drop me home and then head to Scoops. She doesn't mind, said so herself. Poppy loves the shop as much as I do. Have you tried any of her special flavors? I think she's making a new one today, salted caramel bacon."

I wrinkle my nose, shaking my head. "Gross. That sounds awful. Do y'all sit around and brainstorm the nastiest flavors possible? What's wrong with good ol' vanilla, anyway?"

Aunt Jess chuckles, stretching her legs out. "You've never been one to live on the edge, Griffin. You should try some of the flavors—sometimes it's the unique combinations that sneak up and grab you." She cuts her eyes at me, and heat creeps up the back of my neck.

"You never know how good something can be unless you give it a try." She locks her gaze on mine for a long second, the kitchen wall clock ticking loudly through the quiet space.

"I'm going to go start getting ready. Everything takes me three times as long with only one hand."

She stands, then shuffles past me and pats my shoulder. "There's more to life than vanilla, Griffin."

I stare down the hallway at her, wondering when exactly my love life became my aunt's latest passion project.

THE CASTING APPOINTMENT TAKES FOREVER. FIRST THE orthopedic doctor runs late, and then there's an emergency and my aunt's pushed on the schedule. They finally call her back an hour later than scheduled; I hope Poppy doesn't have anywhere she needs to be.

By the time Aunt Jess is done, it's almost dinnertime. I drive her home and settle her in the recliner, then nuke leftover chicken and rice the neighbor brought over. After tossing a green salad, I throw a dinner roll on her plate and deliver the food on a tray.

"Thanks, Griffin. But pretty soon I'm going to need to start doing things for myself again—I can't get too comfortable with having you around all the time."

I set the food down, pull up the TV tray and arrange it for her. Food: check. Water: check. Remote: check.

"I'm here now, so let me help. You good? Have everything you need?"

Aunt Jess nods, propping her freshly casted arm gingerly on the tray.

"I should head over to Scoops. That appointment took longer than I thought. Poppy probably needs to get back to the inn."

Aunt Jess nods. "You're right. Go. And yes, I have everything I need. Thanks for driving me today."

I lean down, squeezing her narrow shoulders in a soft hug. "Anytime. Don't wait up for me. You need to get your rest."

She pats my cheek, like she did when I was a boy, and my heart squeezes hard in my chest. For the first time in my life, Aunt Jess seems fragile, vulnerable. The tables flipped when I wasn't looking, and now I'm the caretaker.

"See you later. Tell Poppy I say hello." Her eyes twinkle at the mention of Poppy, and I don't feel so bad anymore.

The sun's dropping in the sky as I drive over to Scoops, the radio tuned to the baseball channel. Atlanta's playing Chicago and we're up by two runs when I ease into a parking spot close to the shop.

"Adams rounds the base and slides into home!" I pound my fist against the wheel, happy that my boy Trevor scored another run for the team.

Too bad I'm here, shoveling ice cream. A sharp pang stabs me in the chest, but I push it away.

I'll get back. I need to focus on my conditioning, getting stronger, and then I'll be back. Better than ever.

Taking a shaky breath, I adjust my baseball hat, pushing my hair from my eyes and sliding the hat back on my head. Probably a month or two left of rehab, then I'll leave Seaglass Beach for good.

Glancing up, I catch sight of Poppy through the window, her blonde hair spilling over her shoulder in a long braid. Smiling and laughing, she chats with a couple and their two kids. She's a natural, totally at ease.

I'll never fit in here like she does.

Poppy *is* Seaglass Beach. She loves this town and it loves her back.

I never feel that way about anywhere I live. Not Atlanta, not Seattle, not Denver.

Definitely not Seaglass Beach.

The family walks out of Scoops, and Poppy spots me, waving. The last rays of sun slant through the glass, and she stands in a golden pool of light. Every single muscle in my body takes notice.

Not the time, Carter. Don't get involved. Nothing good will come of it.

With a deep breath, I lock my Rover and shove through the bubblegum-pink door.

"Thanks for watching the shop today." My voice is gruff as I take mental stock of the store. Everything's sparkling clean, not one stray drip of ice cream anywhere, and soft music carries through the speaker. I try to find something—anything—to fault her with, but come up empty.

Dammit.

Why's she so good at this? It makes hating her that much harder.

"No problem, it was my pleasure. How's Jess? Everything go okay at the hospital?"

She twirls the end of her braid, her aquamarine eyes wide. I shove a hand deep into the pocket of my jeans, trying to ignore the twitch of my cock.

"She's good. Sorry I'm so late—the appointment took forever." I move behind the ice-cream freezer, sidling up next to her at the register. Close enough to catch a faint hint of citrus from her shampoo. Not helping the whole cock situation.

"It's all good. Everything went great—no customer complaints or meltdowns. And the merch display's still standing." She grins up at me, teasing, and I notice she has a faint splash of cinnamon freckles across the bridge of her nose. Freckles that could be cute if she weren't so damn sunshiny all the time.

"I'm guessing the Mommy-and-me group didn't come marching back in here today is all."

"Uh-huh. That must be it." She bites down on her

bottom lip, drawing my attention to it, and fuck, now I can't quit staring at her mouth.

Get it together, Carter.

"Well, thanks for covering for me." I pin my gaze on hers, and a soft pink blush creeps into her cheeks.

"Sure." She holds my gaze for one long second, then scoots past me, our arms brushing.

And fuck me if a bolt of something I haven't felt in a long time rips through me, my hair standing on end.

Poppy spins and sashays out the door. I keep my eyes trained on her curvy ass until she's no longer in sight.

I'll never admit it, but my night just got a lot less interesting.

8

POPPY

Since Liv's an event planner in real life, I task her with the decorations. Even though King said Roman doesn't need streamers, I know he totally does. *Everyone* needs streamers, whether they're turning five or sixty-five. Besides, we're going to all the trouble of having a party—might as well make it as festive as possible, right?

I did advise Liv not to be too extra. Rome's a low-key kinda guy. I doubt she'll be over the top, though—she's a professional.

Setting the cake down carefully on the passenger seat, I send her a quick text:

> Poppy: Picked up the cake. Should be out at ranch in next 30 min

> Liv: Perfect. Parker and I are here, setting up

Five seconds later, Liv sends me a pic of the party prep in progress, and I grin down at my phone.

True to form, Liv's done an amazing job transforming the backyard. A long farmhouse table's dotted with mason jar centerpieces overflowing with hydrangeas. The head chair's strung with dark blue and white balloons, the huge oak tree in the background twinkles with white string lights, and rustic lanterns hang from the branches.

> Poppy: Looks amazing. Rome's gonna love it

> Liv: Thanks, babe. Hope so

> Poppy: He will. You're the best

> Liv: 🙃

Happy with how the party planning's turning out, I crank Smurfy's ignition and slide into Main Street traffic, heading away from the beach. The wind whips through my hair, and I inhale a deep breath of the cool salty air.

I love all seasons in Seaglass Beach, but autumn here is special. The weather's perfect, humidity's low, and the beach is flat and wide. Summer-season people are gone, leaving only the locals. Everyone has room to breathe again.

"Hey, watch it!" I'm thrown from my daydream, smashing hard on the brakes to avoid crashing into the cherry-red pickup truck that cut me off.

The driver of the truck revs his engine and speeds through the yellow light, flipping me the bird and screaming out the window, "See you around, Princess Poppy!"

I screech to a stop, falling back hard against my seat, missing the light.

"Jagger, that asshole! Oh no. No, no, no!" The cake box is tipped sideways, lying on the floorboard. "If that jerk ruined Rome's cake . . ."

I slam Smurfy into park and lean over to retrieve the box, lifting the cake back up onto the seat. The light changes and there's no time to check the damage; I'll deal with it out at the ranch.

I try not to let Jagger ruin my good mood, but that guy sure knows how to get under my skin. The Capellis are a menace to Seaglass Beach society, that's for damn sure—the only reason to lock your doors here at night. Honestly, it's amazing none of them are in jail. But they're just slippery enough to stay on the right side of the law. That, and one of their cousins works for the sheriff's department.

Motoring down the ranch's long gravel driveway, I pull my car up behind Parker's SUV. I don't see Rome's truck, so I'm guessing he's not yet here. I cut the ignition and run around to the passenger door, my gut twisting.

If that asshole ruined my brother's cake . . .

Lifting the lid, I peer into the box, assessing the damage. The white frosting swirls are smudged on one side, and now the cake reads: *Happy Birthday, Ron.* The *o, m,* and *e* are smooshed together, and the exclamation point's smeared into a period.

"Shit," I mutter, staring down at the mess. Hopefully Liv can work her magic and salvage the dessert.

"Hey, Pops." Parker's mellow voice sounds from behind me, and I spin around just as he runs up and squeezes my shoulders.

"Hey."

"Bakery didn't know how to spell 'Roman'?" Parker stares down at the cake mess.

"No, they did. This cake was perfect thirty minutes ago. Then Jagger Capelli cut me off at a stoplight and, well . . ." I point at the damage.

Parker's jaw clenches, his eyes flashing. "That guy's such a dick. We'll try to fix it, c'mon."

He carefully picks up the cake, and together we enter the ranch, heading straight to the kitchen.

I'm always catapulted back in time when I come out here. This is the house where we all grew up—me, Parker, Rome, King—and before that, my parents and grandparents. The ranch has been in the Montgomery family for generations, and now King lives out here and runs things. Rome stays out here a lot, too, but I prefer living in town with people. If King had his way, he'd probably never leave the ranch and just be a hermit.

"You got the cake?" King's voice rumbles across the massive kitchen, echoing off the high wooden rafters.

"Hello to you, too, big brother." I side-hug him, the scent of fresh hay mixed with his woodsy cologne tickling my nose. "And yes, I have the cake, but it kind of got smashed on the way over. Long story . . ."

"It was that fucking weasel, Jagger," Parker says, and inwardly I groan. I should've kept my big mouth shut. I hate the Capellis as much as my brothers, but I'm not going to get into a bar brawl; there's a real possibility one of my siblings will.

"Calm down, Parks. Let's not ruin our night over some smeared frosting. Is Liv still working outside?"

"Yeah, she's finishing up the place settings. King told her it's buffet-style, but she insisted on folding the napkins." Parker shrugs, clearly not understanding Party Planning with Liv 101.

"I'll help her finish up, so we can get this party started."

I hustle out of the kitchen, banging through the screen door—and run straight into a brick wall of solid muscle.

"Oof."

"Sorry!" My palms splay flat against the soft cotton of a gray T-shirt, and my gaze flicks upward, making out a chiseled jawline and a searing dark gaze. "Oh gawd, Griffin, I'm so sorry."

I feel my cheeks flame, a hot flush creeping up my neck as he stares down at my hands, still resting on his abs.

"I—uh—sorry . . . ," I stammer, and I low-key kinda want to melt into the limestone gravel.

"It's fine. You didn't take out the knee, at least." He doesn't move away, and I'm so close to him I'm sure he can hear the jackhammering of my heart.

Butterflies zoom wildly in my stomach at the rumble of his voice, vibrating against my fingers, and I'm tingly all over.

"Are you going to let go of my shirt or . . ." He peers down at my fingers, curled into the fabric of his T-shirt, and I immediately release him, jumping back.

"Gawd, yes. Sorry, I mean . . . what are you doing here, anyway?" I narrow my eyes at him, as much to take the pressure off me as anything.

"I'm here for the get-together. Parker invited me."

"Oh. Right. He didn't tell me you were coming."

"Should he have? I didn't realize you were in charge of the guest list."

I rock back on my heels, fiddling with a loose string on

my skirt. "I'm not. But yeah—he usually tells me these sorts of things."

"I see."

Griffin locks his eyes on mine, and my mouth goes dry.

"I'm going to help Liv with the rest of the setup. All the guys are in there." I hook my thumb back at the house before sprinting away.

That was embarrassing. Nothing like feeling him up right there on the front porch.

But also kind of worth it.

Griffin Carter may be a grumpy jerk, but he's still gorgeous. Even I can admit that.

"Liv—" I half whisper, half shriek. "You'll never guess who's here."

Liv's dark head pops up from the napkin folding. "Griffin?"

"You knew?" I narrow my eyes at her.

Traitor.

"Mm-hmm. Well, I didn't know if he was coming for sure, but I knew Parker invited him."

"And you didn't even tell me? I thought we were besties!"

Liv rolls her eyes at me. "We are. I didn't think it'd be that big of a deal. You know, since you don't like him or anything." The corner of her mouth quirks up, and I smack her lightly on the arm.

"Shut up! Of course it's a big deal. I could have mentally prepared."

"Or shaved your legs." She smirks, and I'm pretty sure my right eye's twitching.

"Stop. First, I always shave my legs. And second, I'm not interested. I told you that."

"Mm-hmm. Sure." She drapes a napkin over the final dinner plate and peruses her handiwork. "Shall we tell them we're ready?"

"I'll stay here. Make sure nothing happens to the table." I wave my hand over the freshly decorated space.

"Okay." She leans in close to me, whispering, "I put you next to him, don't worry."

Then she winks and heads toward the house, chuckling to herself, her shoulders shaking in amusement.

"Not funny, Liv," I call out, slumping down in my seat. "Not funny at all."

9

GRIFFIN

Not gonna lie, every part of me stood up and took notice of Poppy back there. The pretty flush of her cheeks, the fluttering of her long lashes, the way she ramped into hummingbird mode when she touched my chest.

Kinda cute.

If one's into that sort of hyperintense energy.

Which I'm not.

Not usually, anyway.

The bulge in my jeans tells a different story, but I pointedly ignore that, adjusting my pants so it's not so obvious.

"Griff, yo. Glad you could make it." Parker bro hugs me, slapping me on the biceps. "You want a beer?"

"Sure." I accept the chilled green bottle he hands me straight from the fridge. Popping the top, I take a long, cold swig.

Maybe this will cool things off down below.

"You remember King and Liv."

I wave at both of them across the large granite island. King tips his head at me, and Liv waves back.

"There's the birthday boy." King's serious face cracks into a wide smile as Roman sidles into the room, rolling his shirtsleeves up to his elbows.

"Dude. I told you I didn't want a party." Roman grabs the beer Parker offers, and they tap the glass necks together.

"Happy birthday, bro. And it's not a party, just family and friends. Small and intimate." Parker grins, clearly in his element, as I shift from foot to foot, not at all in mine.

"Where's Poppy?" Roman narrows his eyes, glancing around the room.

"Outside. She's 'guarding the table.'" Liv makes air quotes, and King snickers.

"From what? Horseflies?" King takes a swig of his drink, shaking his head.

"You do have big ones out here," Liv says, defending her friend.

"Happens when you live in the country. C'mon, I'm starving. Let's eat." Parker grabs Liv's hand, dragging her outside, and the rest of us follow.

King lets out a long whistle as he takes in the backyard transformation—the table glowing in soft candlelight, the twinkling oak tree. There's even a photo booth with props. "Man, this is fancy. I told Poppy no decorations."

"No. You told me no streamers. I passed that on to the event planner—our future sister-in-law—and she took it from there." Poppy hops up from her chair, embracing Roman in a huge hug. "Happy birthday, big brother."

Rome ruffles her hair, and she bats his hand away, scowling up at him, although she clearly loves the attention.

"I hope you enjoyed that. I'll let it slide, since it's your birthday and all, old man. And why are you so dressed up?"

"I worked a private security gig for the mayor."

"Ah, got it. Of course he'd want a bad-ass former Marine on his detail. For a second there, I thought you had a date or something."

"Ha-freaking-ha. And if I did, I wouldn't tell any of you. Can we eat?" Roman's gaze flicks to the buffet table, where King's already carving meat.

"Smoked these ribs all night; meat's falling off the bone. Come and get it."

Everyone grabs their plates and heads over to the food. I hang back a little, unsure how exactly I got the invite to this incredibly small party.

"Don't be shy." Poppy circles back to the table, bumping my hip against hers. "My brothers are cool. You can be your usual grumpy self; they won't hold it against you. King's pretty grumpy too. Y'all have a lot in common." She peers up at me through her dark lashes, the picture of innocence.

"Who says I'm grumpy?" I press the beer bottle to my lips, take a sip.

She stares back at me, those aqua eyes wide and unblinking.

"You're joking, right?" Her right brow lifts as she tips her head to the side, the thin strap of her shirt sliding down low on her tanned shoulder. My fingers itch to reach out and fix that strap, feel her smooth skin on mine.

Instead, I swallow and shake my head. "No. I'm not joking. I'm not grumpy. I'm realistic."

"Huh." She folds her arms across her chest, empha-sizing her small but perfect breasts, and it takes a monumental effort not to stare at the silky fabric barely concealing what lies beneath.

"I didn't know *realistic* was a synonym for *grumpy*."

"Listen, just because I'm not spitting sunshine and rainbows every day like you doesn't mean I'm grumpy."

"I don't do that." She nibbles on her plump bottom lip, and my entire lower body stiffens. I shove a hand in my pocket to distract and adjust, praying she doesn't notice.

"You do actually do that."

"Do not. I look on the bright side, is all."

"Not everything has a bright side."

She pauses, then smooths her hair down over her shoulder. "Sometimes you have to look harder."

We lock eyes for a long moment before Parker interrupts, breaking the spell. "You two eating today, or are you gonna keep standing around arguing?"

Poppy screws her face up at her brother, then spins and heads to the food table, her hips swaying from side to side.

"Sorry, my sister can be a real pain in the ass." Parker elbows me. "Go grab a plate. King's the cook of the family, so you're in luck."

Setting my beer down, I follow Poppy over to the food. She carefully ignores me as she scoops mac and cheese onto her plate.

I drop my voice low so only she can hear. "There's no bright side to tearing your ACL. Especially when you're a pro athlete."

The serving spoon in her hand freezes midair, and she glances over her shoulder at me. "That's when you need to look harder. Sometimes the bright side isn't obvious—you have to search for it, like a four-leaf clover."

My breath hitches in my throat as I stare into her

bright blue eyes, glowing optimism practically shimmering all around her like an aura. I'm not sure if that's the dumbest or the most profound thing I've ever heard, and the fact that I'm thinking about it at all has me knocked off balance. The hum of the cicadas fills the long silence between us, a light breeze feathering her hair. I swallow hard, ignoring the hammering in my chest.

"Seems like a lot of work," I finally manage to grumble.

Poppy shrugs, lifting one of her light-blonde brows. "Stay grumpy then. But that kind of mindset's bad for healing."

She pivots on her heel and stomps off through the grass, leaving me standing alone, conflicted, and strangely turned on at the food table.

10

GRIFFIN

Clink, clink, clink.

Poppy taps on her wineglass with a spoon, but Parker and Roman keep talking.

Clink, clink, clink. Louder now, and Roman sits up straighter.

"Attention, please!" Poppy's voice rings through the air, and everyone finally shuts up. "As you all know, it's Roman's birthday."

"Hear, hear!" Parker shouts, lifting his bottle and tipping it toward Roman.

"Ahem." Poppy clears her throat, shooting her twin a pointed look.

"What? Just *cheers*ing the birthday boy." Parker shrugs and holds up his palm.

"Anyway—as I was saying—it's time for the Montgomery family birthday tradition."

Parker grins, King shakes his head, and Roman's brows crush together in a grimace. This oughta be good, judging by the reactions.

"For real, Pops? I think we can retire this tradition—we're grown." Roman scowls from his seat at the head of the table.

"Nope. Never too old for this tradition. In fact, I'm definitely going to continue with my kids when the time comes. So let's hear it, go on." Poppy waves her hand, urging him on.

Roman exhales, folding his arms across his chest and tilting his head up to the inky sky.

"Fine. Here goes. I'm thankful for another trip around the sun, another year done. Blessed beyond measure, so much to treasure," Rome recites, glancing around the table at each of his siblings. "My greatest thing in my thirty-fourth year was . . ." He pauses, screwing his mouth up in thought. "Landing the security gig, I guess."

"You sure? You can't guess at your greatest thing—it's a rule," Poppy says, her fingers thrumming the table.

"I'm sure, Poppy." Rome levels his gaze at her, and she shuts up. "And my greatest wish for next year is . . ."

Another long pause, the wind rustling the trees, the red and yellow tiki flames dancing.

"Dude—you didn't even think about this before now or what? You had a whole year," Parker says, his grin wide.

"Shut up, man. I didn't think y'all would make me still do this." Rome scowls down the table at his brother. "My greatest wish this year is sharing the things I love with the people I love."

"Aww, sweet." King smirks.

"I think that's lovely, Rome. Mom and Dad would've loved that." Poppy's voice falters, but she hops up quickly, running over to her brother and hugging his shoulders.

"Now cut the cake. And sorry about the name—long story."

She slides the cake in front of him, along with the knife, and he cuts through the thick white frosting. Carving a slice, he takes a big bite, and everyone claps and starts singing a very off-key rendition of "Happy Birthday."

And even though the whole tradition is corny as hell, a dull pang aches in my chest. The ease, the camaraderie, the clear bond the Montgomerys have with each other.

It's exactly how I always wanted my family to be.

But we never were. Even before my mom died and definitely not after. No, we were the microwave-TV-dinner family, not the special-birthday-dinner family.

"Excuse me." I push away from the table and stand. "Restroom?"

Parker points at the house, gesturing to the right. "Off the kitchen, down the hall on the left."

"Thanks." I take long, quick strides across the grass, the laughter and chatter of the party growing fainter the farther away I get.

I let myself into the house, the air-conditioning a cool balm to my skin. The kitchen's quiet, peaceful, and I have half a mind to sink into a leather chair in the great room and relax for a minute, but I don't. Instead, I walk down the hall toward the bathroom, glancing at the family photos on the wall as I go.

Poppy and Parker in grade school, sitting on tiny wooden stools, smiling at the camera.

King in a cap and gown, graduating from high school.

An action shot of Roman pitching in a baseball game.

The entire Montgomery clan at the beach for a formal family portrait, all wearing various shades of blue. Poppy and Parker can't be older than freshmen in high school. Poppy's smiling, of course. I've never seen a photo of Mrs. Montgomery before and note how much Poppy resembles her mother—the same bow mouth, small frame, sparkly eyes. I bet they had a lot in common.

Probably like I did with my mom.

A hard lump lodges in my throat as I try to squash the wave of sadness rolling over me out of fucking nowhere.

Get it together, Carter. Go to the john, splash some water on your face. Man up.

I find the bathroom and do my business, thinking about practical stuff like how many runs it's possible for a single batter to score per game. Anything to get my mind off the emotional roller coaster.

Drying my hands, I unlock the door—and run straight into Poppy.

"Oof. Shit. Sorry," she murmurs.

I stare down at her hands, splayed on my chest this time.

"You trying to take out my knee again?" I stare down at her and watch as her cheeks flush a soft shade of pink.

"No, no. Definitely not." She stumbles through the words, and the corners of my lips twitch. She's cute when she's flustered.

"Good. Because I can't afford another setback. Not while my aunt's laid up, anyway."

"Oh, yeah. Right." She still doesn't step out of my space, and we're only inches apart now, standing in the doorframe.

"I was just coming to check on you, make sure you were okay. I thought maybe you left." Her chest rises and falls with each breath. She licks the corner of her mouth, her tongue gliding along her bottom lip, and I can't look away. Every nerve in my body's on edge, tension simmering between us.

I swallow hard, my muscles flexing beneath her hands. "I didn't."

"Good." She tips her head up, those aqua eyes wide, and I don't know what in the hell possesses me in the moment. My hands slide down over her narrow hips, pulling her in even closer, and a tiny gasp escapes her lips right before I press my mouth to hers and swallow up the sound.

She's warm and sweet, tasting like vanilla, her lips soft. She opens her mouth to me, wasting no time. Her hands curl into my shirt as my tongue sweeps in, tangling with hers. Each of us vying for position, wanting to dominate. Be in charge of whatever this thing is between us.

My body thrums like it does when I'm at bat, hyper-aware of every inhale, every exhale. A warm sensation rolls through me, lighting up my skin inch by inch until I feel like I'm glowing—a hot, fiery ball.

Like I'm flying too close to the sun.

I pull away, breaking the kiss.

"Oh." Poppy's mouth forms a perfect pink O, her lips slightly swollen. She's beautiful, standing there, her neck and chest flushed. Still clutching my shirt, as if I'm her life-line or something.

"Sorry. I don't know what just happened there."

She gazes up at me through dark lashes. "I'm pretty sure we just kissed."

"Yeah, I know that."

"Well, what's confusing then? Haven't you ever seen a romance movie?"

"A few. But this isn't that. Right?"

"I don't know what this is." Poppy bites at her puffy lower lip, drawing my attention back to her stupidly kissable mouth.

We stare at each other for a long moment, my heart beating harder and faster than I'd like, with Poppy's fingers hovering just above.

"I should go." I huff out the breath I'd been holding, my shoulders relaxing a little.

"So soon? You didn't even get cake."

"I need to check on my aunt." I shove a hand in my pocket, easing the denim away from my rigid cock.

"Right." Poppy releases my shirt, drawing back into her own space. "Tell her I hope she's feeling better—and I'm looking forward to her return. New flavors to try and all that."

"Will do. Tell your brothers thank you for me."

"Sure. Night, Griffin." She slips out the door, heading back to the party without so much as a backward glance.

"Shit," I mutter to the empty hallway, scrubbing a hand over the back of my neck.

Ever since I tore my ACL and ended up in Seaglass Beach, I have no idea what I'm fucking doing—and that feeling scares the hell out of me, if I'm being completely honest.

And Poppy Montgomery—all five foot nothing of her —only compounds the feeling. Yet I can't seem to stay away, like she has a freaking gravitational pull on me.

The best thing to do here is walk—far, far away. Maybe even run.

So why am I standing still all of a sudden, after a lifetime of running?

11

POPPY

"Where's Griffin?" Parker loops his arm around Liv's shoulders, his fingers caressing her arm. Like his hand is a part of her, one freaking unit.

Casual and annoyingly sweet.

I shrug. "He had to go."

"You scared him off?" Parker teases, grinning.

I scowl across the table at him. "Funny. No. He had to go check on his aunt. Said to tell y'all thanks."

"Uh-huh," Rome chimes in, takes a sip of his beer. "He's cool. I like him."

"Me too," Parker says.

"He's all right." King leans back in his chair, and apparently the vote's freaking unanimous, which never happens—all the Montgomery brothers actually like Griffin.

The man's a damn unicorn.

Not that it matters after what just went down in the bathroom. We kissed, and then he jetted faster than any guy's ever jetted on me before.

I can see how he'd be good at baseball, running around all those bases.

Apparently running's his thing.

"Pops? You wanna help take stuff inside, or you gonna sit out here and keep the horseflies company?" King nudges my shoulder, and I almost fall out of my chair.

"Yeah, yeah. I got it." I stand and grab my plate, stacking several others along with the silverware on top, and start back toward the house.

Liv falls in step beside me, leaning in close and whispering, "What really happened? Did you two have a fight or something?"

"No." I keep my eyes trained on the grass straight ahead of me, avoiding eye contact. I know if I meet her gaze, she'll instantly suss me out.

"He really just left?" Her tone tips up, and my insides churn. I'm not a good liar.

I inhale, the hesitation just long enough to give her pause.

"I knew it!" She jumps up, a little hop, and squeezes my arm. "You kissed him, didn't you?"

"Gawd, how'd you figure that out?" My cheeks burn, a hot flush creeping up my neck, and I'm glad it's pitch black out here now, save for the tiki torches in the distance.

"We've been best friends forever. You always avoid eye contact when you do something you're unsure about. Spill —what's he like? Is he a good kisser?"

"Unfortunately, yes. Very."

"Why unfortunately?" She narrows her eyes at me, her brow furrowed.

"Because I'm pretty sure it was a one-time thing. He

bolted, Liv. Well, first he apologized; then he bolted. Which kinda made it worse." My gut clenches at the memory, even as a delicious shiver rolls over me, remembering the kiss.

"Ouch. But maybe that's more about him, ya know? Maybe he's uncertain. His life's kind of up in the air at the moment."

"Maybe. Or maybe he's really not interested."

"Doubtful. He eyed you all night long."

"Really? You think?" I pause outside the door.

"Definitely." Liv nods, her dark hair brushing over her shoulders.

"Now what?"

"Play it cool. Let him make the next move."

"That could take a while."

"Trust me." She reaches out and squeezes my arm.

I'm not sure when Liv got so wise in the relationship department, seeing as how she's had like one long-term boyfriend in her life besides my brother, but I decide to leave that alone for now.

"Okay. I'll keep you posted."

We head into the kitchen, where Parker's busy loading the dishwasher and King's washing the sheet pans that don't fit, while Roman dries.

"Thought you two got lost. Parker was about to come on a search-and-rescue mission." King hands Rome another pan.

"Y'all left lots of dishes out there." I bend down, loading my plates into the dishwasher and skillfully avoiding eye contact, the familiar prickle of heat climbing up my neck. I really don't want to revisit the Griffin topic.

Instead, I take the offensive and change the subject. "I saw Juliet Capelli in town the other day. She's working over at the Tipsy Taco."

The kitchen goes silent except for the rush of running water in the sink and the clank of dishes being rearranged.

"Huh. I haven't seen her around town much. Not since the Labor Day party." Parker wedges a pot into the dishwasher, and I catch Rome and King exchanging a glance.

"I guess she's back for good. Montana must not have worked out for her." I tuck my hair behind my ear. "Too bad for that. Getting away from her brothers had to be a positive for her. I really thought she'd make it out of this town."

King doesn't say anything, just stares out the window, his back ramrod straight. Rome clears his throat, throws down the dish towel.

"Thanks for the party, guys. But I'm beat. Long day at the office."

"Must be tough scanning all six people who go into Town Hall." I elbow him and he glares at me.

"For your info, I also inspect every piece of physical correspondence addressed to the mayor. And let me tell you—that takes some time. He gets more mail than you'd think."

"Seriously? Who's writing to him? And why don't they stop by and chat? Would be a lot quicker," I say.

"Mostly Maggie McGurty, from what I can tell. Lots and lots of letters, all bitching about the tourists." Rome shakes his head. "Guess she doesn't understand she lives in a beach town dependent on tourism."

"Pretty sure there's a whole lot Maggie McGurty

doesn't understand." King shuts the water off and dries his hands on his jeans. "Liv, you outdid yourself on the party."

Liv blushes—King giving anyone a compliment is a huge deal and she knows it—and Parker leans over, dropping a kiss on the top of her head.

Like I said—sickening. But also, I'm a tiny bit jealous of what they have together. Must be nice to have a guy adore you like that. Parker acts like Liv hung the freaking moon.

"Glad to do it. Happy birthday, Roman." She smiles at my brothers, and Parker grins, wide and proud.

"Thanks. I appreciate it." Rome grabs his keys, and I take the chance to make my exit as well.

"I'm leaving too. Thanks for the party, King." I hug each of my brothers and Liv goodbye, antsy and ready to be home in my bed. "See y'all."

I duck out before anyone can ask me more questions about Griffin.

Besides, there's not much to tell. And I sure as hell don't need any relationship advice from my brothers.

ALL THE NEXT DAY I MENTALLY REPLAY MY KISS WITH Griffin.

The Kiss. With a capital K.

Because that's how freaking good the kiss was.

I'm tingly just thinking about it. Griffin's hard pecs beneath my palms, the clean scent of his cologne mixed with the spicy taste of barbecue on his lips. The heat radiating between us.

Good grief. I'm hot and bothered standing here alone in the lobby.

Stupid Griffin Carter the grump.

And, of course, King Asshole didn't call, text, absolutely fucking nothing.

Ugh.

He probably kisses women all the damn time and doesn't call. Because that's the kind of guy I bet he is.

A runner. A love-'em-and-leave-'em type.

Which isn't my type at all.

So why can't I stop thinking about him?

Honestly, it's getting ridiculous. So far today I've sent room service to the wrong villa, screwed up a guest reservation, and bobbled the laundry-service delivery. At this rate I'm going to single-handedly run the Seaglass Inn into the ground.

All over a stupid Kiss.

I bet he looks amazing naked.

FML.

Now I can't stop thinking about his tight ass, his washboard abs, his stupidly broad, strong chest.

Dammit.

Maybe I should text him. Suggest we sleep together and get it over with so we can both move on. Seems like something he'd totally be up for. Even grumpy assholes like to have sex, right?

I grab my cell from the desk, then scroll through my contacts and find his number. Staring at the keyboard, I finally tap out:

> Poppy: Hey, it's Poppy. About last night
> . . .

I reread the text, backspace, and start again.

> Poppy: Hi! This is Poppy. I had a good
> time with you last night

No. That sounds too upbeat, then morphs into weird and desperate.

> Poppy: This is Poppy. Wanna bang and
> get it out of our system?

I giggle at this message, knowing I'd never send something so audacious, so bold. But it is kind of funny.

"Excuse me? Miss? We're here to check in. Last name's Pierre."

Glancing up, I shoot the family of four standing in front of me my brightest smile, flipping my phone over quickly.

"Welcome to the Seaglass Inn. We're so glad you're here. Where are y'all joining us from?"

"Toronto. We caught the first flight out this morning." The man yawns, dark circles under his eyes.

"Wow, all the way from Canada! That must've been a long trip." I find their reservation on the computer and grab the key from the corkboard behind me. "I have you here for six nights, all checked into villa number three. You'll love that one—it has a great view of the ocean from the patio!"

"Wonderful. This might be an odd request, but do you

have a tailor at the hotel? We're here for a wedding, and my son's suit needs to be altered."

"We don't have a tailor here at the inn, but there's an excellent one in town. Hang on and I'll get the number for you." I reach for my phone, automatically tapping the screen to bring it to life.

Whoosh.

The familiar sound of a text message sending echoes through the lobby, bouncing off the tiles, and my stomach drops.

"No, no, no, no!" I moan, staring at the now-blue text bubble and the dreaded word *Delivered*. A hot prickle of panic tingles up and down my arms as I gape at my cell.

I did not just hit send on a text to King Asshole asking him if he wants to bang.

Oh. My. Gawd.

Honestly, shoot me right now because I'd rather be fucking dead.

"Um—are you okay?" Mr. Pierre's dark brows squish together in concern.

"No. I mean, yes. I'm fine." My hands flutter through the air, my nervous system on high alert. I need to get this dude the tailor's number, then tell Griffin something —anything—to let him know that text was a mistake, a joke.

"Uh—here's the number." I scrawl the tailor's number on a Seaglass Inn notepad, ripping it off and handing it to him, along with the key to the room and the map. "Do you need help with your bags? Here's villa three. You can drive or walk down the path."

"Yes, help with the bags would be great, thank you."

I mash the button for the bell service, and five minutes

later luggage is loaded high on the gold cart and Tristan's walking the Pierre family over to villa three.

Ding.

Oh my gosh. A text.

I'm scared to read it, but also dying to know what it says. Hands trembling, I lift my cell.

> Griffin: Wow. Way to cut to the chase

I stare down at the text, reread it.

He didn't say no.

> Griffin: Not the most romantic offer ever

I can't help it. I giggle, grinning down at my phone. Who knew Griffin would have jokes? A tiny bit of the panic ebbs, and my breathing is only super fast now versus the hyperventilation of a moment ago.

Oh shit. Now I have to text back. Preferably something witty. Which is tough, given the Mach 10 level of embarrassment flooding through me.

I contemplate texting *Sorry, wrong number*, but figure that won't help me reach my end goal. Which is actually banging Griffin, let's be honest.

> Poppy: Well? You in?

I already 1,000 percent embarrassed myself. Laid all my cards on the table. Held nothing back. Might as well go all in and double-down while I'm at it.

Griffin: When you whisper sweet nothings
like that . . . how can I resist?

I giggle at my phone, heat creeping into my face, all the way up to the tips of my ears. My stupid heart's pounding double-time and I'm giddy, my stomach flip-flopping around like a fish on the beach.

Griffin: And here I thought you were a
romantic

Poppy: I can be practical when necessary

Griffin: Sexy

Poppy: Strange turn-on, but okay . . .

Griffin: You gonna analyze me all night?
Or are we gonna do this?

Now's my chance to back out gracefully, pretend it was all a joke, tell him the text was a mistake. The tips of my fingers tingle as I gnaw my bottom lip, bouncing behind the desk, deciding my fate.

Finally, I type:

Poppy: When and where?

Griffin: Meet me at Scoops in twenty
minutes

OMG.

This is happening.

I'm gonna bang Griffin Carter, King Asshole, pro base-ball star. Potentially in his aunt's ice-cream parlor.

I've never been so terrified and so excited at the same time, and I'm not sure what to think about it.

All I do know is I need to log out of the computer and go change my panties. One, because they're not all that sexy, and two, because Griffin doesn't need the physical evidence of the effect his stupid text messages had on me.

12

———————

GRIFFIN

WELL, THAT WAS A SURPRISE.

Can't say I've ever had a text quite like that before.

Sure, I've had women slide into my DMs and ask if I'm single, but I've never had such a blatant proposition.

Guess Poppy wants to cut to the chase. No wining and dining necessary.

Which suits me just fine. Less effort on my part.

Not that I was going to go there at all. But after last night, maybe—just maybe—the thought of going farther with Poppy *might* have crossed my mind.

Maybe.

Fine.

It had.

All night long and half of today, if I'm being honest.

Can you blame me? She might be annoying, but that doesn't diminish her overall hotness. It may even enhance it because some animalistic, barbaric, caveman part of me kind of wants to fuck the sunshine right out of her.

I think she's onto something here. We'll have a quick

bang and get it out of our system. Then we can forget any of this ever happened and move on with our lives.

Because she's obviously not my type. All that cheerfulness and positivity is downright annoying.

Jingle, jingle.

The front door opens and in glides Poppy. And damn if my dick doesn't rise to attention and salute her.

She's every bit as pretty as she was last night, wearing a very short blue sundress with spaghetti straps. Showing off her tanned arms and her long legs, her honey-blonde hair falling in soft waves over her shoulders.

"Hey." Her voice comes out breathy, and the sound makes my dick twitch in my pants.

"Hey." I force the word out, my throat suddenly dry, my palms sweaty.

Which is weird because I'm not really involved here. This is a casual hookup, that's all.

So why the fuck am I so nervous right now?

This isn't a date, Carter. Calm the fuck down.

"You sure about this?" I ask, leveling my gaze at her across the counter, trying to act calm and not give off any anxious vibes.

She nods, standing taller and straighter, her breasts round and perky in the thin, gauzy fabric of her dress.

"Flip the sign and I'll get the lights."

She does as instructed, flipping the sign from OPEN to CLOSED, while I dim the lights. Now the only light in the room comes from the faint white glow of the ice-cream cooler, the two of us shadowy figures in the dark.

"Make sure you lock the door."

The click of the lock is deafening in the quiet, the sound bouncing off the tile floor.

"We can go back into the office." I hook my thumb toward the space behind me, and she crosses the room wordlessly. In the dark, I can't read her facial expression. Is she anxious? Excited? Unsure? I can't tell.

I lead the way to the office, Poppy right behind me, close enough I catch the faint scent of coconuts and something floral. Every muscle in my body is taut and ready to go, leaving me more confused than ever.

"Do you do this often?" I ask, peering over my shoulder as I unlock the office door, holding it open for her.

"No, never. Do you?" One of her brows rises high as she saunters past me, her hips swaying.

"No. I don't." I close and lock the door behind me, and now we're alone in the dark. Fumbling around, I find the desk lamp, click it on. A warm glow fills the small space, soft light highlighting the angles of Poppy's high cheekbones, the curves of her body.

Against my better judgment, I do want to bang her.

Inhaling deeply, I take two large steps forward, backing her up against the desk.

"Oh." Her eyes widen, pupils large and dark, her breathing shallow.

"This is your chance to bail." I lock my eyes on hers. She runs her tongue along her lower lip, considering, as I wait.

"No way," she finally whispers.

Without another word, I lace my fingers with hers, pressing up against her small body, and meld my lips to hers.

It's even better than last night, our connection instant, electric. A zing of excitement shoots through me, from my head all the way down to my toes, and it's as if I'm tumbling through the air, free-falling. There's no net and I'm skydiving, but I'm not worried about hitting the ground. Because the possibility of there even being a ground doesn't seem feasible in this moment.

Everything's floating, the concept of gravity false, imaginary.

That's how fucking amazing this thing between us is.

There's no bottom, no hard earth.

Damn.

She's all white, fluffy clouds and vibrant rainbows and bright sunshine.

Kissing Poppy's like standing in a sunbeam, and I'm glowing from the inside out.

"Griffin," she murmurs into my open mouth, squeezing my fingers tight. She shimmies her hips against me, rubbing on my hard cock, and I don't think I've ever wanted someone this much before.

I want to touch her, taste her, take every ounce of her she's willing to give to me.

"Poppy." I slide one hand up her hip, along her torso and stomach, my fingertips grazing the swell of her breast. She pushes her chest out, and I take that as an invitation, cupping her. She slips her tongue into my mouth as I stroke, bringing her nipple to a sharp peak. I lower the strap of her dress from her shoulders, pushing the fabric down and exposing her bra.

With my other hand, I unhook it and toss the lacy undergarment to the side, all my attention focused on her perky tits. Her cheeks blush pink under my gaze, and she squirms a little.

"What?" I ask, fondling her smooth skin, massaging circles around her nipples.

"Nothing, it's just . . . I'm sure you've seen lots, and mine are . . ." She lowers her eyes, breaking eye contact. "Small."

"They're perfect," I half say, half grunt, gently kneading and pinching her nipples before bending down to rain kisses across her chest. I tip my head up to look at her. "And I wouldn't say that if I didn't mean it."

The vibration of my voice against her flesh causes chill bumps to rise on the bare skin, the lamp behind bathing her in a soft glow, and I've definitely never seen this side of Poppy before. Raw. Vulnerable.

She smiles down at me, her body relaxing as I lick and suck, my teeth grazing the puckered skin. A moan escapes from her lips as her fingers rake through my hair, sending shock waves rippling down my spine. She tugs at the back of my T-shirt, lifting the fabric up and over my head.

"There. That's more fair," she says, as I ease away, chucking the shirt to the ground. Her hands glide across my skin, her fingers tracing the inky patterns of my tattoos.

"What's the bear for?" She runs the pad of her finger along the dark black line on my biceps, looping around and down, then back up again.

"My college mascot."

"I thought maybe you were a big-time camping fanatic. Or a Boy Scout."

I chuckle, skimming my thumb down her soft cheek, then along the line of her jaw.

"No. Didn't have time for the Boy Scouts. I was too busy playing baseball." I cup her face, pressing my lips to hers. She wraps her hands around my neck, pulling me closer to her, and I deepen our kiss, intertwining my tongue with hers. Her fingers tickle my neck, my shoulders, my upper back, pressing and massaging away the tension lying deep in my muscles.

I ease my hand down her arm with the lightest of touches, back down to her hip, then down her upper thigh before tiptoeing under her dress. She inhales a sharp, breathy gasp, but doesn't pull away. I flatten my hand on her thigh, the heat warming my palm, then slide toward her inner thigh. My hand creeping up between her legs, she widens her stance, granting me full access. I don't hesitate, palming her satin panties and rubbing, the silky fabric damp beneath my hand.

She rubs against me, urging me on, and I answer her need, finding her clit through the thin material and pinching it.

"Oh, yes," she moans as I slide her panties to the side, touching her bare skin.

"I guess you don't hate me that much," I tease, nipping at her neck as I stroke her.

"I never said I hated you." The words come out in a staccato, her chest and neck flushed. "Do you hate me?" She arches her back, forcing more friction and contact between our bodies.

I grab her hand, guiding it down to my rock-hard cock. "Does it seem like I hate you?"

She blushes and laughs, shrugging. "I don't know, this could be a hate fuck."

"I don't hate-fuck," I reassure her as she unbuttons my pants, then slides them down until they drop to the floor and I kick them off in a heap. My cock twitches in my boxer briefs, and I pull them off, freeing him.

"Wow. Not a lot of pretense here," Poppy jokes,

reaching out and stroking me, her hand soft and silky, encircling my cock in the exact perfect grip.

"You said bang and get it out of our system. That kind of precludes pretense." I hook my thumbs in the sides of her panties, easing them down her thighs until they pool on the ground. She steps out of them, kicking them to the side; then she lets the dress slide all the way down and off her body.

"Gorgeous," I murmur, my voice deep and husky as my eyes rake over her. She's absolutely fucking perfect, and I don't know how the hell I got here, but I damn sure don't want to stop now.

"Same," she says, stepping toward me, her hands roaming the hard planes of my muscles. I flex beneath her touch, my muscles ropy, taut, ready. I'm wound tighter than a rubber band and feel like I may snap.

"Come here." I grab her round ass, pulling her to me, crushing my mouth to hers. Her breasts smashed up against my chest, my cock twitching on her stomach, every inch of flesh between us hot. I massage her ass, and she moans into my mouth, her tongue tangling with mine. Pressing her thighs up against the desk, I pin her in place, my heart hammering double-time in my chest.

I want this woman. Right here, right now.

Lifting her up onto the desk, I spread her legs, easing her as close to the edge as possible before dipping my finger into her wetness. She bites down on her lip, her head falling back as I slide another finger in, stretching her and getting her ready for my cock. She bucks against my hand, and I pump in and out of her for one minute, two, kissing her neck and shoulders. Nipping at her tender skin, leaving the faintest hint of a bite mark.

"Fuck me, Griffin," she whispers, pushing her body into mine, writhing on the wooden desk. "Please."

I pull out, grab the condom from my wallet, sheathe up. "You're sure?" I ask one more time.

"Yes." She nods, biting down on her lip, and I have consent. Brushing my cock up and down, I slide through her wetness, then into her tight pussy. She wraps her legs around me, and I push deeper into her, her muscles tightening around my cock. We find a rhythm, my hips rocking against her, pistoning in and out. Every muscle in my body contracts, racing toward sweet release. She grips my ass, squeezing me to her, her skin sticky with sweat as I pound into her.

"Fuck, you're gorgeous," I murmur, her tits bouncing, her nipples sharp, pink points. I pinch and roll one of the buds as she milks my cock.

"Oh, oh, oh," she screams, pleasure dancing across her face, and I know she's close. I pound into her, hard, pushing her over the edge. Her nails scratch across the sensitive skin of my back, and I follow right behind, shooting my hot release.

"Fuck," I hiss, clasping her tight against my chest as we both come down. She's so small in my arms, ripples of pleasure still rolling through her tiny body.

I have a strange urge to hold her, stroke her skin, stay just like this and watch her breathe.

Soak in all the goodness my body can hold and she can afford to give.

Shit.

That's *not* how you're supposed to feel after a quick get-it-out-of-your-system bang, and I know deep down that I am royally and truly fucked.

13

POPPY

Wow. Just wow.

That was one hell of a bang.

Felt more like a seismic shift.

An earthquake, a tsunami, and a red-hot fire, all in one.

King Asshole knows how to fuck, that's for sure.

I clear my throat and brush away the sweaty hair clinging to my face. "That was . . . good."

Griffin cocks his head at me, one dark brow raised high. "Good?"

I lick my lips, try to get ahold of my shaky breathing. "Maybe a little bit better than good."

"A little better?" He screws up his mouth, frowning.

"Fine. It was really good."

"The best you ever had?"

"Now let's not go getting cocky. We're in a cramped—and very hot, I might add—office, on a desk. 'Best' might be a stretch. But I'll give you top-five status."

He huffs out a breath, raking a hand through his messy hair. Hair that I messed, twining my fingers in it.

"Damn. Harsh. Only top five?"

"You drive a hard bargain, Carter. Fine—top three."

He holds his palms up. "Hey, I'm not asking for any special favors from the judges. If it wasn't a top-three performance, I understand."

The corners of my mouth twitch, and I can't help but smile. "No special favors. One judge is a little prickly because of past history, but she could probably move beyond the bullshit and concede top three."

"Seems fair and reasonable. You know—since it's a performance-based assessment and all."

I laugh. For a grumpy asshole, Griffin's actually pretty funny.

My gaze drops to his hand running lazily up and down my thigh, and a bubble rises in my chest, followed by a wave of panic.

What the hell did we just do? And what did it mean?

"Um . . . I should go." I gnaw the corner of my lip, and Griffin's hand stills on my thigh.

"Okay." He inches his body away, and a gnawing, hollow feeling lodges in my gut. I hop off the desk, then scoop my bra and panties up off the floor.

Turning toward the wall and away from Griffin, I throw my clothes on as fast as possible, my legs twitchy with the sudden urge to run. When I turn around, he's pulled his clothes back on as well, save for his shirt.

He *is* gorgeous, all strong, hard muscle. And when he smiles? He's a ten. Better than a ten, but I wouldn't ever tell him that. He already has a huge ego—no need to add to it.

"So . . . thanks for that. I'll see you around, I guess." I wave awkwardly at him, and maybe I'm imagining things here, but I swear his face falls. He almost seems disappointed.

"Yeah. Okay." He doesn't make a move as I walk toward the door, unlock it, and step out into the much-cooler main shop area.

I focus on my footsteps—one, two, one, two—heading straight for the door, a wave of emotion washing over me. A little bit of shame, a big bit of disappointment.

It's not his fault, really. I'm the one who suggested a quick bang, so I shouldn't expect more from him.

"Poppy, wait . . ."

I freeze, my hand resting on the metal knob. Glancing over my shoulder, I lock eyes with Griffin. Then he's behind me, his hand at my waist, spinning me around to face him.

He hesitates before reaching out and stroking my cheek with the rough pad of his thumb, tracing the line of my jaw.

"Thanks for texting tonight."

I can barely breathe, staring up into Griffin's deep-blue eyes, our bodies almost touching.

"Um—you're welcome?" I'm not sure what the right response is here; I'm way out of my league.

"I—" He pauses again, swallows hard, his Adam's apple bobbing in his neck. "I'd like a chance to get into the top three."

The pit in my stomach vanishes, a lightness filling my chest as happiness ripples through me.

I squash the urge to screw with him. "Okay. The judges will allow a repeat performance."

His face breaks into a wide smile, his teeth gleaming in the soft light of the freezer.

"Name the time and the place," I say in my most official-sounding tone.

"Do I get bonus points for venue?" He wrinkles his nose as I contemplate.

"Sure, why not?"

"Okay. Challenge accepted. See you tomorrow."

"Tomorrow?"

"No time like the present." He winks at me and my lower body tightens, heat unfurling low in my belly again.

"Okay then. I'll be ready."

I practically skip out of Scoops, looking forward to tomorrow way more than I ever have before.

As soon as I climb into Smurfy, I pull out my cell and impulse-text Liv:

> Poppy: OMG. You'll never guess what just happened

My thumb hovers over the send arrow, but something stops me. I'm not sure what it is, but I don't want to share this thing between me and Griffin right now.

Even with my very best friend.

Instead, I delete the text, letter by letter, until the box is empty. A blank white space.

I click my phone off and drive home with the windows rolled all the way down, the dull roar of the waves calming my jangly nerves.

14

POPPY

For someone who had sex less than twenty-four hours ago, I'm awfully edgy. I jump at a slight breeze tickling my skin, and every jingle of the inn door chime ringing through the air sends a shock through me. At this rate, I may combust before Griffin has his shot at the number-one top-performance slot.

Which he totally already has. But I can't let him know that.

Man's gotta have goals, right?

I check my phone every five minutes, waiting for his text with the time and place.

The morning drags by and no text.

I eat lunch at the reception desk, scrolling through social media, phone in hand.

Still nothing.

When three p.m. rolls around and I'm still waiting, a hot panic starts bubbling through me. *What if he doesn't text me? What if he changed his mind?*

That would be embarrassing. I pride myself on being

able to read a room, and I didn't pick up any not-gonna-call vibes.

Buzz, buzz.

Finally, a text.

> Liv: Want to grab a drink at Manta Ray's tonight?

Argh. It's not even from Griffin. And what am I supposed to say here? Should I fess up to Liv? Evade? Maybe I should say yes and go to Manta Ray's with her, because Griffin might be standing me up anyway.

I thrum my fingers on the desk, staring up at the ceiling fan and weighing my options.

> Poppy: Can't tonight, babe. Sorry

There. I didn't lie. Not really. I mean, I guess I *could* technically go.

> Liv: Bummer. I was hoping to hang out with you. Miss you!

My stomach twists into a tight knot. Truthfully, I miss her, too, and it would be great to see her. And I hate the idea of blowing her off, especially for a guy.

But—Griffin.

Just thinking about yesterday, how he wrapped his muscular arms around me and held me up against his chest, kissed me like I've never been kissed before.

Yeah. Sorry, Liv. Not tonight. I don't want to risk losing my opportunity to be with him again.

Buzz, buzz.

Oh geez. I hope this isn't going to be a follow-up twenty-questions text. I'm not sure how much dodge-and-weave I have left in me.

Griffin: My house. 8 p.m.

A flush rushes over me, every nerve vibrating.

He cut right to the chase. No pretense here. At least he's not standing me up.

Griffin: 118 Driftwood Lane

Heart pounding, I wait a few seconds before tapping out a response. I don't want to seem too eager, like I was sitting around waiting for his text.

Poppy: See you later

I debate a kissing emoji but decide against it. Captain Grumpypants doesn't seem like an emoji kinda guy.

Griffin: Looking forward to it

Hmm . . . wasn't expecting that. Maybe Griffin's not as grumpy as I thought.

Humming to myself, I smile, counting down the hours until I see him again.

AT SIX P.M., I LOG OUT AT THE RECEPTION DESK AND walk the hundred or so steps over to my villa apartment to get ready. Least I can do is shower, maybe blow-dry my hair. I can't make it look like I'm actually *trying* here, but all things being equal, I'd rather impress Griffin than not.

The man is gorgeous, even if he is King Asshole. Definitely worth a little effort.

An hour later, I'm ready—I even put mascara on for the occasion—and I'm wearing my favorite black romper with leather lace-up sandals. I still have an hour to kill, so I pour myself a glass of wine and settle on the couch, flipping the TV to my favorite home reno show.

Knock, knock, knock.

Huffing out a breath, I set my wine down and check the peephole.

Shit.

It's Parker. I hope he doesn't need anything important, and I really hope he doesn't ask a bunch of questions.

I swing the door open and act nonchalant. "Hey."

He squints down at me. "What are you doing all dressed up? Thought you and Liv weren't going out tonight?"

Dammit. And this is why I didn't want my brother to date my best friend. Now he knows all my business, all the time. Versus before when he knew most of my business, most of the time.

"We're not going out. And I'm not dressed up. What are you talking about?" I gesture down at my outfit. "I've had this forever."

"Maybe. But you don't lounge around in it. Usually when I stop by, you're not even wearing pants." Parker shoves through the door, letting himself into my apartment.

Rude.

"Not true, Parks. I always wear pants."

"Ha ha ha—no, you don't. Do you even know yourself?" He scans the room, eyebrows raised. "Seriously —what's up?"

"Nothing." I twirl my hair, my stomach swirling. No way am I telling Parker about Griffin.

No freaking way.

"What are you doing here anyway?" I pop my hand on my hip and shift the focus to Parker's favorite topic —himself.

"I'm covering for Julio tonight, and I need the key to the supply closet. I must've picked up the wrong set of keys at home, because it's not on here." Parker jingles his key ring in my direction.

"Okay, I think I have a spare somewhere around here."

Gratefully turning my back on him, I head over to the junk drawer in the kitchen and rifle around for the extra key.

"Aha! Here it is—one supply closet key for you." I deposit the key in Parker's outstretched palm as he stares me down.

"Thanks. You sure nothing's up? You're awfully antsy. You haven't stopped moving since I got here."

"Parks!" I heave out a huge, dramatic sigh. "You've been here, like, three minutes! And you asked for a key and I found it for you. Stop reading into every little thing. Besides, you're one to talk, sneaking around with Liv behind my back for ages."

Parker runs a hand through his cropped hair, his lips a

thin, tight line. "Yeah, I know. I'm glad that's behind us now and we're all one big happy family. Hey—speaking of family. How's Griffin's aunt doing? Have you seen him lately? Liv was asking me about Jess."

Panic swells in my chest at the mention of Griffin, my cheeks burning under his gaze.

"Uh, I saw him yesterday. Briefly. At Scoops."

Not a lie. We did see each other. Naked. But my twin brother doesn't need to know all the nitty-gritty details.

"And Jess is doing better, I think. She's out for a few more weeks, though."

"Glad she's on the mend. Everything good with Griffin? He left the party so fast, I didn't get a chance to connect with him. Me and Rome were thinking about inviting him to grab a beer this weekend."

"He seemed fine." I work to keep my voice steady, neutral. Nonincriminating.

"You think he'd want to hang out? We didn't scare him off, did we?" Parker shoves his hand in his pocket, shifting from foot to foot.

"I have no idea if he wants to hang out, Parks. Ask him. And no, I don't think you scared him away."

In fact, I'm fairly certain I did, but I'm not confessing that little tidbit to my brother.

"Cool, I'll ask him then. Okay, thanks for the key. See ya."

"Bye." I wave and usher my twin out of the apartment as quickly as possible without raising even more suspicion.

Locking the door behind him, I collapse on the couch.

That was awkward.

This thing between me and Griffin is strictly physical

anyway. No need to get into the details of my sexy times with my twin brother. That would be TMI.

And I hate to admit it, but a tiny part of me wants to keep whatever's happening between me and Griffin private, special.

The last thing I need is any of my brothers weighing in on my dating life. Or banging life. Whatever the hell this thing is.

15

GRIFFIN

As much as Little Miss Sunshine can annoy me, I have to admit she was good last night. I caught myself daydreaming about our time in the office more than once today—her tight little ass, those firm, perky tits as I took her on the desk.

Yeah, I could definitely go for round two of that. This time less frantic, less rushed. Tonight I plan on exploring every inch of her, from head to toe.

She made it clear this thing between us is strictly physical, and that's fine by me. I'm not planning on sticking around in this sleepy beach town any longer than I have to. And once I'm cleared to return to the field, I won't have any free time for dating anyway.

So I'm going to focus on the here and now, the physical, and enjoy my time. Keep it light, nothing serious.

Besides, there's no way someone as carefree and optimistic as Poppy would be a good fit for me.

No way in hell.

We're too different, polar fucking opposites. We have

chemistry, sure, but I know it takes a lot more than that to make a relationship work.

I close Scoops a few minutes early and head home, a nervous energy buzzing through me. Even though it's just casual between us, I can't squash my competitive instincts. I want to be the best. Always. And that includes sex with Little Miss Sunshine. If she doesn't see stars tonight, my job won't be done here.

Pulling into the drive of my rental house, I hustle in to get ready—a quick beard trim and a shower, a splash of cologne. Then I rustle up a few candles, select my special "getting it on" playlist, and uncork a bottle of wine.

I try to ignore the tension creeping into my shoulders, the dampness of my palms. It's not a date. Nothing to stress about.

Knock, knock.

Despite my reaffirming self-talk, my heart pounds a little bit harder as I unlock the door.

"Hey."

Damn. Little Miss Sunshine never looked so sexy before, her honey hair falling in soft waves around her bare shoulders. She gazes up at me through long, dark lashes, and my mouth goes dry, my cock instantly hard.

"Hey. Come in." I step back, opening the door wider, and she glides past me, the scent of coconut trailing behind her, lingering in the air.

I can't help but stare at her cute little ass perfectly showcased in her short black romper, those long, tan legs.

"Good day at work?" She winds a strand of hair around her finger, her eyes darting around the room, sizing the place up. She seems nervous, and for some reason this makes me feel better.

"It was all right. No crying kids, no dropped ice-cream cones, so I'll take it. You?"

"Also fine. No major disasters."

"Want a drink?" I start pouring even before she answers.

"Sure."

When I hand her the wine, our fingers brush, a quick zap of electricity shooting straight up my arm.

"Thanks," she murmurs, taking a quick sip. I do the same, grateful for the cool liquid sliding down my dry throat.

"Nice place. Very coastal chic." Poppy's fingers trace the gray veining in the marble countertop.

"Wish I could take credit for it, but it's a rental. Fully furnished. My stuff's not half as nice. I'm rarely home, so I haven't spent a lot of time decorating."

"Really? Not even in the offseason?"

I shrug. "Baseball season's pretty long. I only have a few months off, and I spend most of that time at the gym, training."

"Oh." She licks her lips, and my cock twitches in my pants, clearly ready for action.

"Are you hungry? Can I get you anything?" I gesture at the fridge. "I probably have cheese and crackers or something."

"I'm fine." She locks her gaze on mine, and I swear there's a red-hot electric current running between us, the tension palpable. Every muscle in my body coils.

We stare at each other for one second, two, and for the first time in a long while, I'm totally knocked off my game. I don't know what it is about this woman, but somehow

I'm twisted up about her. Which is wild. We're practically strangers.

But you don't want to be.

I inhale, trying to slow my shallow breathing and calm the fuck down.

"Oh, I love this song." Her body sways to the beat of a Michael Bublé song—not exactly sure how this got on my playlist, probably a practical joke in the locker room—and she steps toward me, grabbing my hand and pulling me into the center of the room. "C'mon, dance with me."

Normally I'd resist, not being much of a dancer. But I want to touch her, be near her, so dancing is as good of an excuse as any.

Wrapping my arms around her waist, I draw her close to my body, inhaling the flowery scent of her shampoo as her hair brushes my shirt. She feels nice pressed up against my chest, her soft exhale tickling my skin. We move side to side in time with the music, Poppy's hands laced around my neck, her cheeks flushed and rosy.

"This is surprisingly romantic." The vibration of her voice sends shock waves rippling through my muscles, everything tight and tense.

"You didn't think I had it in me or what?" I frown down at her, teasing.

All innocent, she blinks up at me, her pupils wide and dark. "I didn't say that."

She bites down on her full lip, and my cock strains against my jeans as the tip of her tongue darts out, licking along the pink bow of her mouth.

I want that mouth on me. I want to taste those lips. I want that tongue running along my skin.

Maybe more than I've ever wanted anyone before, and that's a real mindfuck, gotta be honest.

With the pad of my thumb, I trace her cheekbone, run my finger down her jawline. She sucks in a sharp breath, her mouth opening just a fraction of an inch, her eyes fluttering closed.

Beautiful, the way the candlelight dances across the planes of her face, the cinnamon freckles splashed across her nose, the upturn of her mouth. I dip my head, dropping my lips to hers, and she moans softly, opening to me. Our tongues entwining, we tangle together, matching each other's pressure. Her fingers tickle the nape of my neck, sending a shiver down my spine. Pressure builds down below, almost to the point of discomfort, and I'm torn between making this last or chasing after a release because this is torturous. Exquisite torture, but torture nonetheless.

"Griffin," she murmurs, voice raspy with desire. She squeezes her body even tighter to mine, her nipples pebbling through the thin fabric of her shirt as she rocks her hips toward me, melding our bodies together.

I want her, every part of her. I want her soft skin on mine, want her tight little body shuddering beneath me as I ride her.

"Poppy."

Her eyes flutter open, wide and wanting. My hands drop from her waist to her ass, bringing her body even closer into me, and now we're not really dancing so much as grinding.

Slowly, I begin to undress her, taking my time and gauging her response to my touch. I slide the thin material of her romper down her arms, inch by inch, until her satin bra peeks out at me. Chill bumps rise on her skin as my fingers trace the swells of her breasts and she shimmies up against me.

I take that as a good sign, pushing the fabric down farther, my palm skimming over her stomach. She wriggles her hips and the clothes pool in a dark puddle at her feet. Now she's standing in only her black bra and panties, my mouth watering at the sight of her.

"Fuck, you're beautiful," I murmur, taking her all in. She smiles up at me, her eyes glowing in the dim light.

"Thanks. But how am I in the same position as last night?" Her fingers curl in my shirt as she eases the cotton up, cool air hitting my bare skin.

Knowing she'll never be able to reach high enough to lift the shirt over my head, I help her out, then chuck it to the ground.

"Very nice, Carter." She tiptoes up my abdominals, her fingers tracing the ridges of muscle.

"Glad you're pleased."

I hiss in a sharp breath when she lands on the button of my jeans, locking eyes with me.

"May I?" She bats her lashes at me—like any guy would say no at this point.

I nod and she undoes the button, then lowers my zipper. A true gentleman, I help her out, kicking out of my jeans as fast as humanly possible.

"I probably shouldn't tell you this for, ya know, reasons. And I'm sure you already know. But you are gorgeous. How tall are you anyway? In real life, not your padded baseball stats." She cocks her head, sizing me up.

"How do you know my stats are padded?"

"Because they always are."

"Mine aren't. I take those sorts of things very seriously. And I'm six two. In real life."

"Shut up!" She punches my biceps and I don't even flinch. "For real? You're a foot taller than me."

"I know. You're tiny."

Wrinkling her nose, she frowns up at me. "Rude."

"Small, but mighty. It's cute."

This comment gets me a solid eye roll. "I hate being called cute."

"How about sexy?" I run my hand down her arm, and she shivers beneath my touch.

"That's better . . ."

Her hair falls across her eyes, and I brush the blonde tendrils away before taking her in my arms and gripping her round ass. I crush my mouth to hers and I'm drowning, but I don't ever want to come up for air. It's terrifying and exhilarating all at once, kinda like making solid contact with a baseball, that moment when you're not sure how far it's going to fly.

But you know with certainty that it will.

And in this case, that's scary as hell.

Shoving that thought out of my mind, I lift Poppy up, her legs wrapping around my waist, and carry her to my bedroom.

I'm going to be her number one, no matter what it takes.

16

POPPY

GRIFFIN'S ON A MISSION TONIGHT. I CAN TELL BY THE tension in his jaw, the serious expression in his eyes.

Fuck, he has nice eyes, clear blue with navy flecks and long, dark eyelashes. And when he locks those baby blues on me, ohmygawd, it's like all the oxygen's sucked out of the room, and I can barely breathe. His gaze is all fiery heat, and I am here for it.

Laying me down in the middle of his king-size bed, he hooks his thumbs in the edges of my panties and eases them down my legs until they're all the way off. Then he inches up my body, kissing the smooth skin of my calves, my thighs, sucking with his hot mouth. I'm instantly wet, my entire body flushed, a throbbing need building between my legs.

I want this man. Multiple times, in multiple ways. I want him to do dirty things to me, and I want to reciprocate. I want him to hiss out my name and never forget me.

He dips his head down, licking the sensitive skin, then swirling his tongue on my clit, and I inhale, a sharp gasp.

"Fuck . . . ," I rasp as he reaches beneath me, cupping my ass and lifting me up slightly. With a firm grip, he holds me still and feasts, even as I squirm under his hot kisses. His facial hair tickles and rubs my tender skin, making me wetter still, every nerve tingling.

The first wave of my orgasm hits me after he sucks my clit into his mouth, hard, and I fall. Crashing down, down, down, relief washing over me.

"Was that good, baby girl?" Griffin smiles up at me.

The jerk knows it was good.

"Mm-hmm," I murmur, barely even coherent. I'm weak right now, and it's all his fault.

He strokes me, up and down, his strong fingers somehow soft and gentle. Then he slides in one, two fingers, pressing his thumb on my core, lighting me on fire. Pulses of desire shoot straight to my belly, everything tightening, and I'm so close already.

I run my palms along the taut muscles of his shoulders, kneading at the ropy fibers. He's fucking strong, all sharp planes and edges. He flexes beneath my touch, and I scratch my nails lightly across his back. A sharp hiss escapes his lips, and then he kicks off his boxers and he's naked, hovering above me, pinning me between his arms.

We're face-to-face and I can't stop staring. He has a faint scar above his left eye, which does nothing to mar his perfection.

"I want you," I murmur, not taking my eyes off him.

"Good."

"Really? That's your response? Good?" I wind my legs around his waist, thrust up to meet him. His dick twitches, hitting my belly.

"It's fine. You don't have to admit anything. Your dick gives you away."

"He always does."

Reaching down, I encircle his long shaft in my hand, rubbing his hard length. He pulses in my palm, his abs contracting with each stroke. Faint wrinkles form around his eyes, his brow furrowing as I slide up and down, pumping, a few drops of hot liquid leaking out.

"If you don't stop, I'm going to explode." He trails his thumb down my cheek, running it across my bottom lip, and I suck him into my mouth.

"Fuck." His dick throbs in my palm as I swirl my tongue around his thumb, applying pressure.

With a pop, he pulls his thumb out from between my lips, reaching into the nightstand for a condom and sheathing up.

"Playtime's over."

He rolls onto his back against the pillows, pulling me onto his chest, and I straddle him.

"The knee still has some limitations." He rubs his flattened palm on my ass cheek, the skin heating up from the contact.

I tip my head down, taking his face in my hands, and kiss him on his full lips. "It's fine. This is good." Then I ease his cock into me, slowly, inch by inch, until he's all the way inside me.

"Oh . . ." A low moan floats through the air as Griffin seats himself all the way back and I start to ride him. He cups my breasts, squeezing and fondling, pinching at my nipples with his rough fingers, and I'm hovering on the edge. Shimmery pleasure pricks at my skin, my body humming and alive.

He smacks my ass lightly as I rock against him, getting as much friction as possible, rubbing against him.

"That's a good girl," he murmurs, kneading the spot he just spanked. His words trickle through my consciousness, sweet and satisfying.

Both of his hands gripping my hips, he thrusts up into me, harder and harder, and now we're trying to get as close as possible, leaving no space between us. I clench and tighten around his cock, milking him, his spasms building.

"Let go, baby." He urges me on, tipping me over the edge, and I comply, shattering around him. He follows right behind, exploding with a long, hard shudder.

I collapse on his chest, our breathing deep and ragged, our bodies slick with sweat. He pushes the damp hair away from my face. I'm warm and sated, Griffin holding me in his strong arms.

Draping my leg over him, careful of his injured knee, I sigh into his chest. The soft thudding of his heart pulsates against my cheek, and I don't think I've ever felt this good.

Calm. Happy. Complete.

But also a tiny bit scared because there's a real possibility that I may be falling for Griffin Carter, King Asshole, and that definitely wasn't in the plan.

17

POPPY

Hungry, Griffin orders food, and we fuck again while we wait for the pizza delivery.

"I thought guys had to wait a while in between rounds." I fall back against the pillows, panting and out of breath. He wraps his arm around my shoulder, bringing me into his chest, and I stroke the heated skin, my fingers running along the outline of his pecs.

"Perk of sleeping with an athlete, babe." He winks down at me, and my stomach swoops—and I'm pretty sure it's not from hunger.

"Nice side bene—"

Griffin kisses me, soft and slow, like we have all the time in the world, and this is not helping the whole "falling for the grump" situation.

At all.

Now's the time to bail. Get out before you do something stupid. Something you'll regret later.

Ding-dong.

The doorbell rings, and Griffin shifts away from me to

get the door, pulling a pair of gym shorts over his naked butt before hustling out of the room.

Shame, that.

He does have an amazing ass. I could stare at it all day long. I bet he looks super sexy in his baseball uniform. I've never been interested in baseball before, but it may become my favorite sport now . . .

The door opens, and there's muffled conversation between Griffin and the delivery dude; then the door closes and Griffin's back in the bedroom.

"Dinner is served." He sets the pizza box on the nightstand, and I sit up, wrapping myself in the sheets.

"Thanks, I'm starved."

Griffin offers me the first slice, and I gladly take it, my stomach growling. Guess I worked up an appetite . . .

We eat in comfortable silence, Griffin scarfing down four slices of pizza in record time. The man can eat, that's for sure.

"That was good. Really hit the spot." I dab at my lips with a napkin, wiping away any stray pizza crumbs.

Griffin leans over, his thumb brushing my cheek. "You missed a spot."

I blush as he licks the tomato sauce from his thumb, his gaze never leaving mine. Heat unfurls low in my belly, and damn if I'm not wet for him again.

This is getting ridiculous. How many times can I possibly have sex with this man in one night?

"C'mon." He grabs my hand, pulling me off the bed, the sheets falling away as I stand.

"What? Where are we going?"

Lacing his fingers in mine, he leads me out of the

bedroom, across the living room and kitchen, all the way out to the backyard.

"Griffin, I'm naked," I screech-whisper, trying to cover myself with one hand.

"So?" He shrugs, dropping his own shorts. "There's a wooden fence. No one can see us unless they work really hard at it."

His hands find my waist, and he grips my hips, pressing his lips to mine. I open to him, his tongue insistent, exploring. My nipples pebble in the night air, brushing against his smooth, firm chest.

"Let's swim."

Before I can protest, he scoops me up in his arms and carries me over to the glittering pool. I fling my arm around his neck and hold on to him as he eases down the steps. The cool water laps at my skin, sending chill bumps skating across my flesh. Griffin sinks lower, moving into deeper water, until my body's fully submerged except for my face and neck. He holds me tight against him, his hands splayed across my ass and stomach, and a dull ache throbs between my legs. I press my thighs together to ease the pressure, but it doesn't help much.

I don't think anything will help when I'm rubbing up against this gorgeous man, all rock-hard muscle and testosterone.

"Fuck, you're sexy." He nuzzles my neck, sucking gently on my tender skin, ripples of pleasure rolling down my spine.

Tipping my face up, I crush my lips to his, and he tastes sweet and spicy and delicious. His tongue plunges in, and the water laps around us, the ocean waves pounding the shore in the distance.

Everything about right now is perfect and romantic, and I cannot believe this is the same King Asshole I met three months ago.

This man is different, less edgy. Sensual and seductive, and it might be the hormones talking, but I want more.

I need more.

"Griffin?"

He pauses, inching his head away to peer down at me. "Yeah?"

"What are we doing?"

"Kissing."

"Yeah, I know that. Obviously. I mean, on a bigger level."

He squints at me, his deep-blue eyes narrowed, but he doesn't answer the question.

I bite down on my lip, suddenly hyperaware of the situation. My feelings swirl around, alternating between my gut and my head.

"Because this is feeling like more than a quick bang to me."

Griffin licks his lip, swallows. Silence stretches between us, and a cold slither of regret slides through my stomach.

Finally, he clears his throat and I hold my breath, waiting for his response. Certain I'm about to be shut down.

"Do you want it to be?" His voice is low and serious, his eyes searching mine for answers.

I screw my mouth up, his hand running light circles on my bare ass.

Hell yeah, I want it to be.

I nod. "Yeah. I do."

"Okay then." He presses his mouth to mine, laying the most gentle kiss on my lips, sealing the deal.

It sounds stupid and cheesy, but in this moment my heart soars, straight up into the starry night sky.

I'm not exactly sure how I got here—in the strong, capable arms of this incredibly sexy man—but I know I sure as hell don't ever want to leave.

18

GRIFFIN

Tonight was . . . unexpected. In the best way possible. Who would have thought the two of us would actually be good together, have anything in common? We talked for two hours straight—I didn't know I had that many words in me.

And she was funny, and charming, and cute, and witty.

Also, fucking hot as hell.

Thinking about her naked breasts pressed up against me in the pool, the way she rode my cock.

Damn. I'm hard all over again.

And I can't believe it—would never in a million years have guessed I'd be feeling like this—but I actually really like this girl.

I understand exactly what she means when she says this thing between us feels like more.

Because I feel the same way.

Holy hell.

Falling for Poppy Montgomery is not part of the lineup.

But lying here in the dark, her breathing feather soft on

my skin, our legs tangled together in the sheets, I can't imagine being anywhere else.

Holy hell.

How is this going to work? I'm eventually leaving Seaglass Beach and going back to baseball. Baseball's my life. And her life is here—this town, her family, the inn.

I can't stay, and she won't leave.

A heavy pit settles deep in my gut, my chest tight. This is why I don't get involved. Feelings are messy. I don't like messy.

Poppy's arm stretches out, wrapping around my biceps, and she snuggles in closer to me. She's so peaceful, asleep in my arms. I've never seen her still and quiet before, and she's even more beautiful, the dark fringe of her lashes fluttering on her cheeks with the rise and fall of her breath.

I know deep in my heart that she could be different, special. And that thought scares the hell out of me.

With a long inhale, I shove down my thoughts, my fears, my doubts, and make the conscious decision to focus on the present. I'm going to live in the here and now for the time being.

I can only hope Poppy will be good with that decision as well.

NEXT THING I KNOW, LIGHT'S STREAMING INTO MY bedroom, and I have a serious case of morning wood. Partly because I have to pee, partly because I have a gorgeous, naked woman draped over me.

I smooth my hand over the silky strands of her hair, and she sighs contentedly, wiggling her body up against me.

"Hey, beautiful."

Her eyes blink open, a smile lighting up her face.

"Hey."

Dropping my lips to hers, I kiss her long and slow. She responds, shimmying her hips on my thigh.

"What time is it?" she murmurs, breaking the connection.

"Almost eight."

"Eight? Oh shit. I have to go." She tries to spring out of bed, but she's tangled in the sheets, our legs wrapped up together.

"Hang on, just a sec." Reaching down, I unwind the cotton bedsheet, and she pops out of bed, scrambling around trying to find her clothes. She hooks her bra, wiggles into her romper, then slides on her sandals.

"I'm supposed to be at the inn by eight. Shit, shit, shit . . ." She's flying around the room, searching for all her belongings, and my gaze follows her in awe. Poppy goes from zero to sixty faster than anyone I've ever met. She should really be a sprinter.

"Guess you're not staying for breakfast, huh?"

"Not today, sorry. Maybe next time." She fastens her earrings, runs a hand through her tousled hair.

I casually stretch, then sit on the edge of the bed and watch her flutter around the room.

"You forgot these." I scoop her lace panties up off the floor and dangle them in front of her. She swipes at them, snagging them and shoving them into her pocket.

"Thanks. See you later?" Her brows raise in question, and I nod, grabbing her by the hips and holding her still against my naked body. I press my mouth to hers, satisfied when she gasps, then relaxes into the kiss.

"I'll call you."

"Okay."

Two minutes later, she's gone, and this house has never felt so quiet, so empty before.

Yeah, I'm in deep. Way too deep, but I have no desire to get out now.

19

POPPY

Well, that was the hottest night of my life. Like, totally, 100 percent unbeatable.

If Griffin didn't have the top spot before—which, to be clear, he did—he'd certainly have it now.

The man knows what he's doing in the bedroom, that's for sure.

Those hands. Those lips. That mouth. That rock-hard body, long and lean and ripped from years of training.

Who knew baseball players were so freaking gorgeous?

It's official: Griffin Carter has ruined me for all other men.

Dammit.

This is not good. We were supposed to have a quick bang.

That's it. Period, end of story.

But no.

What we had was a fucking amazing marathon sex session, and I already want to do it again, an excited shiver rolling down my spine as I drive down A1A.

Shit.

How is this going to work? He's leaving.

I know it. He knows it.

We have no future.

So what in the hell am I doing?

I'd love to lie to myself here and say we're having a fling, but I know in my heart of hearts this is more.

Bigger.

Deeper.

It's real between us.

I shared stuff with him last night that I don't tell other people. Deep stuff, like the loss of my parents in the car crash and how it feels to be alone, responsible for the inn. He's a surprisingly good listener and easy to talk to. He's funny, genuine. Open. Thoughtful.

I never expected King Asshole to be like that.

And now I'm falling for him—already fallen is probably more accurate—and I know I'm going to get hurt.

Not on purpose. Griffin doesn't seem the type—at least that's my impression after spending time with him.

But my heart will be collateral damage.

Because he's not going to stay. And I can't leave.

Way to go, Poppy. Of all the guys in the world, you fall for the one who will never, ever be able to settle down.

Fucking perfect.

But maybe he'll stay?

The selfish part of me wants to hold on to my optimism. So you know what? I will.

I fly into the parking lot, slamming into the closest open spot, and glance at the clock on the dash. Only ten minutes late, no biggie.

Hopping out of Smurfy, I half jog into the inn, taking a

few deep breaths of the citrusy air as I slide behind the front desk. Luckily the lobby's still empty, and the message light on the phone isn't blinking. I power on the computer, and cool relief washes over me—crisis averted. Everything's fine—no angry guests, no missed reservations.

The adrenaline rush from my mad dash seeps out of me slowly, like helium from a balloon, and I sag against the front desk. As wonderful as it was hanging out with Griffin, I didn't get a whole lot of sleep last night.

Coffee. I definitely need coffee.

I head over to the coffee bar set up against the back wall and pop in a purple pod, then hit the power button. The machine roars to life, the dull whir filling the quiet lobby. Steam rises from my Seaglass Inn mug, the sweet scent of dark roast hitting my nostrils and instantly perking me up.

"Hey, Poppy."

I jump at the familiar baritone rumble behind me, spinning around. "Hey, Rome. What's up?"

"Heading over to Town Hall again. Just grabbing coffee." He saunters across the tile floor, fiddling with the button on his shirtsleeve.

"I got you. Medium roast, right?"

He nods, and as soon as my coffee's brewed, I switch my mug out for his stainless-steel cup.

"Here you go." I hand over the cup, then stir creamer into my coffee before heading back over to the desk. Trying to play it cool and act nonchalant. At least Rome doesn't know I wore this romper yesterday.

"Thanks for the coffee." He tips his head at me and I nod, staring straight ahead at the computer screen, avoiding eye contact.

There's no way he knows anything. Relax.

"You dropped these."

Black, lacy fabric hits the mouse pad, and my face flames, heat creeping up my chest and winding around my neck like kudzu, choking me.

Ohmygawd. Kill me now.

Somehow my panties managed to slip out of my pocket. And my freaking brother picked them up.

FML.

I swallow hard, my mouth dry as red-hot embarrassment pulses through my veins. "Uh, thanks."

"Uh-huh." Rome doesn't ask any questions, just smirks to himself and sidles out of the inn, leaving me stewing in mortification.

MY DAY DOESN'T GET ANY BETTER. IN FACT, IT CRAWLS by, which almost never happens. Usually I'm happy working the reception desk. I love helping guests with special requests, giving upgrades and making their events memorable.

Today, though, all I can think about is Griffin.

His deep-blue eyes, all serious and reserved. The way his face crinkles when he finally breaks a smile, the low chuckle that vibrates his abs.

Those abs, let's be real.

I could spend an entire lifetime thinking of those abs, and it still wouldn't be enough time.

I stare at my cell, willing it to ring. He said he'd call. Why hasn't he called?

Maybe he won't call. Maybe I'm reading too much into this whole thing.

I don't want to be that girl, but right now—I'm that girl. I want him to call, need him to call.

Maybe I really was just a quick bang, even though he said otherwise.

Tapping my fingers on the desk, I google his name and "girlfriend" for the fifth time today.

No results.

Unless he's leading an uber-secret life, it appears he is indeed single. And also very good at baseball, judging by his stats. Granted, I don't know what many of them mean, but they seem impressive. From what I read, third base is one of the hardest positions to play too.

Basically, Griffin Carter's a superstar athlete, and any team would be lucky to have him. So there's like zero percent chance he's not getting called back. No coach in their right mind is going to cut someone with his talent, even if he is injured.

This thought hits me hard smack-dab in the center of my chest, and I swear my heart squeezes harder than normal, followed by a deep pang.

Oh, come on, Poppy. Y'all haven't even been on a date yet, and you're already freaking out about him leaving. Get attached much?

Buzz, buzz.

My hand darts out and grabs my cell so fast I knock over my water bottle, droplets splashing the keyboard.

"Shit!" I swipe at the water with a napkin as I snatch up my phone to read the text.

Griffin: Last night was fun

I grin down at the screen, warm and tingly all over.

Poppy: I had a great time

Griffin: I forgot to ask you this AM . . .

The text bubbles pop up, then swirl, my heart hammering hard.

Griffin: Did I make it into your top spot?

I laugh out loud, shaking my head.

Poppy: Happy to report you're officially number one

Griffin: Good. Not that I had any doubts . . .

Poppy: Sure . . .

Griffin: Listen—I have to work late tonight. The high schooler I hired quit on me via text this morning. Want to stop by and help later?

Griffin: I might get another crying kid and I kind of bobbled that last time

Poppy: LOL. Kind of?

Griffin: Customer service isn't really my thing

Poppy: You excel in other areas, don't worry. And yes, happy to pop in later. I have a new flavor to whip up anyway

Griffin: Should I even ask?

Poppy: Maple pumpkin spice popcorn. I think you're going to like it

Griffin: Doubtful

Poppy: Sometimes you've got to live on the edge

Griffin: I do. Every once in a while I ditch the cone and get chocolate sauce instead

Poppy: You're a wild man, Griffin

Griffin: I'll prove it to you later tonight

Poppy: Challenge accepted

Griffin: I like the sound of that. Time for PT. Gotta run. See you later

I type out *Bye*, but that's too formal. Then I tap XXXX, but I think it's too much, too soon. Kissing emoji? Doesn't feel right. Finally, I settle on the heart eyes smiley face and throw my phone down on the desk.

What is it about this guy that has me obsessing over him?

Everything.

Every damn thing.

My thighs clench as I think about him, heat pooling in my belly.

I can't wait to see Griffin again tonight.

20

GRIFFIN

ALL DAY LONG, I THINK ABOUT POPPY.

While I'm running through my exercises at PT.

Poppy.

When I'm in the shower.

A naked Poppy, covered in white suds in here with me last night.

Eating lunch.

Poppy's tinkly laugh, the way she reached out and touched my arm every time I said something funny.

When I stop in and check on Aunt Jess.

Poppy and how great she is with people. And have we tried any new flavors lately?

"Funny you should ask, Aunt Jess, because Poppy texted me a new one she wants to try today."

"Really?" Aunt Jess props her casted arm up on the TV tray, pushing her glasses up with her good hand. "What flavor?"

"Pumpkin maple popcorn or something. I can't

remember exactly." I set the plate of grilled cheese and baby carrots down in front of my aunt.

"That sounds yummy."

"No. Sounds gross. But she wants to try it out, so . . ." I shrug, and my aunt's mouth quirks up at the corners.

"What?"

"Nothing." She tucks into her sandwich, the tiny smile still tugging at her lips.

"Okay, you good here? I'm going to head over to Scoops. I told you the girl I hired quit? I'll put another ad up on the community message board today, see if I can find someone."

"Sounds good, honey."

I lean down and gently hug my aunt, then head toward the door.

"Griffy?"

"Yeah?" I glance over my shoulder at Aunt Jess in her recliner.

"Have fun tonight." She winks at me over her sandwich, the skin around her eyes crinkling into the familiar lines, etched over a lifetime of joy and love and laughter.

I half-heartedly roll my eyes and walk out the door, doubtful I'm even fooling Aunt Jess at this point.

One thing I will give Seaglass Beach—the weather in the autumn is pretty damn nice. Beats Atlanta's weather for sure. The sun's shining, with a slight breeze blowing in off the ocean, and I roll my windows down for the few-block drive into town.

I make a quick stop at the town community center, pinning a HELP WANTED flyer to the large corkboard filled with brightly colored announcements and a variety of other job openings. A red poster announcing the Fall Fest catches my eye—apparently fall at the beach is more than pumpkins and hayrides. The Fall Fest boasts the "tastiest blue crabs on the coast!" along with the more standard pony rides and carnival games. I make a mental note to ask Aunt Jess about the festival and whether she wants to have a booth or something.

Buzz, buzz.

I fish my cell out of my pocket and read the text from my teammate Danny.

> Danny: Hey, man. How's the knee?

> Griffin: Getting better. We making it through the playoffs?

> Danny: Prob not without you

My gut twists, a flash of adrenaline surging through me.

> Griffin: Doubt that. Wish I could be there

> Danny: You should come watch the games. Cheer us on. Yell at Dickerson when he sucks on third base

I chuckle, picturing poor Dickerson trying to play third base. He's not as tall as me, and he's definitely not as fast.

> Griffin: Would love to, but my aunt broke her wrist. I'm helping her out for a bit

> Danny: Damn, tough break. Hope she gets better soon

> Griffin: Thanks. I'll watch you boys on TV though. If you make the Series, you know I'll be there

> Danny: Wouldn't book your plane ticket just yet. Like I said—Dickerson is no Griffin Carter. Miss you, man

A dull ache spreads through my chest. I do miss baseball. My team, the cheering crowd, that exhilarating rush when a ball's flying at you through the air, the thud as it slams into your glove.

Damn.

I've been pushing through—specifically avoiding all thoughts of baseball—because of this right here. This terrible panicky feeling, clawing at my throat, threatening to pull me under.

What if I can't go back?

Ignoring that worst-case scenario, I text back:

> Griffin: Yeah, me too. Give Dickerson hell for me. And remind him not to get too comfy on my bag

> Danny: Will do. Take care

I shove my phone back in my pocket and hustle back to the Rover. A few hours at Scoops will be plenty of motivation to get after my knee exercises and rehab my way right out of this town.

By the time Poppy shows up, it's dark outside and I'm ready to close up shop for the night.

"Sorry I'm late." She bustles through the door, her hair blowing around behind her like a honey-blonde cape. "The pool heater's on the fritz at the inn, and I had to get the pool company to come out for an emergency repair."

She whirls around the counter, her cheeks a soft pink, and she's moving so fast she's practically a light blue streak.

"It's fine." I grip her hips, stopping her. Her eyes flutter up to meet my gaze, and she takes a breathy inhale, her body humming beneath my hands.

Bending down, I press my mouth to hers, and she relaxes against me, frenetic energy radiating off her.

"Hi," I murmur against her sweet lips, and the bow of her mouth curves into a smile.

"Hi."

I slide my hands from her hips to her ass, the slippery fabric of her skirt cool on my palms. She arches her back, pressing into me, and my cock takes notice, bulging in my shorts.

"Looks like you survived without me. Make any kids cry?" She leans back, narrowing her aqua gaze up at me.

"Not today. Maybe tomorrow."

"Griffin!" She smacks my biceps, giggling, and now I'm rock hard. That laugh gets me every time.

"It's inevitable. I'm sure I'll run out of gummy bears or mint chocolate chip or waffle cones at some point, and there will be tears."

"That's the spirit." Even as she teases me, she loops her arms around my waist, moving in closer.

I shrug. "Hazard of being in the ice-cream biz. Is what

it is. I'm gonna go ahead and close up. It's a school night, so it's not like we're losing business. Hang tight."

Smacking her playfully on the ass, I stride across the shop and flip the sign to Closed before locking the door and cutting the lights. The room goes gray, the white light from the cooler beaming out into the darkness.

"Oh, I was going to make that new flavor for your aunt to try." Poppy leans against the counter and bites at her bottom lip, the contours of her face highlighted in the soft glow from the freezer.

"I have way better ideas than that." I move behind her, my palms gliding down her arms. She shivers and wiggles her bottom against my midsection, and my balls tighten. Leaning down, I kiss along the smooth column of her neck, my mouth barely brushing her velvety skin. A whisper of a moan falls from her lips as I nip and suck, peppering kisses lower still. One hand splays at her hip, while the other snakes around and caresses her breast.

"Perfect," I whisper into her ear, her pulse drumming fast in her neck.

Giving her away.

I continue to fondle her, tweaking her nipple through the thin fabric of her dress. She's so responsive, pebbling in my fingers. I inch my hand up her skirt, my fingers tiptoeing up her thighs until they find her hot center. Spreading my hand wide, I slide in between her legs, cupping her.

"You're already wet." My voice comes out a husky rasp as I struggle to maintain control. I want to spin her around and fuck her—hard—right here, but I figure I should take my time.

Her head bobs up and down, and an image of Poppy down on her knees, lips wrapped around my cock, springs into my mind. I twitch in my briefs, every muscle flexing.

Thumbing her clit through the satin of her panties, I play with her most sensitive spot while she writhes against my hand. Her breaths are shallow, staccato pants as she squirms against me.

Sliding the scrap of satin to the side, I ease one finger, then two, into her, and she inhales, clenching around my fingers. I move in and out, slowly, warming her up for my cock.

Abruptly I drag her panties down her thighs. She wiggles them off her ankles, and I spread her legs wide with my knees before unbuttoning my pants and freeing my cock.

I nip and kiss at her neck, alternating between licking and sucking, while I stroke my hard shaft. Ripping open the foil packet, I sheathe up. Poppy steadies herself against the freezer, anchoring herself with open palms on the cool glass.

Then I sink my length all the way into her until I'm balls deep and stars shimmer in my peripheral vision.

"Baby, you feel so fucking good," I murmur, running my nose along the shell of her ear. Chill bumps rise on her delicate skin as I caress her chest, pulling the top of her dress down until her breasts spill out. I stand still, letting her get used to the feeling of me inside her, before rocking my hips forward.

"Oh, Griffin," she moans, her nipples sharp points as I twist and pinch.

"Do you like that?" I breathe against her heated skin,

and her pussy clenches around my cock, milking me. "I'll take that as a yes."

She nods, and I thrust into her, harder and deeper, our bodies slapping together and hitting against the ice-cream freezer.

"Fuck me, Griffin," she moans, and I'm rocketing toward my release, trying to hold on a little while longer for her. I pound into her, harder and harder, until she finally cries out, the sound bouncing off the tiles. Waves of pleasure roll through her body, and only then do I release my climax, exploding inside her.

I squeeze her tiny body to mine, giving her every last drop, pulsing inside her before my muscles finally relax.

"Fuck. That was good." I kiss her hair, the floral notes of her shampoo tickling my sensitive nose. "I've been wanting to do that all day."

"That was one hell of a greeting." She tips her head back, and I seize her mouth in a hot kiss, slipping my tongue in and sweeping around. Claiming her.

"I thought we might get a little farther than the cooler, but that worked." I reach down and trail my fingers over the lacy edge of her bra. "I didn't even get you naked."

"You're right, that is a shame." She swivels around, unhooking her bra and tossing it to the ground beside her panties. "Better?"

I bite down on my lip, tip my head and appraise her. "Yes. But I still want more."

"Well, aren't you a greedy boy?" She eases her dress down her arms, over her hips, down her thighs, until it rests next to her undergarments. "How about now?"

"Much better." My gaze rakes over her body, taking her

all in. She's absolutely stunning, standing there in only her sandals.

Headlights flash and shine into the shop, Poppy's face beet red as she ducks down quickly behind the cooler.

"Ohmygawd, do you think they saw me?" She pokes her head up, peering through the glass of the freezer out into the darkness.

The lights fade and recede, the car turning around and retreating down the road. I chuckle, taking my shirt off and laying it down on the floor.

"No, I don't think so. Here, sit."

She curls her legs up underneath her and sits on my T-shirt. The glow from the cooler illuminates her face, highlighting her cheekbones. Her eyes meet mine, and I'm hard all over again as she stares up at me through her thick fringe of lashes.

"What?" She blinks, licking her bottom lip.

"You're beautiful."

Even in the dark, I can see the rosy blush bloom on her cheeks. I kick off my shorts and lay them down, joining her on the floor.

"Your aunt doesn't have cameras, right?" Poppy's eyes flick nervously to the corners of the room.

"Kinda late to be asking that question, don't you think?" I arch a brow at her, and she shrugs.

"Yeah, probably. I'm kind of an act-first-think-later kinda girl."

"You don't say." I trace my thumb over her jaw and watch as she sucks in a breath and her nipples harden at my touch.

"I wouldn't complain about that too much. Seems to be working to your advantage."

"Truth. You hungry?" I ask, my own stomach growling.

"Yes."

"We could get dressed and try to find something to eat. I don't think I have any leftover pizza."

She smiles at me, her eyes glittering in the white light. "I have a better idea."

21

POPPY

I HOP UP FROM THE FLOOR AND HURRY OVER TO THE toppings bar to the right of the ice-cream freezer. There's a selection of miniature candies—gummy bears, M&M's, chunks of candy bars. Plus, crushed sandwich cookies, sprinkles, chopped-up fruit, and the ever-popular sauces: chocolate, caramel, a signature citrus syrup. I grab a plastic cup and squirt chocolate sauce into it, then snap up the whipped-cream dispenser and a few gummy bears, because they're my favorite. Then I spin back around to Griffin, his dark brows raised high on his forehead.

"What are you doing?" His voice rumbles through the dark, low and deep, sending a tingle straight through me.

"Having dessert first." I drop down to the ground, setting my toppings to the side. Then I straddle him, being careful to avoid the red, angry scar marking his injured knee. He's beyond gorgeous, all smooth, hard muscle, his skin tanned from the Florida sun. I trace the dark lines of his tattoos swirling over his broad chest, my fingertips skimming over the warm skin. The clean, masculine scent of cologne and soap mixes with vanilla and envelops me.

Being this close to him, heat radiating between us, my body's on fire. Every nerve ending aware of his presence, his power. His hand finds my ass, holding me close to him, our pelvises pressing together, and I feel his erection. I tip my head, sealing my lips to his in a searing kiss, and the entire world stops. Right now it's just me and Griffin, here in the sweet darkness of the ice-cream shop, and everything's wonderfully, wildly perfect.

He could be The One.

I deepen our kiss, sliding my tongue into his mouth and pushing that thought straight out of my mind.

I don't want to think.

I only want to feel.

I want to feel Griffin's hands on my body, his lips on my skin.

I want to be so close to him that we're not separate anymore.

I want to be with him, no space between us at all.

Pulling away slightly, I reach around him and pluck up a gummy bear, popping the little red candy into his mouth. His eyes widen in surprise, then he chews, his serious gaze locked on me. I lift the plastic cup and use a spoon to drizzle chocolate sauce over his pecs. Dark brown streaks roll down his chest, and I lean forward, licking at the sweet, shiny river. Chill bumps skate across his skin everywhere my tongue touches as I suck the chocolate from his body.

"Poppy," he hisses, his voice strained even as he entwines his fingers in my hair, holding me to his chest.

"Don't worry, I'll clean up my mess." I bat my eyelashes

at him, and he sucks in a breath, his cock hard against me, pushing insistently against his briefs. "I think you should lie back and get more comfortable, actually."

I push against his shoulders, urging him down, and he does as instructed, kicking out of his briefs until he's as naked as I am.

"That's better. Now I can have dessert." I grab the shiny silver dispenser, depress the nozzle and squirt a line of white cream from his navel all the way down the shaft of his dick. With a flourish, I put an extra dollop on the tip, and he groans.

"Fuck." He lifts his head up, staring at my handiwork, and I shoot him an impish grin.

"I love cream." Then I ease down his body, licking my way down the thick white line, lapping at the cool sweetness. His dick bobs, and I reach down, massaging his balls, before taking the tip between my lips and swirling my tongue around the crown. I lap up all the whipped cream, sucking his hardness deep into my mouth. His skin's hot and salty as I draw him farther in, hollowing my cheeks to take him all the way. His hands twist in my hair, holding me to him as he pulses in my mouth, and I know he's close.

"Unless you want me to finish, you should stop now." The low vibrations of his strained voice undulate his abs beneath my hand, and I shake my head no.

I want to finish him off, feel his release.

With a deep breath through my nose, I take him that much deeper, his cock hitting the back of my throat.

That does it. He explodes, hot, salty spurts shooting and hitting my tongue. I swallow, then swallow again as he convulses, spilling into me. His body's tense and sticky with sweat, and I stroke the hard, defined planes, a happy glow filling me up from the inside.

"Fuck, Poppy." He huffs out a breath, reaching down and pulling me up and onto his chest, smoothing down my tangled hair. "That was fucking hot."

I grin, wiping at my mouth. "I wanted you to have the house special."

He chuckles, a low, deep laugh, stroking my back lightly with his large, calloused palm.

"You're a dirty girl and I love it."

"I have three brothers. I know how y'all think."

"I'm happy to return the favor, but I'm kind of old and broken for the tile floor. How about we move somewhere a little more forgiving?"

"Okay. Besides, I should probably eat dinner. And now I'm sticky too."

His hand travels down my back, massaging my bare ass. "Let's clean up and get out of here."

He presses a kiss to my lips, and I can't remember a hotter, happier time than right this very instant.

"C'mon."

I ease off him; then he rises, reaches his hand down, and pulls me up off the ground. He cups my face, staring down at me, his pupils dark.

"You're something else, Poppy Montgomery."

He drops another kiss on my lips, my lower belly flip-flopping at his slightest touch.u

I have no idea where this is going, but right now I don't want us to ever end.

THE SAND'S COOL AND WET BENEATH OUR BARE FEET AS the ocean waves roll onto the shore, recede. In, out, in and out, the moonlight shining on the rippled surface of the water.

"What's it like living at a hotel?" Griffin asks as we stroll down the deserted beach, our fingers interlaced.

It's well past ten p.m. now, and even the vacationing guests are tucked into their cozy beds, asleep or at least watching television.

A breeze ruffles my damp hair, and I shiver. He drops my hand, instead wrapping his strong arm around my shoulder, bringing me in close. The scent of my orange-and-bergamot bodywash drifts off his skin, mixing with the salty air, and I nestle into his warmth.

"It's good. I like being on the beach. Plus, I always have the chef at the restaurant, so I never have to cook if I don't want to. And the commute's awesome." I grin up at him and he laughs.

"But I thought you loved driving your car?"

"I do. But I hate dealing with traffic."

"There's no traffic here, from what I can tell."

"Every once in a while, there's a fender bender and we get a jam. Also, summer traffic is way worse."

"Have you been to Atlanta? Traffic's out of control."

"Are you there very often? How much do you travel?"

"I'm not home a lot. We're on the road almost six months of the year. I drive to and from the airport a ton."

"Have you always played in Atlanta?"

"I started out in Colorado, then got traded to Atlanta. Been there ever since."

"And you think you're going back?" I tip my head to read his expression. A flicker of something crosses his face, his brow furrowing, but I'm not sure exactly what it is.

"Planning on it. I'm making good progress in PT. The knee's still tight, but we added strength and conditioning into the rotation now. I figure that's a good sign."

I nod, knowing how important it is to stay positive when you have an injury. "For sure."

Silence stretches between us, the only sound the waves splashing against the shoreline. I swallow hard over the lump in my throat, shoving down the panic licking up my chest.

I don't want Griffin to leave.

"Have you ever thought about what you'll do after baseball?"

Griffin's hand stills on my shoulder, pressure from his fingertips bearing down on my arm.

He shrugs. "Not sure. Before the knee, I didn't worry too much about it. I'm not that old, and a lot of guys have long careers in baseball."

I exhale, air hissing through my teeth, the sound swallowed up by the wind.

"I suppose I should come up with a backup plan. For after. But I'm going back. No question."

My heart seizes at the thought of him leaving Seaglass Beach, but I don't want to crush his hope.

For one of the first times in my life, I have to force trilling optimism into my voice. "Definitely."

He squeezes my shoulder, lacing his free hand in mine,

and I'm so conflicted my stomach rolls even as a ribbon of excitement winds through me.

Eager to change the subject, I ask, "Do you have more family, besides Jess?"

Griffin nods, his lips pressed together in a tight line. "Yeah. I have a brother two years younger than me. And a dad and stepmom. They all live in Colorado, along with my half brother and sister. They're in high school now."

"Oh."

He swallows, the only sound the waves hitting the shore. Clearly family's a sore subject.

"My mom died when I was in middle school. My dad moved us out to Colorado, and he met my stepmom. He started over, family round two. Hence the half brother and sister."

"I'm sorry." My voice is quiet, barely carrying over the wind.

His shoulders rise, then sag. "It's whatever. Kinda sucks. Aunt Jess is—was—my mom's sister. Me and my brother always spent a lot of time with her. When my mom died, my dad shipped us off to be with her every summer. One August we came home, and—surprise!—we had a new stepmom."

I rub my thumb over his, wishing I could do or say something—anything—to lessen his loss. "That must have been hard."

He glances over at me, and we stop walking, the waves rolling over our feet. "It wasn't awesome. But I get it—he wanted a fresh start. And me and my brother reminded him of her."

Reaching up, I take his face in my hands and kiss him, soft and slow on the lips. Trying to ease his pain. He relaxes into me, winding his arms around my waist and pulling me to him.

We kiss for a long time, standing beneath the stars at the edge of the ocean, just the two of us.

We kiss until the air grows cold, the waves rising and licking at my calves.

Finally, we head back to the inn, a little bit rawer, a little more exposed. And a whole lot closer than we'd been only three days ago.

22

GRIFFIN

I DIDN'T INTEND TO UNLOAD ALL THAT STUFF ABOUT MY family on Poppy. And I certainly didn't expect her reaction. For someone who comes off as flighty and perpetually upbeat, she handled that conversation way different than I thought she would.

I think I underestimated her.

She's a lot deeper than I gave her credit for. I probably shouldn't have been such a dick to her.

But I suppose that's behind us now. She doesn't seem to be holding any grudges, so . . .

Parker: Hey man. This is Parker. Wanted to invite you out with the boys tonight. Tipsy Taco. You in?

I scrub a hand over my neck, reread the text. *Is it wise to hang out with Poppy's twin brother?* I'm not sure how she'll feel about that.

> Griffin: What time? Let me check the schedule at Scoops and I'll let you know

> Parker: 8-ish. It's casual, you can swing by whenever. Me, Rome, King, Smitty

> Griffin: Cool. Thanks for the invite

> Parker: You bet

He shoots me a thumbs-up emoji, followed by a funny GIF of a man drinking an oversize margarita, and I have to laugh at that. He and Poppy are pretty similar, although I'm sure they'd both argue that point.

> Griffin: Hey, babe. Parker asked me to go to boys' night with him and the rest of your brothers. What do you think?

I hit send, frowning at my cell, my gut tense. It's kinda strange asking Poppy what to do—like I'm asking her permission or something—but I'm not sure how she'll feel about me buddying up with her brothers. Maybe that's crossing some invisible line I don't know about.

Five seconds later, I have a response.

> Poppy: Really? I wanted to hang out with you tonight

> Poppy: Parker always steals all my toys

> Griffin: Ha ha. I promise I won't let him steal me. I can swing by afterward?

Poppy: Obvs you haven't gone out with the boys of the beach. I'll be sleeping by the time y'all are done

Poppy: Unless you duck out with King. He always leaves early. Has to take care of the animals bright and early

Griffin: I'll dip at the same time as him then. If you don't mind me waking you up

Poppy: I'll never mind you waking me up

Maybe I should ditch boys' night altogether and skip to the good part . . .

Griffin: You sure you want me to go?

Poppy: Yes. My brothers NEVER invite anyone to boys' night. That's like a huge compliment

Griffin: OK, I'll go. But I'll miss you

Oh geez. Now I'm getting sappy. What the fuck's wrong with me? *Dial it back, Carter. You don't have to propose just yet.*

Poppy: I'll miss you too. Just out of curiosity—and they probably won't ask or anything—but if they do ask about me and you, what are you going to say?

Oh fuck. I hadn't thought about that yet. What am I going to say? *Hey, banging your little sister and she's great. Best I ever had and sexy AF.*

Even worse, what if they grill me about my intentions? Poppy and I haven't even had a proper date yet.

Griffin: What do you want me to say?

I mean, they're *her* brothers. This should totally be her call.

The phone vibrates in my hand, the screen lighting up with Poppy's name.

"Hello?"

"Hey. So, you don't have to, like, commit or anything, but, um . . ." Poppy's voice trails off, a heavy silence hanging between us. My gut twists and knots, and I swear my heart rate shoots up ten extra beats a minute.

"Is it cool if I say we're dating?" I run a hand through my hair and stare down at the bright red scar on my knee. I'm oddly nervous to hear her answer.

"Are we dating? I mean, I'm good with that. But I don't want you to feel pressured."

I scrub my damp palm on my shorts, a cool shot of relief running through me. "I'm good with it, yeah. They're not going to want to kick my ass or anything, are they? Because I'm gonna be way outnumbered."

Poppy giggles, a light, melodic tinkle, and my muscles unclench.

"No, I don't think so. But they'll probably try to scare you off. Don't listen to anything they say—it's all lies, I swear. Well, except I really did cut up all the T-shirts of a guy who cheated on me. That part's true. But everything else is a lie."

"Okay. So what I'm hearing is your brothers will be cool with us dating, and never cheat on you. Check and check.

For the record—I've never cheated on any of my girlfriends."

"That's good. Because I'd hate to have to destroy your T-shirt collection."

"I'd hardly call it a collection. But I do have one or two that I really like."

"Well, don't cheat on me then, and your T-shirts will be safe."

"Anything else I should know about your brothers before tonight?"

"Not really. They're pretty cool. But don't tell them I said that. I like to keep them guessing."

I chuckle, a lightness replacing the knotted tension in my chest. "If you think of anything later today, text me."

"Will do. Listen—I'm going to tell Liv then. Just in case you do end up talking about it with my brothers. I don't want her to think I'm holding out on her."

"Okay."

"And Griffin?"

"Yeah?"

"Whatever you do, don't make any bets with Parker. He always wins."

"Got it. No bets with Parker, check."

"Have fun tonight."

"Later, babe."

I disconnect, then shoot Parker a quick text.

> Griffin: I'm good for tonight. See you at 8

> Parker: Awesome. It'll be a good time. See you then

Shoving my phone in my pocket, I wonder belatedly if this is a good idea. Either way, it's happening, so I better get my head in the game. I have a feeling that tonight matters more than Poppy thinks if the two of us are going to have any kind of future together.

23

GRIFFIN

The Tipsy Taco is bumping at eight p.m., the lot jammed full of cars, and every table is taken when I stroll into the dim restaurant. Glancing around, I search the room for a familiar face, praying I'm not the first to arrive for boys' night. I intentionally left a few minutes late to avoid that very scenario.

A hand shoots up from a table in the back corner. Parker, waving me over, a wide grin on his face. I wave back, heading in his direction, weaving my way through the clusters of tables haphazardly spread throughout the room. A live band plays a bad cover of Journey's "Don't Stop Believin'," and a table of college-age girls warbles along with them. I silently pray they're almost done with their dinner, because I'm not sure how much of the impromptu drunken karaoke I can take.

"Hey, man. Glad you could make it." Parker stands, slapping my hand in a side high five. Rome shoots me a wave, and King nods as I take one of the two empty seats.

"Thanks for the invite."

A waitress stops by, and I order a beer and the Beach Taco special—three shrimp tacos, nachos, and a side of beans and rice.

"Good pick. The shrimp tacos here are great." Parker takes a swig of his beer, his fingers drumming on the table to the beat. "So, Griffin, what's good?"

He trains his eyes on me, and it's like staring at a male version of Poppy, which is kind of bizarre. They have the exact same color eyes and make the same facial expressions. You can definitely tell they're twins.

"Not much. Managing the ice-cream shop until my aunt's back on her feet."

"How's she doing? Was it a bad break? Not that there's such a thing as a good break." Rome squeezes the lime into his beer, takes a sip.

I shrug. "She's all right. On the mend. She'll probably be cleared for light work soon."

"That's good. I'm sure you're tired of scooping ice-cream cones," Rome says.

"Kind of. I never knew how terrible I am at customer service."

"Don't feel bad. It's not my thing either." Rome swipes at a droplet of condensation on the table. "Not like Poppy and Parker. They're the ones with that gift."

The mention of Poppy kicks my heartbeat into overdrive, my mouth drying up, all the fluid in my body rushing to my sweat glands. I'm burning up, and sweat beads on my palms. I reach for my beer, take a long, hard pull, and fervently hope her brothers don't ask me any questions.

"Thanks, man." Parker smacks Rome on the back, and then their cousin Smitty shows up, taking the focus off me.

He places his order, and I try to relax. *Pretend you're out with the team. It's all good.*

"Griffin, your team gonna make it to the World Series?" Parker shoves a tortilla chip into his mouth, crunching.

"Not sure. They're down a few guys, including me. My buddy Danny said it's not looking likely. But he may have been trying to make me feel better."

"Me and my crew have a bracket going. I pegged y'all for the big win." He dunks another chip into the salsa.

"Thanks for the vote of confidence. A W would be nice."

"You think you'll be back by spring training? Maybe we can catch a game. Y'all train here, right? I mean, obviously not Seaglass Beach, but down farther south?"

"Yeah, in Vero. I'm hopeful I'll be back, and I can definitely get tickets, sure."

"Cool. Road trip!" Parker and Smitty high-five, and my mind flashes to an image of Poppy sitting in the stands, wearing a team jersey with my number, cheering me on. Then I take a hard left turn, and now she's wearing *only* my jersey, nothing underneath, and I'm fucking her up against the orange metal lockers in the locker room.

"Griffin, has Poppy been a huge pain in your ass?" Parker raises his brow, and I plummet back down to Earth, leaving my scorching-hot fantasy behind.

"No, not really." More sweat beads on my back, and I swear Rome snickers, but the table of college girls is singing so damn loud I can't be sure. "She was pretty helpful the other day. Kind of saved me from a gaggle of crying kids."

The corner of Rome's lips twitch, and now I'm pretty sure I'm not imagining things. He and King exchange a look, and I shift in my seat, debating if I should escape this line of questioning and hit the head.

"Oh, Poppy loves kids. She used to make me play house with her when we were little, and she always made herself the mom and had, like, ten babies." Parker groans at the memory and Smitty laughs.

"That sounds about right. At least you didn't have to be one of the babies," Smitty says, shaking his head. "She always made me be one of her kids. She was so bossy."

"Not much has changed." King swirls the ice in his glass, the large, square cube clinking against the side. "Whoever decides to take her on is gonna need a whole lot of patience and an extra heaping of prayer."

I swallow, my throat tight. I'm unsure if I should mention anything or just let it be until someone asks me the direct question.

"You up for the challenge?" Rome levels his gaze on me, and my stomach rolls, the beer swirling around like a hoppy whirlpool. My gut tells me he somehow knows, so I may as well be honest and man up. This isn't going to get any easier.

"Yeah. Yes. I am." I straighten up in the wooden chair and square my shoulders. We have nothing to be embarrassed about; we're two consenting adults having appropriate sexual relations. Not that it's any of her brothers' business, but no way am I going to tell them that.

"Wait—what?" Parker narrows his aqua gaze. "You and Poppy? I thought y'all hated each other?"

"Thin line between love and hate, Parks." King's voice is serious, like he speaks from experience.

Honestly, he's right. I never would have thought that before, but here we are.

"Dude. Mad respect. My sister's a real hellcat. Good luck." Parker clinks my beer bottle with his and takes a long swig of his drink. The rest of the table drinks, too, like a *Godspeed* moment or something, and I try not to let this freak me out.

"Thanks. But we're good." I run a hand through my hair, shifting in my seat again, trying to get comfortable.

"Give it time." Rome smirks and snags a chip.

Our food arrives, and I'm grateful for the distraction.

"Oh, you've gotta be fucking kidding me." Rome practically growls under his breath, and I glance around, confused.

"Oh fuck," Parker chimes in, and Smitty shakes his head, all three of them staring at the waitress standing directly behind King. She's clearing tables, her back turned away from us.

"Juliet fucking Capelli. Poppy did mention she saw her here. I totally forgot." Parker's knuckles turn white as he grips the edge of the table, his jaw tense.

I have no idea why this is a huge deal, but it clearly is. King glances over his shoulder to see what has the rest of the table staring, and his face pales. At the same moment, Juliet spins around, her tray stacked high with dirty plates. She flushes a deep crimson, her mouth forming a silent *oh* as her gaze travels over our table, then locks straight onto King. The two of them stare at one another for one moment, two, before she flips her hair back over her shoulder and strides away.

King doesn't say anything, just swivels back around and takes another big slug of whiskey, downing the rest of the drink in one gulp. The table falls silent as our waitress hands out the food, and King orders a double. She hustles off to the bar for the next round of drinks, and we all eat, the band's rendition of "Livin' on a Prayer" shaking the table, the bass is so loud.

"Oh, fucking hell." Rome cracks his knuckles, his eyes glued to the bar.

"They had to come here tonight." Parker rolls his shoulders, taking in the three stocky guys wearing all black and standing at the bar.

"You had any run-ins with those assholes yet?" Parker tips his head at the dudes.

"No. Why?"

"Those are the Capelli brothers. The thugs of Seaglass Beach," Rome says. "Jagger, Cash, and Damon. Jagger fancies himself the brains of the operation, although that's debatable. Pretty sure between the three of them they might have one solid, functional brain. Juliet's their baby sister. Hundred bucks they're going to swagger over here and try to pick a fight."

Right on cue, the Capelli brothers pivot away from the bar with their drinks and spot us.

"Oh shit," Rome mutters, sizing up the situation. The Capellis saunter over, shoulders square and muscles flexed, leering.

This can't be good.

"Well, well, well. What do we have here? A Boy Scout meeting?" the shortest, stockiest of the three says.

"Shut the hell up, Jagger. Why don't you slither away, back to your snake hole, where you belong?" Parker says, the vein in his neck throbbing.

"Very funny, pretty boy. How's little Livvy doing? You enjoying your little love nest?" Cash says, and Parker's jaw tenses, the vein popping even more.

"None of your damn business, Jagger. How's being a slumlord treating you?" Parker spits back, and Jagger's nostrils flare.

"Would have been better if your little girlfriend stuck around. She could have seen how a real man operates."

Rome guffaws, and Cash and Damon both crowd in closer to the table, flexing their muscles.

"I see you picked up another pal." Jagger gestures his beer bottle in my direction. "You boys telling him all about how the Montgomerys stole half of Seaglass Beach from us?"

"Shut the fuck up, Jagger. Our family didn't steal anything from yours." King levels a flat gaze on Jagger.

"That's not what the paperwork says, Prince." Cash and Damon both snicker at Jagger's dumbass joke. My fingers itch to knock the stupid smirk off Jagger's face myself, and I don't even know the dude.

"What the fuck are you talking about?" Rome says, leaning back in his chair. Calm and unaffected by these goons.

"You didn't see the petition I filed up at the courthouse, Roman? Thought you'd be in the know, what with your fancy-pants new job and all." Jagger's lips curl around his beer bottle as he takes a slug.

"I work private security, asshole. I'm not a damn clerk," Rome snarls, his eyes flashing.

"You may want to see if you can boff a secretary then and figure it out. Because we're gonna sue your asses." Jagger sneers at each of the Montgomery brothers in turn, and Damon and Cash bob their heads, perfectly in sync, like two stick-on dashboard buffoons.

"What?" Parker frowns.

"That's right. The sun's setting on the Montgomery regime. There's about to be a new sheriff in town, boys. So saddle the fuck up." Jagger's mouth twists into a perverse smile, and a chill runs down my spine.

"Get outta here, Capelli. Have a nice night, tipping cows or bashing mailboxes, or whatever the hell it is you clowns do for fun." King scowls at them, then turns back to the table and starts eating his taco.

Damon lunges at King, gripping his shoulder, and before I even know what's happening, Rome has Damon's arm twisted behind his back and that goon's squealing like a damn pig. Cash goes after Rome, trying to help his brother, and King's out of his seat, knocking him away. Cash flies into the empty table behind him, plastic menus spilling off, and Jagger makes a dive at King. Parker stands up so fast his chair crashes to the ground, and then Smitty's up and in the mix too. I'm not sure what I should do—I just know I can't afford to hurt anything. As much as I'd love to help out, I do have a major league career hanging in the balance.

"Guys, stop!" Juliet runs over, throwing her tray down on the empty table behind us, rushing to get between King and Jagger. She's not as petite as Poppy, but the two hulking men dwarf her as she tries to wiggle between them. Jagger shoves her out of the way, clipping her shoulder with his meaty paw, and King absolutely snaps. His face turns fire-engine red, nostrils flaring, his gaze dangerously dark.

"Don't you fucking touch her." King's voice is low, deep, and menacing—anyone in their right mind would back the fuck up.

Instead, Jagger puffs out his chest and sneers, "Or what? She's my sister, so this is family business."

And because Jagger is obviously one stupid mother-fucker, he shoves his sister again, this time a little harder, and she reels backward. Smitty catches her right before she bounces up against the table, and King loses it. He rears back, then sends a sharp right hook straight into Jagger's nose. Blood splatters out of his huge nostrils, and he staggers, clutching his face.

"Stop it!" Juliet screeches, her fists balled at her sides, but no one pays any attention to her. Cash and Damon try to bum-rush our table, coming after Parker and Rome, but Rome holds them off. The band's still playing, but people have stopped eating, instead staring intently at the bar fight.

Jagger's nose must hurt pretty bad, because he twirls a finger in the air and retreats, Damon and Cash following behind him like the obedient attack dogs they are. Juliet crosses her arms over her chest and leans against a table, her eyes wide, her entire body trembling. Parker and Smitty sit back down at the table, acting like it's a normal dinner and nothing extraordinary happened. Rome leans down and picks up the menus Cash knocked to the ground and rights a few chairs before he cracks his knuckles again and sits. King shakes his hand out and stretches his fingers before crossing over to Juliet, his back turned to us. He reaches out, touching her elbow, but she recoils as if scorched by his palm. Her cheeks flush, and she shakes her head no, but the room's too loud, and I can't hear what either of them are saying. She's biting down on her lip so hard it's white, and the vibrations of King's deep voice rumble over the music, although I can't make out any of the words. Then Juliet storms off, untying her black apron and tossing it onto the bar before she shoves through the employee exit.

King stomps off toward the bathrooms, muttering under his breath, "unreasonable" and "mistake" the only words I'm able to make out.

Parker clears his throat. "Well, that was fun."

He picks up his beer and takes a long slug. Smitty shakes his head, and Roman taps the table with his fork, clearly distracted. Then Rome pushes away from the table and stands.

"I'm gonna go check on King. Make sure his hand's all right. We all know Jagger's hardheaded as fuck."

Parker grimaces at his brother's bad joke, and I wonder how soon I can leave without seeming rude. This night took a decided turn for the worse, the easygoing vibe from earlier evaporated.

"So—are you and my sister officially dating then? Not that I'm into labels or anything. I'm just surprised she hasn't mentioned it to me or Liv." Parker reaches for the salsa, his eyes sliding up to meet mine, and I shift in my seat.

"Yeah. I mean, I guess." I clear my dry throat, wishing I hadn't eaten any of the salty chips.

"Interesting." He chews, slowly and thoughtfully, his eyes trained on me. But he's not really looking at me at all, his gaze glassy.

My skin prickles, and I get the sense I should try to protect Poppy here, but I'm not sure exactly how to do that.

I swallow hard over what feels like an entire tortilla chip lodged sideways in my esophagus. "It's kind of a new and developing situation. We're keeping it casual, seeing where things go."

"Always a solid plan." Parker tips his chin in agreement.

"Anyway . . . thanks for the invite. This was fun, but I have to jet." I pull out my wallet and drop some money on the table.

"Already? We were gonna head to Manta Ray's next." Parker juts his thumb to the left, presumably in the direction of Manta Ray's.

"Maybe next time."

As fun as it is hanging out with Poppy's brothers and getting grilled on my love life, I'd much rather spend time with the woman herself. I can't wait to kiss her, touch her, hold her in my arms.

Turns out, going back to Atlanta and baseball might not be as easy as I thought it was gonna be.

24

POPPY

Since Griffin's out with the boys (a.k.a. my brothers), I invite Liv to Seaglass Sips. I figure we can grab a light bite, enjoy a bottle of wine, and wrap things up by nine so I'm home in plenty of time to meet Griffin. No need for her to be over when he shows up at my door later tonight.

"Hey, girl, hey!" I bounce up, embracing Liv in a hug, like I haven't seen her in years versus days.

"Hey!" She smooths her hair down over her shoulders, settling herself onto the barstool.

"I went ahead and ordered a bottle of chardonnay. What do you think about splitting a cheese board?" I squint at the menu, trying to decide between the Manchego and the brie.

"Perfect. I'm ravenous. Diane had me running all over town today, getting ready for Fall Fest. I love my boss, but sometimes..."

"Why were you running around?"

"She had the brilliant idea to cosponsor the event with

the town. Great idea, except I'm the one doing all the legwork. And there's a lot of legwork. We have swag packs I put together—Parks helped—"

I giggle, finding the visual of my brother sitting on the couch bedazzling tote bags downright hilarious. There's only one person in the entire world he'd do that for, and it's Liv . . .

"Plus, I'm in charge of the vendors. I mapped out the location of each booth, coordinated the food-prep sites; it's been a lot." Liv relaxes back against the stool with a heavy sigh. "You're going, right?"

"Next weekend?" I gratefully accept the wineglass the bartender slides across the granite counter and watch as she uncorks the bottle and pours straw-colored wine into each of our glasses.

Liv takes a delicate sip. "This is nice. Good choice, Pops."

"Thanks. I've been talking to the chef at the Seaglass and picking his brain on wines. I think we might start rotating ours out more, make them more seasonal."

"Oh, that's a good idea." Liv sets her glass down, the pendant lights catching her diamond engagement ring, and bright, sparkly prisms beam down on the smooth surface of the bar.

A tiny pang fires in my gut.

I should tell her about Griffin.

Especially after this past summer and everything that went down between us.

I take another swallow of wine and a deep inhale.

Just do it, Poppy. This is Liv. She's still your best friend since grade school. Even if she is marrying your brother.

"I slept with Griffin," I whisper, my gaze fixated on her ring.

"What?"

I cast my eyes over at her. She's scrunching her perfectly shaped brows together, frowning.

"I slept with Griffin." I emphasize every syllable, my voice fractionally louder.

"What?"

Unbelievable. Does she want me to broadcast it?

"I. Slept. With. Griffin. Well, technically, I'm sleeping with Griffin. Present tense." I force each word out in a sharp—very clear, very audible—tone.

Her lips curve up into a huge smile, and she pumps her fist. "Yes! I knew it. I just made you say it again so I could be certain I heard you correctly."

She leans over and rummages through her purse, coming up with her cell. She taps on the screen, clickety-click-click, then *whoosh* and my cell vibrates.

Liv: September 26. Poppy declares she will never get with Griffin Carter. Ever

I read the text, my cheeks burning.

Dammit. She got me.

"Fine." I set my cell down.

"Fine what?" Liv smirks, swishing the wine round and round in her glass, gloating and victorious.

"Fine. You were right."

"OMG. I never thought I'd hear those words." She grins, then hunches forward, our noses almost touching. "Now the good bits—is he so amazing? I bet he's amazing." Her eyes glaze over as she stares off into the distance, and I punch her on the arm, a tiny splash of wine flying out of her glass.

"You're engaged to my brother! Stop fantasizing about my man. And yes—he's freaking gorgeous and so, so good. He has all this ink, and my god, those abs." I shiver, remembering our little whipped-cream tryst at Scoops. "Like, ten out of ten."

"Nice. I'm so happy for you!" Liv wraps her arms around me in a hug, and my chest lightens.

I'm glad I told her.

"You can't mention any of this to Parker, though. Seriously—swear. I do not need him knowing about my sex life. That is where we draw the line."

"Pops! Of course I won't. I'd never. He wouldn't want to hear about it anyway. He won't even watch *Real Housewives* with me anymore." She rolls her eyes and I laugh.

"I'm impressed you got him to watch it at all. Count that as a win."

"I take it Griffin's not as grumpy as you thought, then?"

"Oh, he is. But now he turns his grump on other people instead of me, which works out just fine."

Liv laughs, and it's nice hanging out with my bestie again, having girl time. It's been so long I almost forgot what this is like.

"This is nice. We should do this more often."

She reaches out and squeezes my arm. "Agree. Listen—I wanted to talk to you in person. . ."

My heart stops for a split second, buzzy panic racing through me.

"Nothing bad, Pops, promise. Will you be my maid of honor?" Her emerald gaze finds mine, her eyes wide with earnestness.

"Liv! Of course I will! You didn't even need to worry for one second." My arms fly out to crush her in a tight hug, almost knocking over both the wineglasses. "Silly, you know I love you. Thanks for asking."

"Whew. That's a relief."

"When are you thinking of having the wedding? I mean, maybe I should have checked my calendar first . . . ," I tease.

"Not sure. I'm still looking at venues."

My palm flies up into the air. "Hold up—venues? You're not getting married at the inn?"

"Parker did mention something about a reception at the tiki bar."

"Perfect!" I clap my hands together, my mind already cranking on the details. "Come by tomorrow and we can look at the event calendar, see what's available. I suppose I can even give y'all the friends-and-family discount. But not a double, just one discount."

"Great. Parker will be happy. Not that he's going to be too involved. Between me and you, I'm sure we'll manage to cover most everything."

"Since you're the bride, does that make Diane the assistant who has to do everything?" I scrunch my nose up, thinking through the logistics.

Liv snorts. "Doubtful. Pretty sure that's going to fall to you, as the maid of honor. There's still time to bail . . ."

"Never. I've got your back. And I may even have a plus-one." My entire body heats at the idea of having Griffin by my side at Liv and Parker's wedding. Someone to escort me, dance with me, hang out with me when my brother and best friend ride off into the sunset, leaving me behind to pick up the grains of rice or rose petals or whatever thing they decide we should all chuck at them as they begin their lives together as Mr. and Mrs.

Yes, it would be very nice—amazing, really—to have Griffin with me at the wedding.

"Any chance you can plan the wedding around the baseball schedule?"

25

GRIFFIN

WHEN I GET TO THE INN, I PARK MY ROVER NEXT TO Smurfy and grab my to-go box. Due to the dustup, I didn't get a chance to eat all my food, and now I'm kind of hungry. I lock the car and amble up to the door, trying to act calmer than I feel inside.

Knock, knock.

My stomach flip-flops—maybe the shrimp tacos weren't a great choice after all—and now I'm not hungry anymore.

"Hey, handsome." Poppy opens the door, wearing only a T-shirt, and fuck if it isn't the sexiest thing I've ever seen.

"Hey." I drop my lips to hers and kiss her like I haven't seen her in a decade, slipping my tongue in and claiming her mouth. Wrapping her arms around my waist, she leans into me, and I step all the way into her apartment, closing the door behind me.

After a few minutes, I pull away and shake the white Styrofoam box. "I have tacos."

Poppy grins up at me. "Amazing, because I'm starving. Also, I want to hear all about boys' night. How'd it go?"

She breaks away, heading into her kitchen to fetch plates, and I follow behind, admiring the round globes of her ass peeking out from the bottom of her shirt.

"Eventful, actually."

Her blonde head swivels back around so hard I'd swear she's an owl. "Whaddya mean?"

"Well—" I rake a hand through my hair, debating how much I should say. I don't want to throw fuel on the fire, but I figure she'll hear about it from one of her brothers anyway. Honestly, I'm surprised she doesn't already know.

"Everything went great with your brothers—they're cool. But then the Capellis showed up."

"Oh no." Poppy shakes her head, reaching up into the cabinet and pulling down plates. "All three of them?"

"Four."

"Oh yeah. Juliet works at the Tipsy Taco now. Slipped my mind. I'm so used to her being out of the picture."

"It was kinda weird."

"How so?" Poppy's aqua eyes narrow, one eyebrow tipped high on her forehead.

"The one guy—Jagger, I think—came over and started shit with your brothers. Egging them on. But all your brothers stayed cool. It was impressive. Then he started talking about land and how the Montgomerys stole from them and how the Capellis are going to sue."

"Hold up." Poppy's palm flies into the air, a five-digit stop sign. "They're suing us? On what grounds?"

"That's where things get fuzzy. He told Rome he should know about it because he works at Town Hall, but Rome hadn't heard anything. Then Jagger shoved Juliet, and King lost it."

Poppy licks her bottom lip, frowning. "What? What do you mean? That jerk laid hands on his own sister while she was working?"

"Yeah. He didn't hit her, but he pushed her hard enough to knock her over. That's when your brothers and the Capellis had a full-blown bar brawl. I'm sorry I didn't jump in—you can tell them that for me—but I can't afford to get hurt."

Poppy huffs out a breath, honey hair falling down over her forehead. "Boys, I swear. . ."

"King got really pissed. I'm pretty sure he broke Jagger's nose."

"Serves him right. Jagger's a real asshole." She crosses her arms over her chest, her bare foot tapping a mile a minute on the tile.

I set the to-go box down on the bar and grip her narrow hips, pulling her to me.

"Hey. It's fine. Your brothers definitely won that round."

She gazes up at me, eyes wide with worry. "The Capellis are gonna sue us?"

"Probably all talk. They seem like blowhards."

She heaves out another sigh, then rests her head on my chest, just above my heart. I run a hand down her back, trying to comfort her. "It'll be fine."

"I hope so. My family's been through a lot in the last few years. We don't need any more trouble."

"I'm sure Jagger's full of shit."

Poppy tips her head, gazing up at me through her dark lashes. "Fuck Jagger. Let's eat."

She untangles from me and snags the to-go box, popping the tacos onto plates and heating them up in the microwave. We eat the rest of the nachos cold, standing at the bar, then move to her couch to polish off the tacos and rice.

"Thanks for dinner round two." Poppy dabs her lips with a napkin. "That was great."

"No problem. Listen—" I clear my throat, take a big gulp of water. "Parker asked me if we were dating."

"Oh?" Poppy's eyes slide up to meet mine, but her expression's blank, unreadable.

"Yeah."

"What did you say?" Her gaze is steady as I silently trace the faint cinnamon freckles on her nose.

"I told him we were. But I didn't go into any details."

A flush creeps up her neck, moving straight into her cheeks. "You didn't mention that I made you my personal ice-cream sundae?"

Now my cheeks burn. "Uh, no. Didn't bring that one up."

She giggles. "Good. I told Liv, too, so Parker would find out one way or another. What about the others?"

"I intimated that we were involved, but I didn't go into specifics. I think they got the point, though."

Her face breaks into a smile as she climbs into my lap, straddling me and twining her arms around my neck. "Thanks for hanging out with them. I appreciate it."

She cups my face, pressing her lips to mine in a spicy kiss. My hands trail down her spine, settling on her ass cheeks, and I squeeze lightly. She opens her mouth to me, and I slip in, claiming her.

I could do this every day for the rest of my life.

The thought pops up out of nowhere, and I shove it away, my heart jackhammering in my chest so hard I'm vaguely concerned about a heart attack.

Simmer down. One play at a time, Carter.

I grip her harder, deepening our kiss. At the very least, I want her to remember me.

Even if this thing between us doesn't last—because nothing ever does.

26

POPPY

Griffin Carter's the best thing that's ever happened to me, hands down.

Better than making prom court back in high school.

Better than acing my statistics class in college.

Even better than the Seaglass Inn being voted "Best Beach Stay" in the state of Florida last year.

He's that damn good.

My fingertips lightly trace along the inky swirls covering his broad chest. I outline each abdominal muscle, silently counting as I go—one, two, three, four, five, six. Dropping lower still, I run my hand along the deep V at his hip, the line pointing directly to his dick, and he stirs, wrapping his strong arm around me tighter.

"Be careful what you start . . . ," he murmurs, his voice deep and gravelly, still thick with sleep. The vibrations tickle my ear, sending a hot tingle rolling through me. His hand splays on my backside, cupping my ass and kneading the bare flesh.

"Now who's starting something?" I tug at the elastic of

his boxers, and he sheds them with one hand, his dick springing out. I encircle him, stroking up and down his hard length.

"How much time do we have?" Griffin caresses my breast, thumbing at my peaked nipple.

I peer at the window, the first rays of milky sunlight filtering through the shades.

"Probably about thirty minutes, I'd guess. At least I don't have too far to go."

"Not enough time for all the things I want to do to you, but I can make it work." He pulls me onto his chest, and I straddle him, his impressive erection bobbing between us. I lean down, sealing my lips onto his, and he groans, opening his mouth to me.

Griffin's an amazing freaking kisser.

I'd love to kiss him all day long, love for his tongue to plunder me like a pirate searching for gold.

He finds my breasts, squeezing and pinching, my skin hot beneath his large, rough hands. His touch is just right —firm and self-assured—as he wrests pleasure from my body. I'm so wet for him, rocking up against him. He reaches down, his fingers finding my clit, circling until it's hot and swollen for him.

"I'm on birth control, you know," I whisper between kisses.

He gazes up at me, his eyes dark and hazy with lust and sleep. "You sure you're okay with that?"

I nod. "Yes. If you are."

He answers by spreading my legs wider, then easing into me. Slow, so slow, a sharp hiss escaping between his teeth.

My eyes flutter closed as he stretches me, filling me all

the way up, and I adjust to the pressure of his cock inside me.

"Fuck, you're so tight. You feel so good."

A warm glow of pleasure rushes over me, a golden balm, sweet like honey running through my veins. I shimmy against him, taking him all the way in, as deep as he can go. He thrusts up, hitting my pleasure spot, and a moan falls from my lips.

"Griffin."

"You like that, baby?" He thrusts again, this time harder, and my body flushes, hot and wanting.

I move with him, and we find a good rhythm, our hips undulating together to a beat only the two of us can hear.

Being with Griffin like this, feeling him inside me, nothing between us at all is fucking magical. I don't want to ever stop, but the waves of pleasure rolling through me are coming fast and hard, and I know I'm close.

His hand finds my nipple, and he pinches it hard, then releases, the blood rushing into my chest. Pain, followed by rippling pleasure, and I've never been with someone so skilled, so attentive.

"Griffin . . ." My voice comes out strangled, half moan, half cry, and my orgasm rocks through me, my muscles contracting around his dick. He smacks my ass, thrusting up harder into me, chasing his own climax. Hot jets of his release stream into me, his body tense and shuddering.

"Fuck . . . ," he hisses, tensing, driving into me one last time before his body relaxes. His breathing's fast, the vein in his neck popping.

I place my hand on his heart, the thudding hard and rapid. "I take it that was good for you." I roll off, twining my leg around his.

He lazily strokes my back, his breathing slowly returning to normal. "Yeah. That's one helluva way to start the day."

I want to start every day like this.

My breath catches in my throat, my heart pounding hard again. I bite down on my lip, focus on the smooth skin beneath my outstretched palm, and try not to freak at all of these forever thoughts.

"Hey—what's wrong?" Griffin peers down at me, his pupils dark, still wide with desire.

"Nothing." Not a lie, exactly, more like a half truth.

"You sure? Are you having second thoughts about what we just did? If you are, don't worry. I have a physical every six months, and I'm clean."

"No, it's not that." I inhale, exhale, blinking hard and debating what to say. I don't want to freak him out with my feelings and come on too strong. I'm kinda known to do that.

"What's going on, Poppy?" He strokes my back, urging me to open up to him.

I sigh, scrunching my eyes shut tight, the words spilling out of my mouth. "I'm falling in love with you."

His hand freezes on my back, and a heavy silence fills my bedroom.

I knew I shouldn't have said anything. Too much, too soon.

"Uh . . ."

Dammit. Why didn't I keep my mouth shut? This is so embarrassing.

My skin's burning, and I want to dive into the cool comfort of my sheets and hide. Maybe forever.

"Wow. I wasn't expecting that."

"Yeah, me neither. I'm sorry, I shouldn't have gone

there. It's too fast, I know."

To my surprise, Griffin reaches down, tipping my chin up and locking his eyes on mine. "I feel the same way. It's just complicated. I usually work through things in my head before I talk about them."

My jaw drops, shock hitting me square in the chest, my heart pounding so loud I can barely hear over the thudding.

"You do?"

"Yeah, I do." He traces his thumb along my jaw, his touch so soft, so gentle. Dipping down, he presses his lips to mine, an electric current humming between our naked bodies. Relief and desire mingle in my veins, a powerful aphrodisiac.

"So now what?" I trace the curve of the Celtic knot inked on his chest.

"I don't know. This wasn't part of the rehab plan."

"We can make it work, though, right?" Hope filters into my voice, bright and shiny.

"Let's take it one day at a time. I'm not going anywhere right now."

My gut clenches, but I focus on the positive. "Okay."

He kisses me again, soft and slow, and I melt into his hard body. Steady, calm, strong enough for the both of us.

Eventually I come up for air. "I have to shower and go to work. See you later?"

Griffin presses his lips to mine again. "Yes. See you later."

I leave the comfort of my bed and hit the shower, shoving all my doubts out of my mind and letting them wash down the drain.

Surely we can make this work. Because now that I've been with Griffin, I don't think I can live without him.

27

GRIFFIN

I didn't expect Poppy to lay it all out on the line like that. I felt it too—humming between us, strong and intoxicating—but I didn't want to label it. Make it even more real.

Because what can I do? Even though I don't hate Seaglass Beach anymore—it's kinda growing on me—my life isn't here. It's back in Atlanta, with my team, playing ball. I can't give that up. Not yet.

Even for Poppy, as much as I like her. Love her.

Maybe.

Maybe.

The word echoes in my head, banging around, getting louder and louder until my breathing's shallow and my chest aches.

And damn if I'm hyperventilating, right here in the middle of Scoops, the sweet scent of vanilla winding around me, twisting and choking me.

I sink down onto the stool, pain from my knee radiating up my thigh, lodging in my quad muscle.

Fuck.

Why is my life so complicated all of a sudden? Before I blew out my knee, I had a schedule, a routine, a plan for every last second of my day, my week, my month.

And I liked it. Practice, play, rinse and repeat.

No complications. No feelings. My only worry winning the next game.

But now I'm floundering, trying to figure out the future and how I can have it all. Have a life outside of baseball.

Sure, other guys do it. But none of their girlfriends or wives run a business like Poppy. They can travel with the team, attend the games. Be there a lot of the time.

Poppy can't do that. She *is* the Seaglass Inn.

Quit baseball.

Nausea rolls through me, acid rising up my throat, burning my tongue. I never thought about quitting before. Not when my ACL ripped right there on the field, not when I met with the surgeon and he broke down the reconstructive surgery necessary to repair the damage, not the day I went under the knife.

I always knew I'd be back on the field, the crowd cheering as I whaled the ball home, saving our team from another run.

Quitting's not an option.

Right?

Before I met Poppy, my kneejerk response would have been "hell no." Walking away from the game—from my life, from my dream—is an impossibility.

Right?

Right?

Now I'm not so sure. There's more to think about.

How long can I realistically play? How much more can

my body take? I'm in my thirties now, so maybe it's time to settle down. Move on.

I slump down on the stool and stare at the shiny white countertop, an icy cold washing over me.

Am I done with baseball?

I have another year left on my contract. I have to go back. It'd be ludicrous not to.

I have to go back.

I only hope I can make Poppy understand.

Buzz, buzz.

The vibration of my cell in my pocket shakes me out of my thoughts.

> Poppy: Want to go to Fall Fest with me?

I swallow hard over the lump in my throat, even as my heart hammers hard against my ribs.

> Griffin: Sure. When?

> Poppy: Saturday. Maybe around noon?

> Griffin: I'll try to get someone to cover the shop

> Poppy: OK

The text bubbles pop up, then disappear. I stare down at the screen for what feels like five minutes—and nothing.

> Poppy: I hope I didn't scare you this morning

I roll my shoulders, trying to ease the tension between

my shoulder blades. A dull thud pistons in the back of my right eye as I tap out a lie.

Griffin: You didn't. All good

I've never been one to back down from a challenge, so why start now?

She texts me a GIF of a cat wiping his brow in relief, and I smile down at my cell.

Maybe we can make long distance work . . .

I'll bring it up when we're together, in person, at the right time, and feel her out on the situation. I know it's not ideal, but maybe short-term it'll work?

Poppy: Gotta bolt. Teeny-tiny kitchen emergency. See you later?

Griffin: See you tonight

I'm excited to see her and be with her, but also nervous as hell, knowing she's not going to love my answer. But it's the best I can do.

Life's never perfect, even if you try to spin everything in the golden beams of sunshine Poppy dances in.

28

POPPY

Fall Fest is one of my fave events of the year. The celebration marks the official kickoff of the holiday season in Seaglass Beach. After Fall Fest, Halloween's right around the corner; then we're all in full holiday mode—Thanksgiving, Christmas, New Year's. Fall Fest is the first of the festive dominoes, and I absolutely live for it.

This year I'm loving it even more because I'm going with Griffin.

We'll get to spend an entire day together, not just a few stolen hours after work. Today we'll get to talk, be with friends and family.

Solidify our relationship out in the open.

An excited tremor ripples through me.

Who would have ever imagined me and Griffin together, a real live couple?

Probably not too many people. But together, we do work. He's serious and I'm playful; I lighten him up and he brings me back to reality when necessary. Which is rare, but I'll admit, sometimes I can get a little whimsical.

Right now everything between us is perfect. When he slips his fingers through mine, it's like putting on my most comfortable and best-fitting yoga pants. I'm right at home with him, and being with him feels so, so right.

Even though we haven't been together very long, I'm madly in love with Griffin Carter and can't imagine my life without him in it. When I'm not with him, I'm daydreaming about being with him, and when I am with him, I feel complete.

He's definitely The One.

I spot him from across the lawn, his broad frame and dark head towering over most of the crowd. Waving, I walk quickly across the grass to the Seaglass Scoops booth Liv and I helped set up yesterday.

"Hey." My voice comes out breathy, and my cheeks burn as Jess smiles at me, then Griffin.

Oh geez. How much has Griffin told her? And there's no way she has cameras inside the ice-cream shop, right? Because that would be trés embarrassing.

"Hey, Poppy. Great to see you. Griffin tells me you've been real helpful at Scoops. Thanks a bunch."

"Oh my gosh, no problem at all." I wave off the good deed. "He's a natural, barely needed any help, really."

Griffin guffaws at this, a deep, hearty chuckle, sending vibrations straight to my core.

Damn, he's sexy. That jaw, those corded forearms. I'm never going to get enough of this man, and now I kinda wish we were going back to my place instead of hanging at the Fall Fest.

"Well, you kids go have fun. I can manage the booth on my own for a bit, and then Hailey'll be here to help out."

"Oh good. I'm glad she's working out for you." I helped

Griffin find Hailey; she's the younger sister of a valet at the inn.

"So far, so good. Even Griffy needs some downtime. And with my cast off now, I'm almost back to normal."

Griffin's brow furrows. "Not really, Aunt Jess. Your wrist's still weak. You'll need a lot of PT before you can start scooping ice cream full-time."

It's sweet how much Griffin cares for his aunt. A warm, fuzzy feeling spreads through my chest, and I lace my fingers through his.

"Enough worrying about me—go have fun!" She shoos us away with her good hand, her gray bob bouncing on her shoulders.

"Where to?" Griffin glances down at me as we walk, my heart flip-flopping under his gaze.

"Games, rides, or food? You choose, since I'm the home team."

He chuckles, his teeth gleaming white in the autumn sunshine. "Rides first. Then games, then food. Least chance of vomiting."

"Solid strategy." I lead the way to the far side of the common area, closest to the beach. A pirate ship swings high up into the cloudless sky, whooshing up and back down again while riders scream.

"You afraid of heights?" I size him up as he stares at the ride.

"Me? Nah. I'm fearless."

"Okay then. Let's do the pirate ship, then the bungee-drop thingy. After that we'll hit the go-karts."

"Is that the technical name, the bungee-drop thingy?" he teases, ribbing me with his elbow as we wind our way in the line.

"Yes. Actually, it is."

He snickers, pulling me back against his hard body by the hips. I rest against him as we wait our turn, the sun warm on my face, the air a cool balm to my wild emotions. His clean scent rolls off him, tickling my nose and mixing with the salt air, and my thighs clench.

I'm in deep.

"Ready?" He squeezes my waist, and the dull ache between my legs pulses, intensifying.

"Mm-hmm." I squeak out my response, thinking I'm more ready for something else, but the pirate ship ride will have to do in a pinch.

We fasten our seat belts, and then Griffin reaches over and double-checks mine's tight enough that I won't fly out. He's protective, just like my brothers. When they baby me, it's annoying; when Griffin does it, it's thoughtful and sexy.

He takes my hand, and I notice his palm's sweaty.

"You nervous?"

"Me? Never. I told you—I'm fearless."

"Uh-huh." I purse my lips, trying not to laugh, as the vein in his neck pops.

The ride kicks, the ship groaning as we inch up into the air. Slowly at first, pausing at the apex, then we oscillate backward. Gravity takes over and Griffin drops my hand, gripping the metal safety bar for dear life. Now we're flying through the air and I can't help it: I scream and scrunch my eyes shut tight. A rush of adrenaline courses through me as we swing through the sky, the wind whipping my face.

"Ohmygawd!" I cry.

Inching my eyes open, I peep over at Griffin. He's pale,

and he's got a death grip on the bar, the skin on his knuckles translucent.

"Griff. Griff, it's okay," I shout over the screams of the other riders, my hand finding his and squeezing.

His pinkie locks onto mine, but he still doesn't open his eyes.

I think it's safe to say Griffin's scared shitless.

So much for fearless . . .

After a few minutes, the ship slows and comes to a rocking stop. Only then does he open his eyes, his face now flushed.

"It's over, right? There's not some sick encore or something?" His head swivels around, taking in his surroundings.

I giggle. "Yeah, Mr. Fearless. It's over. Thanks for going with me—I can tell it wasn't your jam."

He rolls his shoulders back and exhales a long breath. "Probably not going again. But you seemed like you were into it, so . . ."

I lean over, brushing my lips against his. "Thanks, babe. But you could have told me you didn't want to go."

Bright spots of color stain his cheeks. "You wanted to go. I wanted you to have fun and be happy. What's five minutes of torture anyway? No big deal."

"Griff!" I punch his arm, unhooking my seat belt now that we're safely back on the ground. "You can be honest with me. About anything." I drop my voice. "You can even tell me if you're scared—I won't broadcast it."

"Thanks. So, special request then. Let's skip the bungee thingy. I might have a clause in my contract that prohibits that anyway."

"Mm-hmm. But that's fine." I grab his hand, hauling

him off the ride. "C'mon, let's head straight to the games. I'm sure you're going to slay."

We head over to the games area, and I make a beeline for the "Strong Man" contest, the brightly colored barometer stretching high into the sky. "I've been wanting to see you wield this hammer ever since it showed up on this square. Show me what you got."

Griffin cracks his knuckles, stepping up to the big silver button and handing over the tickets. His jaw flexes, parallel lines of concentration furrowing between his brow. He's so damn sexy, staring that multicolored pole down, that my panties dampen.

Wrapping his hands around the mallet, he squares his shoulders and raises the hammer. He hesitates at the top, then swings down hard. The puck flies up, all the way to the top, and the bell rings out loud and clear.

"Yes!" I clap, jumping up and down. "I knew you'd do it. On the first try too."

The guy operating the game shoots Griffin a wary look, one brow cocked as if he doesn't believe it can be done.

"What?" Griffin meets his gaze, challenging him.

"Nothing, bro. It's just—no one ever wins this game. I've been working it for a few years now, and I can count on one hand the number of people who've managed to ring that bell. That was impressive."

"He *is* a major league baseball player." I wind my hands around the back of Griffin's neck, grazing my lips with his.

"Oh, y'all are so cute."

I recognize that nasty voice even before I see him. Jagger.

FML.

"Piss off, Jagger." I mince the words out, swiveling around to verify his presence. Yep, it's him.

"What's up, ball boy?" Jagger tips his greasy head at Griffin, his nose swollen and his eyes rimmed with dark rings. Griffin presses his lips together, not taking the bait.

"You a permanent resident now? Or you gonna bolt once you're tired of banging Princess Poppy?" Jagger's eyes rake over my body, a cold shiver skittering down my spine.

I hate this dude.

"None of your damn business." Griffin spits out the words, pulling me behind him and putting more distance between me and Jagger.

"But Princess Poppy is my business." Jagger steps in, his oily voice oozing over me. His gaze rests on my chest, and I can practically feel his meaty hands on my skin.

"No, Jagger, I assure you I'm not your business. Buzz off." I straighten up to my full height, even if it doesn't amount to much past five foot. Better than nothing.

"Aww, sweet little innocent princess. I'm about to rock your world." His lips curl into a sneer and my insides quiver.

"No way, Jagger. You've been trying to best the Montgomerys for years now. Whatever it is you're planning, I'm sure you'll fail. You always do." I grip Griffin's hand tight, wishing we could go back to a few seconds ago, before this weasel showed up.

"I've got y'all now. And you're gonna pay. Hotel Capelli has a nice ring to it, don't you think?" He winks at me, and my skin crawls, my stomach roiling.

What the fuck is he talking about?

"C'mon, Poppy." Griffin drags me away toward the food stands, although eating is the furthest thing from my mind.

My entire body's shaking with anger—there's zero chance I can eat right now.

"Ohmygawd, Griff! What's he talking about? He's going to try to take the inn?" Total panic sets in, hot and pressing, and I'm struggling to breathe.

"Shh, relax. He's trying to get to you. We'll figure it out, don't worry." Griffin's voice is calm, soothing, helping to center me.

"I need to call King, tell him what happened." I'm already fishing my cell from my pocket.

"That's fine. But I'm sure it's nothing." He rests his hand on the small of my back, rubbing in slow circles as I catch my breath.

I call King, but he doesn't answer. Leaving a message is futile—King never listens to messages. So I shoot him a text:

> Poppy: Call me. Urgent

> Poppy: It's about Jagger

Five minutes later, my cell rings.

"Hello?"

"What's up?" King's deep voice vibrates down the line, and I already feel better. My oldest brother will know what to do, how to handle this.

"It's Jagger. We ran into him at Fall Fest and he said he's gonna own the inn!"

"Hogwash. The Seaglass Inn's been in our family over three generations. We have the deed to the land, and we own it free and clear. Plus all the surrounding land. Jagger's full of shit."

"Then what's he talking about, King? I agree—he

usually is full of shit. But he sounds pretty convincing this time. Like he knows something we don't." I nibble at my fingernail, still low-key panicked.

"It's probably nothing. But Rome's looking into it. Stay calm and don't engage with him."

"Do you think we should get a lawyer?"

"Maybe."

Shit. This is bad. If King thinks we might need a lawyer, we could be in real trouble.

"Don't worry about it now, Pops. Have fun at Fall Fest. Like I said—Rome's on it."

I blow out a breath, some of the tension draining from my body. "Okay. But I want to be kept in the loop. Got it?"

"Got it."

King hangs up without saying goodbye, and I tuck my phone back in my pocket, only slightly less stressed than before the call.

"You want to get out of here?" Griffin tips his head, sizing me up.

"No. Let's stay. I don't want Jagger to think he got the best of me. Besides, we haven't even hit the highlight yet—the blue crab."

Taking Griffin by the hand, I drag him toward the food tents, determined to have a good time.

Jagger Capelli is not ruining my date.

29

GRIFFIN

Running into Jagger was a real buzzkill. Even though Poppy's trying her hardest to stay sunshiny and optimistic, she's jumpy as fuck. At the sound of any male voice, she spins around, her eyes scanning the crowd for a Capelli. And if she keeps up the assault on her fingernails, her cuticles are gonna be bleeding soon.

"Poppy, we don't have to stick around. We could swing by that noodle place you like and grab takeout."

"No way." She crosses her arms over her chest, physically and mentally digging in her heels. "The best part of Fall Fest is the food, and I'm not letting stupid Jagger Capelli ruin that for you. C'mon."

She reaches for my hand, dragging me across the vast food tent. We pass booth after booth, all offering their signature dishes. The Orange Grove has everything citrus —jams, jellies, marmalades, freshly squeezed orange juice, key lime pie. There's an Everything's Coming Up Mac booth, serving all types of mac and cheese; a peanut butter vendor with different peanut-based dishes—I could go for the homemade dark chocolate peanut butter pie.

Finally, Poppy stops in front of the most crowded booth, a huge banner waving in the air announcing *"Florida's Tastiest Blue Crabs!"* A long line stretches down the side of the tent, moms and dads trying to entertain their antsy kids while waiting. Mercifully, the line's moving quickly, the servers taking and filling orders in record time.

Poppy's uncharacteristically quiet as we inch our way up to the front, and I wish I talked her out of staying. I think we'd have a lot more fun back at the house, skinny-dipping and eating dumplings. But she's hell-bent on being here, so I shuffle behind her in the line, trying to think of a way to take her mind off Jagger.

"The team won last night."

"Really? That's great." Her head bobs in acknowledgment, but she's staring off in the distance, only half listening.

"The mascot played shortstop."

"Nice."

"Pops—you're not even listening. Let's go." I rub her thumb, urging her to look at me and stop scouring the crowd for Capellis.

"I am listening." She folds her arms over her chest, her foot tapping on the grass.

"I just said the mascot played shortstop and your reply was 'Nice.' It's not nice—mascots don't play baseball."

"So now you're quizzing me on my baseball knowledge?"

"No, not at all. I'm saying you're distracted, and it's cool. But just admit you're upset."

"I'm fine." Her cheeks puff out; then she blows out a heavy breath.

"You're not fine. And that's okay."

"Dammit, Griffin, I said I'm fine!"

The people in front of us spin around at her raised voice, giving us a mean case of side-eye. Tears shimmer in Poppy's aqua eyes, and now I feel like an asshole.

"Babe." I pull her in close, wrap my arms around her. She stiffens, then relaxes as I rub her back in circles, like my mom used to when I lost a game.

"You don't always have to be up, you know. It's okay to be stressed or worried. That's very relatable."

"I just wanted to have the best day with you, and now I'm worried about the inn." Her voice quivers, and I want to kick Jagger's ass myself.

"Tell you what—let's grab food and see if we feel better after we eat. If not, let's jet."

She nods and sniffles, her face rubbing against my chest. But she seems to be at least a little calmer now.

"Are you gonna buy a shirt?" I point at the merch to our left, a tall stack of T-shirts with the catchy phrase "I got crabs at Jimmy's!"

She gives me a wan smile. "No, I already have one."

"Shut up! You don't."

"Yeah, I do. So you should get one; then we can match."

"I'm not wearing it in public." Now it's my turn to fold my arms across my chest.

"Oh, come on. Don't be a spoilsport."

"I do not need to go viral for that. Nuh-uh," I say, shaking my head.

Poppy's face brightens in a genuine smile, and at least I'm getting somewhere.

"Fine. I swear I won't post the pics anywhere."

I squint down at her. "I'm gonna need that in writing."

"I'll do you one better than that." She lifts up on tiptoe, pressing her mouth to mine in a slow, sweet kiss. "I promise."

"Fine," I murmur into her lips. "You're a tough negotiator, Miss Montgomery."

"I've had a lot of practice. You've met my brothers."

"Next!" A man wearing an "I'm crabby, don't ask!" T-shirt waves us up to the counter. I defer to Poppy, the local, and she orders for us.

"We'll take two steamed blue crabs, an order of fries, and two beers."

I pay for the food; then we shift to the side to wait. Poppy pushes me toward the merch display, so I buy a T-shirt to make her happy.

Five minutes later, we have our food, beer, and merch. We head out to the lawn to snag a place to eat, and Poppy spies Liv and Parker at a picnic table in the distance. She waves, and a few minutes later we're deeply engrossed in the fine art of cracking crab. Apparently there's a special Montgomery method of crab deshelling I need to catch up on.

"The first thing you do is crack the sucker and peel off the top shell, like so." Parker demonstrates, using his metal cracker. "Then you take off the dead man's fingers." He removes the razor-sharp gills carefully, which is kind of revolting.

"Next, dig out the meat like so . . ." Parker excavates the little bugger like a damn bear foraging before winter. "I like to leave the claws for last because they're the best part. Claws are meaty, not fishy. Dip it in butter and"—he holds up his hand, pressing his thumb to his fingers—"chef's kiss!"

He slurps the claw meat from his hand while Liv stares over at him. I can only guess they've not eaten crab together very often, because she looks a little traumatized.

Being a savvy woman, she shoves her plate his way. "Babe, would you mind cracking mine for me? You're so good at that." She bats her eyelashes at him, and Parker falls for it hook, line, and sinker.

"Sure, babe. You got it." He happily takes over cracking duty, while Liv sits back and sips her chardonnay.

Sadly, I don't think I can foist my crab cracking onto Poppy. I pick up the silver cracker, then the crab, holding the bright-red-orange shell up to the light to figure out the best angle to hit for maximum effect.

"It's not rocket science, Griff." Poppy clucks at me, twisting first one claw, then the other, off her crab with ease. "Dive in."

I follow her lead, rotating the claw in a slow circle. The appendage breaks off easily, so I do the same to the other side.

Success.

Then I remove the spindly legs, shoving them over to the far side of the paper basket. Now for the hard part—breaking the shell.

"You want help?" Poppy leans over, examining my progress.

"I can do it."

"I don't want you to hurt yourself." Her pretty bow of a mouth tips up in a smile, teasing me.

I inch closer to her, our legs touching beneath the table. Tilting my head toward her, my lips brush her ear.

"You worried about my baseball career? Or is it more about what these hands can do to you later?"

Splashes of pink bloom on her cheeks as she peers at me through her dark lashes.

"Yeah, that's what I thought."

With my knife, I flip the crab over onto his back and slice through the apron. Peeling off the shell like Parker showed me, I pull out the gills and the innards. Disgusting, but I try not to think about it. Then I get to work parsing the meat, piling all the white bits into a neat and tidy heap.

"Aren't you going to eat it?" Poppy bites at the corner of her lip, staring at the pile of crabmeat.

"Yeah. But I want to get it all out first."

"So methodical." Her voice is teasing, and she winds her foot around mine beneath the picnic table.

"There's a best method for everything."

"Such patience. I can never resist." I take in the red shards of shell mixing with the white chunks of meat mingling with the yellow butter patches in her basket.

Feels on brand for her.

"Delayed gratification, babe. Makes everything taste that much better."

Her pupils darken and she licks her lips—and damn if I'm not rock fucking hard in my pants.

I drop down close to her and whisper in her ear. "We can practice that later tonight."

Her chest rises on a sharp inhale, the bare skin flushed. I pick up a chunk of crabmeat, dip it in butter, bring it to her lips. I hover, her breath warm on my fingers. Then I slide the meat into her mouth, her tongue flicking against my fingertips. An electric impulse shoots straight to my dick, and I shift on the bench, my pants uncomfortably tight.

She licks her full bottom lip, her aqua gaze locked on mine. "Thanks."

"My pleasure." My voice comes out thick and gravelly, and I'm grateful Parker and Liv are deep in wedding talk. They don't seem to notice me and Poppy at all, now that the crab lesson is over and they've moved on to more important topics, like how many attendants they'll have.

"Want to get out of here?" Poppy asks in a breathy whisper, fixing her eyes on me. She's biting her lower lip, and all I can think about is kissing that mouth until it's pink and swollen, not letting up until she's clawing at me and screaming my name.

"I thought you'd never ask."

30

GRIFFIN

Poppy and I bolt from the table with a quick goodbye, practically jogging out of Fall Fest.

"You sure you had enough fun? We didn't drive the bumper cars." Poppy points at the primary-colored mini vehicles whizzing around the smooth surface to our left.

"More than enough fun here. I can think of other things I'd rather be doing." I smirk at her and she blushes, the autumn sun catching the golden highlights in her hair.

She's fucking gorgeous. And wearing entirely too much clothing right now.

I unlock the Rover, opening the door for her, and she slides into the passenger seat. I'm jealous of that leather, caressing her tight, round ass.

Hustling around the car, I swing into the driver's seat and fire up the ignition. The Rover roars to life, and I ease out of the lot, being careful of the families coming and going from the festival. Chris Stapleton's voice belts from the speakers, talking about how he should probably leave, and damn if that sentiment doesn't ring true right now.

I should probably leave.

I am leaving.

But there's no way I'm stopping this now.

Not when Poppy's sitting next to me, her intoxicating floral scent floating on the air, every nerve ending in my body humming and alive.

No fucking way.

Instead, I reach over, laying my palm flat on her warm, smooth leg. Caressing her soft skin, dusting my fingertips up and down her upper thigh.

"Take off your panties."

Her head swivels to stare at me. "What? No!"

"Take. Off. Your. Panties." I emphasize each word, my gaze sliding to meet hers.

She bites down on her bottom lip, and I return my grip to the steering wheel. Then she unbuttons her shorts, shimmying the denim down her legs.

"All the way off. I want full access."

"Bossy," she says in a teasing tone, but complies with my request.

"Keep going. Panties off." I watch out of the corner of my eye as she slides the tiny scrap of satin down her thighs, down her calves, until they hit the floorboard of the SUV.

"That's a good girl."

A pink blush spreads from her chest, creeping up her neck, bright spots of color staining her cheeks, and I know she likes the praise.

Keeping my eyes on the road, I reach over and slide my hand from her outer to her inner thigh. Then farther still, like a heat-seeking missile until I find her warm pussy. I run a finger straight down her slit, and she arches her hips toward me. Just fractionally, but I notice.

"So wet already. Aren't you a dirty girl, getting naked in the front seat here in broad daylight?"

Her chest rises and falls, her breathing rapid and shallow, as I play with her. Finding her clit, I apply a slight bit of pressure, and she gasps.

"You like that, don't you?"

She nods, biting down on her lip, her eyes glazing with desire. Damn if she's not the sexiest thing I've ever seen, her legs spread wide on the buttery leather.

We stop at a red light, and I circle her clit, pinching and rubbing.

"The man next to us is definitely looking over here. Just act normal. Hell, even better—give him a wave."

"Griffin," she moans, grinding down on my hand. I stop my movements and she whimpers.

"Do it."

She huffs out an exasperated breath but shoots the man a smile and a friendly wave.

"Good girl. See, you're so good at this."

Before she turns back around, I thrust two fingers into her slick heat.

"Oh. My." She hisses and presses back into the seat as I crook my finger, hitting all the right spots. She gyrates on my hand as I move inside her. My balls tighten, and I'm hard, watching her chase her pleasure.

"Green light." I slip my hand out as I hit the accelerator, and she whines in frustration.

"I do not like this game." She pops her lip out in a pout, and I chuckle.

"Patience, Poppy."

One hand on the wheel, I lick the fingers that were

inside her a few seconds ago. "Fucking delicious. You're going to be my dessert this time."

I park in the driveway, and she unbuckles her seat belt in a rush, reaching for her panties and shorts.

"No. Those are mine." I pluck the panties out of her hand, stuffing them in my pocket. "And don't bother with the shorts. We're taking everything off as soon as we get in the house."

"Griffin! It's not even dark yet. The neighbors will see."

"Cover up with my crab T-shirt." I toss the dark blue shirt to her, and she rolls her eyes.

"When did you get to be so demanding?"

"Tell me you hate it." I level my eyes on her.

She opens her mouth, then shuts it again.

"Exactly what I thought. Now do you want me to fuck you right here in the driveway in broad daylight, or do you want to go inside?"

"You're incorrigible."

"Thank you very much, Little Miss Sunshine." I shoot her a wicked grin before jogging around to get her door. She hops out, then wraps the T-shirt around her waist and high-tails it to the house. I saunter up, taking my sweet time, chuckling as she shifts from foot to foot on the front porch.

"You're a real asshole, Griffin Carter. Did anyone ever tell you that?" she hisses at me.

"All the damn time. But I like it the best coming from you." I wink at her and unlock the door, stepping aside. "Ladies first."

She races into the dim living room, and I kick the door shut behind me.

"Now where were we? Oh yes—dessert." Two broad

steps later, I'm face-to-face with Poppy, my new T-shirt already a blue pile on the floor. I claim her lips, possessing her, and she opens her mouth to me. "You're so damn tempting," I murmur, my tongue sweeping in.

I'm never going to get enough of this woman.

Instead of delving deep into my thoughts, I cup her bare ass, kneading the flesh. Then I scoop her up, and she wraps her legs around me. We never break our kiss, and it's like I need this woman more than I need oxygen.

I carry her to the couch, gently laying her down on the brown leather. She gazes up at me with hungry eyes as I drop down next to her. She lifts her feet, and I spread her legs wide, sitting between her thighs. I palm her with one hand, thumbing her clit, and she sucks in a deep breath of air. Lowering, I lick her slit, tasting her arousal.

"So sweet," I murmur before lapping at her juices, swirling my tongue on her sensitive bundle of nerves. She lifts her ass, craving more contact, and I suck harder until a low hum escapes from her lips.

Gripping her hips, I pull her in closer to me, increasing the friction between my mouth and her pussy. She writhes and bucks as I dip into her with my tongue, not letting her move away from the intensity.

Her legs begin to tremor, and I know she's close. Only then do I loosen my grip and pull away.

"Ohmygawd, Griffin . . ." She pushes down on my shoulders, urging me to finish what I started.

"Nope. Not yet. Remember that whole patience thing we talked about? I'm going to take you so close to the edge, a puff of air will send you rocketing off the cliff."

She stares down at me in disbelief. "What? No. I never signed up for a crash course in patience!"

"It's actually called edging, and trust me—you're going to love it." My mouth tips up in a sly smile as she frowns at me. "Give it a try. I promise it'll be worth it."

She huffs out a breath. "Fine. But this better be amazing. Because I was super close."

"Aww, babe. I'll have you screaming my name before you know it. How do you feel right now?" I run my hand up her inner thigh, trail my fingers over her belly. Her muscles contract at my touch, and I know she's wound tighter than a TheraBand right now.

"Hot."

"Get naked then." I inch the hem of her shirt up her abdomen, and she sits up, lifting the flimsy fabric over her head. Unhooking her bra, she drops the lacy garment to the floor, and now she's naked on the couch.

"This isn't fair. You're fully clothed." Her eyes roam over my body, her hands following close behind. She tugs at my shirt, so I oblige, chucking it to the floor. Then I stand up and unbutton my pants, kicking them off until I'm wearing only my boxer briefs.

"Keep going." She waves her hand at me.

"Awfully demanding for someone who wants to come . . ." But I lower my briefs, my erection springing from the cotton prison.

Poppy licks her lips, staring at my hard length. I step forward, and she loops her arms around my legs, pulling me in close to her. She licks the crown of my cock, circling the hot flesh with her tongue. I grip her shoulders, my shins flush with the couch. Then she takes me into her mouth, sucking me in while massaging my ass, and it's heaven. Hot, wet heaven, her lips on me as I leak precum into her mouth.

"So good," I murmur, my eyes barely able to focus. She uses one hand to play with my balls, and they tighten, building up for their release.

After a few minutes she pulls away, cold air hitting my cock. I lift a brow, staring down at her.

"I believe it's called edging." The corners of her pretty, swollen mouth lift in a smile and I groan.

"Fine. I guess two can play at this game. Stand up."

She flips her hair back over her shoulders, rising to her full height but only bringing her about three-quarters of the way up my chest.

"You're such a petite little fucktoy." I smack her playfully on the ass, and she squeals, surprised. I rub my palm over the spot I just spanked, goose bumps rising on her heated skin. With my other hand, I trail a finger all the way down her belly until I find her core.

"Just as I suspected. Wet. Little Miss Sunshine likes that."

Her face flames, but she nods her consent.

"I knew you would." I smirk at her, trailing my thumb over her cheek. The tip of her tongue slips from between her lips, and she sucks my thumb into her mouth, slurping hard, massaging it.

"Fuck, Poppy," I groan, my cock bobbing against my abs. I roughly pop my thumb out of her mouth, her teeth grazing my calloused skin, and I'm not sure how long I can make this last. Now I'm jumpy, every muscle ropy and tense. She can definitely give as good as she gets.

Pursing her lips together, she stares up at me through her thick lashes.

"Walk over to the sliding glass door. Don't turn around."

She blinks, unmoving.

"Go on," I urge, waving my open palm at her. When she spins around, I smack her on the ass, harder this time.

"Ow!" She clutches the hot spot, staring at me over her shoulder.

I follow behind, watching her sashay across the room, the round globes of her ass bouncing with each step. My cock throbs, and I reach down, stroking the hard shaft.

At the window, she stops and waits for more instructions. I press up against her, pulling her to me by the hip, her soft curves hugging my hard chest. She relaxes into me, her head lolling back and exposing the long line of her neck. I lick at the tender skin, watch as bumps rise and her nipples peak. I cup her breast, pulling at the rosy point.

"Oh . . ." A low moan vibrates deep in her throat, and I keep up my assault, her body melting into mine.

"Very nice," I murmur into her ear, nipping at the lobe. She squirms, so I clutch her hip more firmly, preventing her from wiggling.

"Be still while I pleasure you. Close your eyes." Her eyes flutter shut, and she stands quiet between my arms. I drop my hand from her breast to her core, dipping inside her. She contracts around my fingers, and she's ready for me. I thrust in and out a few times, stretching her.

"Put your hands on the glass. Anchor yourself, just like that." She stretches her arms out on the window, and I move in closer to her, pressing her body up against the cool window. I kiss down her neck, raining kisses over her skin, down her spine. I'm rewarded with a shiver, and I know she likes this. I nudge her feet apart with my foot, kicking her legs open wider, before I run a flattened palm over her ass.

Smack.

She starts and whimpers, and I soothe her skin. Her peaked nipples press against the glass, and I kiss up and down her arms.

Smack.

More whimpering. I soothe and kiss, trailing my mouth across the sharp ridges of her shoulder blades.

Smack.

"Griffin . . ." She pants my name, and I don't hesitate any longer, plunging my cock into her wet pussy. She cries out, her palms lifting off the glass, but I circle her wrist and hold her in place.

"Uh-uh. I didn't tell you to turn around. Or move your hands." I purr into her ear, and she trembles against me, her orgasm already building as I thrust into her harder. She contracts around me, squeezing, and I'm close too. Seeing her like this—splayed against the glass, my cock driving into her—tingling pressure builds inside me.

"You're so fucking tight like this." I pound into her, her feet lifting off the ground with the force.

"Oh . . . oh . . . Griffin . . ."

With one more hard thrust, Poppy unravels, shaking and trembling on my shaft. I keep driving into her, not letting up, milking every last drop of her release from her body and chasing after my own. Finally, I explode inside her as she sinks back against me. Supporting both of us, I wrap my arms around her, kissing down her warm neck.

"That was so perfect. You're so perfect," I murmur into her hair.

"That was amazing." She tips her head up, her ocean-blue eyes hazy, and kisses me gently on the lips. "You're amazing."

"I'm going to really miss this when I'm back in Atlanta."

She stiffens in my arms, and silence hangs heavy in the air between us. My gut clenches, then roils.

Definitely the wrong thing to say.

"But we can talk about that later." I skim my hand over her curves and watch as her body responds to my touch.

For the first time since I got here, I really and truly don't want to leave.

But I have no choice. Once I'm cleared by the team doctor, I need to go back and fulfill my contract.

I only hope Poppy will understand.

31

—————

POPPY

THAT WAS THE HOTTEST SEX I'VE EVER HAD IN MY entire life. Like, five-chili-pepper hot. Nuclear hot. Call-the-damn-fire-department-because-I'm-pretty-damn-sure-I'm-burning-from-the-inside-out hot.

Even after a cool shower, my skin's still heated, my muscles sore from all the contracting. Now we're lying in Griffin's bed in the dark, the ceiling fan whirring overhead. I drape my arm across his sculpted chest and listen to the rhythmic beat of his heart.

Thud-thud. Thud-thud. Thud-thud.

His breath fluffs my hair with each exhale, and I try to will myself to sleep.

Everything's fine. We're all good.

Except it's not—and we're not. Griffin actually mentioned leaving, and a hard pit's been lodged in my stomach ever since.

"Griff?" I whisper.

"Mmm . . . ," he murmurs, his hand running up and

down my back. Slowly, so slowly. He's drifting off to sleep, blissfully unaware of my anxiety.

"Do you have to go?" The words come out so small, so quiet, I'm not even sure he hears.

After a few seconds that stretch out for eternity, he answers. "Yeah. I do."

An awful ache grips me, squeezing my chest so hard, so tight, I can barely breathe. Hot tears prick at the corners of my eyes, and I fight back the urge to cry.

How can I be this upset over someone I hated only a few months ago?

But we've been through a lot since then. I feel differently about him now—obviously. And I thought he felt differently about us too.

I wait for him to say something—anything—but nothing comes.

"When are you going? You'll be here for Parker's wedding, right? In February?" My voice is needy, a pleading edge to it, and I hate it. Hate myself for sounding so . . . pathetic.

Griffin sighs, his chest rising and sinking, my head undulating with his breathing as if I were riding waves in the ocean.

"Spring training usually starts the end of February."

Good. We still have loads of time.

Enough time for me to change his mind, convince him to stay.

"So as long as the wedding's before spring training starts you'll be here?" I lift my head, peering up at him. His mouth is a thin line, his jaw tense.

"No. I'll be gone by then."

"What?" I shoot up in bed. Panic races through me, my

heart hammering hard in my chest. "But you just said spring training's at the end of February!"

"It is." He lifts himself up on his elbows. "But the team workouts start January second."

I frown, my brows squishing together as I try to calculate how many days we have left together.

Not very many is the official answer to that question.

"So what's spring training then, if you have to go back January second anyway?" I jut my chin out, a low boil of resentment simmering in my gut.

He scrubs a hand over the back of his neck. "Spring training is when we start playing practice games. Against other teams. The only real break from baseball is the mandatory four-week block after the Series. Then unscheduled workouts by the trainers usually begin in December. Come January, we're back in the gym; by February, we're out on the field again."

"Oh." My voice falls, and I slump back against the pillows.

"It's okay." He runs his hand up and down my thigh. "We'll work it out. I'm playing ball, not going off to war. I'll at least have weekends until spring training."

"And then what?" I whisper, almost afraid to ask.

"Then you'll have to come see me, because I'm off once every twelve days or something. Depends on the schedule."

Gawd, this sucks. How am I going to survive seeing him once every other week? Or less?

I should have gone with my gut and not gotten involved with Griffin Carter at all.

But it's too late now—I'm in deep.

I let King Asshole get under my skin.

Into my head.

Even worse, I let him wheedle his way into my heart—the biggest risk of all.

And it looks like I'm about to lose big.

After what feels like forever, Griffin tips my head up and presses his lips to mine. A soft, tender kiss that feels different somehow.

"I'm sorry, Poppy. Baseball can be a rough life. I get it if you want to bail."

Dammit. That's not the reassurance I need from him, the words I want to hear right now.

Why didn't he say he can't imagine living life without me? Fuck baseball. All I want—all I need—is you.

Tears pool in my eyes, but I will them not to fall.

Because I know—*there's still time to change his mind.*

32

GRIFFIN

I sleep like shit, even with Poppy lying in my arms, her even breaths whisper soft on my chest. Just before sunrise, I slip out of bed and get dressed, lacing up my sneakers. I have to get out of the house and clear my head.

Creeping out of the bedroom, I'm quiet as I unlock the door and step outside. The salty air's chilly, the sun not even up yet. I stretch my calves and quads, then ease into a slow jog. I'm careful not to push, although my muscles fire up, ready to perform. I have to pull back, remember to go easy on the knee.

I take a right off my street, then run out of the neighborhood toward the beach. It's my usual path, but I'm never out this early. The quiet's kind of nice—not having to swerve around moms pushing strollers, avoid dog walkers, or dodge kids on bicycles. Right now I have the sidewalk to myself, giving me space to think.

Because I can't stop replaying yesterday.

The date, the sex.

Poppy's questions.

And the realization there's no way I can avoid letting her down.

I've put both of us in an untenable situation, and no matter what one of us is going to get hurt.

I should bail now.

Fast and clean, like picking a man off second base as he's trying to make a steal.

Hesitation gets you nowhere. In baseball or in life.

The longer I stay—the more involved we get—the harder it will be to leave.

Even though I don't want to go.

A sharp pang hits me in the chest as I jog down the wooden boardwalk leading to the beach. My chest aches with every inhale, every exhale, and I don't think it's from running.

I'm going to miss Poppy.

Her tinkly laugh, that cute little thing she does with her tongue when she's thinking, her sense of humor and quick wit. Hell, even the way she manages to always find the bright side of everything.

But I can't steal her away from her life, as much as I want to.

And I can't walk away from mine.

I slow my pace down, my knee stiff and achy as my feet pound the packed sand. The ocean's dark blue, the waves frothing and churning—white, angry. A sharp contrast to the bright pink and orange of the sun rising, streaks of color splashing across the dusty blue sky.

Poppy dances in the light, always. I love that about her, but it's just not how life works.

Real life's choppy, like the Atlantic, with peaks and

valleys, sandbars. Hell, even riptides, tidal waves, hurricanes, and the occasional tsunami.

I had the chance to dance in Poppy's sunbeam, and it was magnificent.

Bright and shiny, happy.

But nothing this perfect lasts forever.

As much as I care for her—love her, if I'm being honest with myself—the right thing to do is set her free. I can't be there for her, be what she needs.

She can do better than me.

The pang in my chest amplifies, swelling to a full-blown ache, and my heart physically hurts.

I hated coming to Seaglass Beach—and now I hate that I'm leaving.

But it's for the best.

Hard as it's going to be, I know what I have to do.

As soon as Aunt Jess gets enough help at Scoops, I'm gone.

33

—————

POPPY

GRIFFIN'S BEDROOM IS ABSOLUTELY STILL. DIM AND quiet, as if the entire world's fast asleep.

Too quiet.

No breathing, no soft thudding of a heartbeat.

Turning over, I see only a tangle of sheets where Griffin used to be.

Hot panic rolls over me, and now I'm fully awake, like I already drank three cups of coffee.

Griffin's gone. I scared him off.

But then a door creaks open, followed by footsteps. He's back.

He didn't leave me.

I take a deep breath, snuggle back down into the covers. Maybe we can get this day started right, with a little morning sex. I gave myself the morning off, so I've got time.

Griffin's broad frame fills the doorway, and I smile, happiness blooming in my chest. He's so gorgeous as he rips off his shirt, a slight sheen of sweat glistening on his tanned skin. He crosses to the bed, perches on the edge. Reaching out, he trails his fingers along my arm, and a delicious shiver shoots down my spine, heat unfurling low in my belly.

"Morning, sunshine. How'd you sleep?" He gazes down at me with those serious deep-blue eyes.

"Good." I stretch my arms over my head, the sheet riding down and revealing my naked breasts. His eyes skim my body, but he doesn't make a move.

"I'm gonna hit the shower. I promised Aunt Jess I'd be at Scoops by eleven today. She's interviewing someone, so I'm gonna need to run the shop."

"Oh." Disappointment washes over me; I thought we'd at least get to spend a few hours together before I had to go to the inn.

"Want me to join you in the shower?" I work to keep my tone light and flirty, even though I'm bummed.

"Nah. You keep sleeping. I know you don't get many mornings off."

My heart sinks as he rises from the bed and heads to the bathroom, shedding his gym shorts on the way.

What changed between last night and this morning? I can't put my finger on exactly what it is, but Griffin seems different.

Distant.

Not cold, really. More like lukewarm, but it still sucks.

He turns the shower on, the sound of the water deafening in the silence.

Then he closes the bathroom door, effectively shutting me out.

Hot tears well in my eyes, the wall across the room

shimmering, and then the tears leak out, wetting Griffin's pillow.

I hate feeling sad. I hate feeling shut out. And I hate when people don't tell me the absolute truth.

Well, fuck this.

With shaky legs, I climb out of bed, grabbing one of Griffin's many team shirts out of his drawer and throwing it over my head. Then I march into the bathroom.

Steam swirls around me in the small space, the room warm and humid. The clean, crisp scent of Griffin hits my nostrils, and it's like a physical blow to the chest. That smell electrifies my senses, my thighs already clenching, my core throbbing.

I want this man. I need this man.

I love this man.

The water cuts off, and Griffin pulls back the shower curtain, the hard planes of muscle shiny and wet, droplets of water beading and magnifying the dark ink covering his chest.

My mouth waters as I devour his body with my eyes.

"Hey. You gonna shower? Want me to leave the water running?" He reaches out and snags the towel hanging on the metal bar.

I shake my head no, words failing me. Which rarely happens.

He steps out of the shower, our bodies inches away from each other as he towels dry. I long to run my palm over his taut muscles, feel every ropy cord as he pulls me up against him.

Instead, I take a deep breath and forge ahead with my mission. "What's wrong?"

He shrugs, rubbing his dark hair with the fluffy white towel. Leaving his erection fully visible.

Not helping me focus.

"Nothing."

"Really?" I bite down on my lower lip and search his face for signs that he's lying. But his expression's neutral. "Because you seem—I don't know—distant."

He wraps the towel around his waist, covering up his most precious body part. Now only his upper body's exposed.

"I'm fine, Poppy. Just woke up in a bad mood, I guess."

"Why?"

"I don't know. Sometimes it happens. I'm grumpy, remember?" He locks his heated gaze on me, and a frisson of desire skitters through me.

"So you're in a bad mood for no reason?" I fold my arms over my chest, pressing the issue even as Griffin's jaw tenses.

But I can't help myself. I know I'm waving a red flag in front of the bull, but I deserve answers.

"Dammit, Poppy," Griffin growls, spinning to face me head-on. "Life's not always sunshine and fucking rainbows, okay? I'm entitled to a bad mood every once in a while."

I step back as if he's slapped me. Reeling from the anger rolling off him in hot waves, his body flexed and tense.

"Fine. Be in a bad mood. But I know you, Griffin. And even grumpy you doesn't get in a bad mood for no reason."

I pivot to storm out of the bathroom, but then Griffin's strong hand claps down on my shoulder. He spins me around to face him, his lips pressed into a thin, tight line.

"Fine. You want to know what's up? I'll tell you. I'm leaving."

All the air's knocked out of my lungs, and my knees go weak. Luckily, Griffin's strong grip is enough to keep me standing upright.

"What? When?"

"As soon as I can. My aunt's got Scoops under control; she's hiring more people to help her. I have to go back."

"But . . . why? You have more time before you have to be back in Atlanta with the team."

Griffin shrugs, and his nonchalance pisses me off. "It's for the best."

"No, it's not. We could have more time together!" My shrill voice bounces off the shower tiles, a screechy echo ringing over the rush of blood pounding in my ears.

No, no, no!

"What about yesterday, when you told me we could make it work? 'We'll work it out, Poppy. I'm not going off to war.'" I air quote his words, and anger flares in his eyes, his jaw clenched.

"I changed my mind. I need to go—like I said, it's for the best." His voice is flat, firm, brooking no argument.

Wrong.

He's clearly never fought with a Montgomery before.

A red-hot fire burns in my belly, acid rising in my throat. I straighten up, standing as tall as I can, squaring my shoulders.

"Bullshit, Griffin. You keep saying it's for the best. But the best for who? You?" I spit the biting words out of my mouth, my hands flying through the air. He stays perfectly still, absorbing my anger.

"No, Poppy, not for me. For you. I'm doing the best

thing for *you*." Flinty eyes lock on mine, and my heart stutters before revving back up again.

"You don't get to decide what's best for me!" Now I'm shrieking, the words flying around the tiny bathroom, fists balling at my side. My entire body's shaking, I'm so pissed off.

"I already made my decision. I'm sorry, but it really is for the best."

Tears spill onto my cheeks and I hate that I'm crying.

I hate that I let him see me cry.

I hate that Griffin doesn't do anything to make the tears stop. He just stands there, a pained look on his stupidly gorgeous face.

Most of all, I hate that I let myself fall for King Asshole in the first place. In this moment, I loathe the man standing in front of me with every fiber of my being.

Swiping at my face, I turn and run out of his bathroom.

I grab my clothes, my bag, and race out of his house.

Out of his life.

Unlocking Smurfy, I fling my stuff into the car and fly out of Griffin's driveway. Huge sobs rack my body, tears flowing freely now, as I get as far away from him as possible.

I knew I should never have given my heart away to grumpy Griffin Carter.

34

GRIFFIN

My number-one rule in baseball. My number-one rule in life.

And I do usually trust it. I usually follow the rule.

I don't know why the fuck I didn't this time around.

I knew Poppy was too good, too pure, but I went there anyway. Let myself get swept up in her rose-colored world, a world where people fall in love under a clear-blue sunny sky in a quaint little beach town and everyone lives happily ever after.

Well, maybe that's her world, but it sure the fuck isn't mine.

My world can be cold and rainy, or hot and arid. Sweaty or freezing-ass cold. In my world, there's no happily ever after. And the only thing I can damn sure count on is ending up alone.

Every fucking time.

I slump against the bathroom counter, my body bone

tired, my knee hollering in pain. I need to ice it, pop some Advil.

I need to get to Scoops.

But my legs are lead pipes attached to rusty hips, and I can't muster up the motivation to move at all. Let alone go run a damn ice-cream shop holding a thousand and one memories of Poppy.

Poppy smiling at a customer, then grinning over her shoulder at me, her ocean eyes laughing at some inside joke we share.

Poppy helping people, always ready to pitch in. Sure, her *pitching in* might be closer to taking over, but I never minded.

How could I have hurt her like that?

The way she looked at me, like I shoved my hand inside her chest and ripped her heart out, still beating.

I know leaving's the right thing to do, but I still feel like shit.

She'll forget about me after a while, move on, find someone new.

She's Princess Poppy. And she's practically perfect. It's bound to happen.

A lightning-sharp stab hits me in the chest.

I don't want her to be with anyone else.

I close my eyes, shoving the shadowy image of Poppy and Mystery Man far away from me.

It's for the best. Leave her alone. Take the high road.

And that road is for sure headed straight out of Seaglass Beach.

The sooner I can leave, the better.

I text Aunt Jess:

> Griffin: On my way. See you soon

> Jess: See you soon, hun

I have to break the news about leaving to Aunt Jess now too. This day's shaping up to be all-around stellar and it's not even ten a.m. yet.

I PUSH THROUGH THE BUBBLEGUM-PINK DOOR, GIRDING myself for the tough conversation ahead of me. The now-familiar scent of vanilla hits me as soon as I step into the sunny, cheerful shop, and it's a sucker punch to the freaking gut.

All I can think about, all I can see, is Poppy.

She's everywhere and nowhere all at once, her presence so strong, so visceral in this space that the wind's knocked out of me. I catch my breath and try to ignore the dull ache in my chest, the pounding in my head.

You're doing the right thing.

She needs more than you can give.

"Griffy!" Aunt Jess waves at me from one of the white metal bistro tables over in the corner by the window. A college-aged brunette woman is with her, presumably the potential hire.

"This is Lynessa. She's going to start working the evening shift. That'll give you more time off to go out and do things." Aunt Jess smiles at me knowingly, and I'm certain she's talking about me spending time with Poppy.

Tension creeps into my muscles, my shoulders inching up to my ears. *This is gonna be awkward.*

"Great. Let me know if you need me to show her how anything works around here. Happy to help bring her up to speed."

Lynessa's sizing me up, her eyes roving over my body, and I've never been less interested in a pretty female in my life.

Because all I can see is Poppy. Her honey-blonde hair, the splash of freckles across her nose, that pink-bow mouth.

It's going to take me a long time to get over her. Maybe an entire lifetime.

Maybe never.

"Griffy? Can you show Lynessa how to clean the drink machine?" Aunt Jess peers at me over the rim of her glasses, one gray brow arched high.

I clear my throat, scrub a hand over the back of my neck. "Sure. Come on."

Leading Lynessa back behind the counter, I demo the cleaning routine for the drink dispenser. She watches in fascination, like I'm building a rocket ship or something instead of the basic manual labor task I'm actually doing.

"It's pretty simple, really, once you get the hang of it. I can write instructions for you. Might be helpful for Hailey too. And anyone else that's hired."

Lynessa's dark head bobs. "Would you? That would be super great." She reaches her hand out, caressing my biceps, and my entire arm stiffens.

I glare down at her hand and she pulls it away so quickly Aunt Jess doesn't even notice the contact between us.

"I'm gonna dip into the office. I'll get those instructions done." Without another word, I retreat into the back, happy to be away from the overly enthusiastic new hire.

Sitting down at the computer, I tap out procedures for the drink machine and the ice-cream freezer. Then I move on to payroll and inventory, making notes about timing of payments to vendors and preferred suppliers, and the dates when we last received shipments of various items. I stay tucked in the office until I hear Lynessa call out her goodbye and the door jingles closed.

Good riddance.

I stand and shake out my stiff knee, then walk back into the chilly shop.

"There you are! I was wondering if you crawled out a window." The skin around Aunt Jess's eyes crinkles in amusement behind her glasses, but I don't smile.

"No. The window's too small; I won't fit."

She chuckles at my joke, beaming up at me, and for the second time today, my heart squeezes, aching.

I'm going to miss Aunt Jess.

"Listen—" I lower myself into the chair opposite hers. "I've loved being here with you. But now that you're back on your feet, it's time for me to go."

"What?" She frowns at me, her brow furrowing. "Now? It's early still. You've got time before you have to be back with the team."

"I know. But I need to get to Atlanta. I have an appointment with the team doctor next week." The lie rolls smoothly off my tongue, like the creamy caramel sauce I drip over ice-cream sundaes.

"Oh, I see. Will you be coming back after the appoint

ment?" Aunt Jess purses her lips and waits for me to respond.

"I don't know. Probably not." I shrug, acting a lot more lackadaisical than I feel.

"What about Poppy?" My aunt squints at me, like she's trying to stare deep into my soul.

"What about her?" I force myself to sound neutral, callous even.

"I thought the two of you had something going. You seemed so happy with her."

My chest tightens and my stomach rolls. I hate lying to my aunt, but I don't want to get into the details with her.

"Nah. It was casual. She understands. Baseball's my life. And her life is here. At the inn with her family."

"I see." My aunt nods sagely, understanding finally dawning. "The situation got complicated, so you're running away."

I bristle, my skin prickling at her accusation. "No. I'm not running. I'm leaving. There's a difference."

"Tomato, to-mah-to." She waves her hand through the air. "I'm not a damn fool, Griffin. I see how you look at that girl. Like she hung the damn moon and the stars too. And you know what? She probably could if she put her mind to it. Now, do what you want, but in my oh-so-humble opinion, you're making a huge mistake. Girls like Poppy are one in a million."

"So is a professional baseball career," I say, pointing out the obvious, my index finger raised high in the air. "And I still have a year left on my contract. I can't ask Poppy to leave Seaglass Beach and follow me all around the continental US. She belongs here and I belong there." I tap the left and the right sides of the table, demonstrating how far apart we'll be. "End of story."

"Hmmph." Aunt Jess crosses her arms over her chest, clearly aggravated with me and my life choices. "Baseball-schmaseball. I get it—you're a hotshot all-star third baseman. But baseball won't last forever, Griffin. And when it's over, you'll be kicking yourself for losing out on love. I promise you that."

I scowl at my aunt, trying my best to reject her words of wisdom. "I'm not done with baseball, though. I could have years left of my career. It's not fair to Poppy to ask her to wait."

"Did you ask her?" She frowns at me, her lips scrunched.

Shrugging, I mumble, "No."

I sound dumb, even to myself, but my aunt doesn't get it. I've been alone since I was a teenager, and everything's been fine.

Not great, but fine.

"It'll be better this way. Trust me, Aunt Jess. Poppy doesn't need a complication like me."

"Think about it. That's all I'm saying, Griffy. Baseball lasts a little while, but love can last forever."

"Thanks for the advice." I rise, folding my aunt's narrow shoulders into a gentle hug, trying to absorb all her goodness and push aside my aggravation at the same time.

I know she's trying to help, but it's still annoying.

"When are you leaving?" Aunt Jess's eyes glitter under the fluorescent light, tears shimmering behind her glasses.

Dammit. I'm making everyone cry today.

"Tomorrow, I guess. I have to pack up, clean out the fridge—that kind of stuff."

She pats my hand. "One more unsolicited piece of advice, if you can stand it?"

My eyelid twitches, but I nod. "Okay, shoot."

"Keep the rental. Just in case you change your mind."

I hold my eye roll in check. "Thanks. I'll see what I can do. I'll call you when I'm back home."

Leaning down, I kiss my aunt on the top of her head. Then I push out the door of Scoops for the last time, heaviness crushing my chest.

35

POPPY

I send Liv an SOS text as soon as I get home.

Poppy: SOS. Beyond urgent

Poppy: I NEED you

Liv: What's wrong?

Poppy: Come over. Please

Liv: Be there in five

And this is why I love Liv. Thank god we made up, because I can't live without her. Clearly.

I curl up into a ball on my couch, crying softly into my "Life's a Beach" throw pillow; at the moment, it should say "Life's a Bitch."

Knock, knock, knock.

My body's tired and heavy, and it's a monumental effort to stand up and open the door, but I somehow manage.

"Babe." Liv steps inside, wrapping me up in a warm hug. Just what I need at the moment.

Too bad it's not Griffin telling me what a dumbass he is.

But I'll settle for my bestie, I guess.

"What happened? Sit. Let me make you some tea." Liv ushers me to the couch, and I resume the fetal position, hot tears leaking from my eyes. I cannot stop crying, and it's pissing me off.

"Griffin's an asshole." I mutter the words into the pillow, hot anger bubbling inside me.

"What? Why? I thought you guys were getting along great at Fall Fest. You seemed so happy together!" Liv fills the rose teakettle with water and puts it on the stove to boil.

"Yeah, I thought so too." I sniff and wipe at my nose. Always observant, Liv brings me a napkin.

"Thanks." I blow my nose, swiping at my tears. "We had an amazing night—I won't go into details, but let's just say it was a little kinky and super freaking hot."

"Oh." Liv's mouth forms a perfect O, but being the good friend she is, she doesn't dig for more specifics.

"But then I mentioned your wedding, and he said he won't be here in February."

"Really? I thought he would be, according to the schedule you gave me."

"Right?! Like, how am I supposed to know there's barely an offseason for baseball? And did you know spring training is, like, the official start of the season? And he has one million games and is only off four stinking weeks? All year long! And here I thought running the Seaglass Inn was a 24-7, 365-days-a-year job!"

Liv shakes her head, her dark braid swishing on her shoulder. "I had no idea."

"Me neither." More tears fall, saturating the aqua pillow, a dark circle growing with each teardrop.

The kettle whistles, and Liv pops up from the couch to fix the tea.

"You want apple cinnamon or chai?"

"Apple, please." I always like to stay seasonal, but especially if I'm in the depths of despair.

"Okay, here you go." Liv hands me the steaming mug of tea, and I sit up, the spicy scent of cinnamon buoying me a little.

"I can't believe it, Liv. Why did I let myself fall for King Asshole? I mean, yeah, he's hot. Beyond amazing in bed and a good listener. Funny. And apparently a complete dick." I blow on my tea, creating tiny waves on the tan liquid.

"What happened exactly? Give me the play-by-play." Liv peers at me, her grass-green eyes wide.

"Like I said—I asked about the wedding, and he said he'd be gone. So I dug deeper, and turns out the training season actually begins January second. So he's due back in Atlanta by then for sure. But there's a bunch of extra shit before then . . . it sounded kinda optional, but Griffin feels like he needs to be there."

"Oh-kay . . . I mean, he has been out a long time. He might need extra time with the trainer, the coaches. I get that."

"Fine. I could understand all that. But last night he talked about doing the long-distance thing. And that sucks, but okay, I guess we can at least give it a try. But then this morning when I woke up, he was gone. And when he got back, he basically ended things."

"What? I have whiplash here." Liv rubs her neck for effect, and I smile a teensy bit at her dramatics.

"Right? I don't get it. One minute we're madly in love, and the next he's leaving forever and never looking back."

Liv narrows her eyes, her mouth twisting up to the side. "It does seem odd. You sure nothing else happened?"

"Positive. We were sleeping, for fuck sake." I take a sip of my tea, thinking back over the whole night, then this morning. "Nothing else happened. It's like he flipped a switch and that's it. Done deal."

"Well, I know what I would do." She sits back, tucking her legs up under her.

"What?"

"I'd go over and try to talk to him. At least understand why he's leaving and if he's planning on ever coming back. Maybe float the long-distance thing again. He probably thinks you wouldn't be game and didn't want to put you in that position."

I stare into my mug, contemplating.

"I don't know, Liv. He seemed pretty adamant about leaving."

"At least try, Pops. The worst that can happen is he still leaves. You have nothing to lose."

She does have a point there.

"Fine. I'll give him one more chance. But if he blows it as spectacularly as he did this morning, we're done."

I set my mug on the coffee table and stand up, already feeling better.

"I can appreciate that. But Poppy?"

I gaze down at my friend.

"Listen to him."

"What's that supposed to mean? I always listen."

"But you don't always hear. No offense." She holds her palms up, a pink blush tinting her cheeks.

"Imma let that one slide. Since you made me tea."

"I just think Griffin's a little more—complicated—than the guys you usually date. You might have to dig deeper to get to the issue. But he'll be worth it."

I flip my hair over my shoulder, buoyed by Liv's pep talk. I can totally do this.

"Got it. Listen and hear what he's saying. I can do that. I'll text him, then take a quick shower. Surely he hasn't left yet."

"That's the spirit!" Liv pumps her fist into the air. "This is going to work out for you, Poppy. I can feel it."

I'm not so sure, but I hope she's right. Grabbing my cell, I text:

> Poppy: Did you leave town yet?

I wait a few minutes, then the text bubbles pop up, swirling.

> Griffin: I'm still here

> Poppy: Can we talk?

> Griffin: Probably not the best idea

My heart sinks reading those words, but I forge ahead anyway.

> Poppy: Please

Kinda desperate, but what do I have to lose?

Griffin: I'll be home all day packing

"Okay, Griffin's still home and he agreed to talk. What should I wear?"

Liv eyes me up and down, assessing the situation. "Something slightly sexy, but nothing that screams you're trying too hard. Maybe the floral V-neck and your white skirt?"

"I like it. Perfect. Thanks, Liv—you're the best." I give her a quick hug, and she pats me on the rear.

"Hit the shower! You need to go change Griffin's mind."

36

POPPY

ANXIETY CHURNS MY STOMACH, THE TEA SWIRLING around like a maelstrom. I fiddle with the radio, switching stations again and again, until I finally give up. Everything sounds so peppy and upbeat, and I'm just not in the mood. Sure, Liv pumped me up back at the apartment, but the closer I get to Griffin's house, the less confident I feel.

Get it together, Poppy. Or this is definitely not going to work out.

I drum my fingers on the steering wheel, remembering all the times my mom bolstered my confidence when things were hard.

You're smart. You're capable. You're beautiful. You're a Montgomery. And most importantly, I love you.

Hot tears prick behind my eyes.

Dammit. Not helping.

I wish I could talk to my mom right now; she'd know how to handle this situation. She was great at dealing with people. Hence, the success of the Seaglass Inn. But she's gone, and I'm the only female Montgomery left.

I'll have to do what I can with Liv's advice.

Listen, Poppy. Hear.

What the fuck is that supposed to mean? I *always* listen.

I swing Smurfy in behind Griffin's shiny Range Rover and cut the engine. Taking a long, deep breath, I center myself.

Be upbeat. Positive. We can work this out.

Slowly, I walk to the door, focusing on the salty marine breeze in my hair, the warm sun shining on my face. It's a beautiful day to work out any issues we have.

Knock, knock.

I wait a few seconds, shuffling from foot to foot, wishing we could rewind and go back to a few days ago. Before all this BS happened between us. Before I brought up baseball and weddings and the future.

"Hey." Griffin startles me out of my regrets, swinging the door open. He looks rough, dark shadows under his serious eyes.

He steps aside, so I take the cue and enter. We stand in the den, staring at one another; then Griffin heads back to his bedroom.

He glances over his shoulder at me. "I'm packing. You're welcome to watch."

Super.

With a heaviness in my heart, I follow him back to his room. A suitcase lies open on his bed, tidy rows of T-shirts and gym shorts lined up like soldiers, ready for battle. He turns his back to me and yanks a drawer open, continuing his task as if I'm not even here.

What an asshole.

"You want to talk, talk." His gruff voice is matter of fact, devoid of emotion.

I clear my dry throat, trying to remember what it is I came to say.

"Um . . . I want answers, Griffin. I deserve answers." I force the words out, barely keeping my voice steady. Inside, I'm shaky, but I don't want him to know that.

"About what?"

The jerk doesn't even turn around, just keeps stacking fucking T-shirts like he works at the Gap.

"Us, Griffin! Obviously." I press my tongue to the side of my cheek, try to tamp down my aggravation at this man.

"There is no 'us,' Poppy. I have to leave and you have to stay."

The room grows darker, my peripheral vision blurring, and I'm lightheaded.

"What do you mean, Griffin? What happened this morning that made you like this?"

He spins around, taking two giant steps toward me, and grips my shoulders. "This is how I am, Poppy. You knew that when we started hooking up. I'm an asshole. You said it yourself—more than once."

I blow out a shuddery breath, his hands large and strong on my arms. "You changed, Griffin. You're not as big of a dick as you pretend to be. I've seen you take care of your aunt, run Scoops even though I know it's not your thing. You grounded me, calmed me down when Jagger taunted me at the Fall Fest. Deep down, you're a good guy."

Griffin shakes his head. "I'm not. You called it right in the beginning. I'm an asshole. I'm not good with people. I'm not you, Poppy."

He locks his eyes on mine—dark, wide, and sad—and the room shifts beneath my feet.

I'm losing this battle.

"You don't have to be me, Griff. That's what I'm saying. We work together—yin and yang, vanilla and strawberry." I demo with my hands, palms up and flying through the air. "I don't want you to change. I love you just how you are."

Griffin sucks in a breath and I freeze, every muscle tensing.

Why did I just say that?

"Poppy—"

"You don't have to say it back. I'm sorry, I shouldn't have said it right then. It just flew out . . ."

He loosens his grip on my shoulders, scrubbing a hand over the back of his neck, and I want to die right now. My cheeks flame while I wait for him to say something, anything.

"I can't stay. You knew I couldn't stay; I told you that from the beginning."

Cool. So no response to my declaration of love.

Awesome.

A hot tear slides down my face, and Griffin reaches up, brushing it away. "I'm sorry."

I channel my sadness into anger because that seems like the less embarrassing option. Shoving his hand from my face, I pummel him on his stupidly strong chest.

"Don't be sorry! Sorry doesn't *change* anything, Griffin. Sorry doesn't help."

"I don't know what you want from me, Poppy." He huffs out an exasperated breath. "I never lied to you. I was always one hundred percent up front about how much I have to give. You want it all—and I can't give that to you."

"Dammit, Griffin!" I stomp my foot, my fists balled at my side. "Let me decide what I want. That's not your call! Yesterday you were all—let's try the long-distance thing. So why can't we? Why are you giving up on us?"

Griffin steps away from me, putting distance between us again, and my body physically aches at the loss of contact.

I'm losing him.

"You deserve more. You deserve better. You deserve sunshine and rainbows and cake and fresh-cut flowers. And that's not me."

"You're wrong, Griffin. That is you; you just don't see it." I reach out to him, cupping his face with my hand, his beard scratchy on my palm. He stares at me, and he looks so sad, so lost. I want to hold him in my arms and tell him everything will be okay, but I can't.

His pupils darken as he slams his wall back into place, shutting me out.

"I have to go, Poppy. I can't stay; I have baseball and a contract. My life isn't here. And yours is."

Tears blur my vision, and my throat's so tight my voice comes out squeaky as I plead with him. "We're good together, Griffin. Don't throw that away—we can at least try. Give us a chance. Please."

He clenches his jaw and locks a steely gaze on me, his eyes now cold. "It won't work out. Trust me. We'll end up hating each other. Let's call it before either of us gets hurt."

"It's too damn late for that, Griffin." I spit out the words, sharp and bitter, anger and sadness mixing together inside, rolling through my veins like poison.

Knowing it's over, I spin and race toward the door. I need to get out of here, need to get air, need to be alone.

I need to get the fuck away from Griffin Carter once and for all.

My hand freezes on the metal doorknob, hot tears streaming down my face, every nerve in my body humming with jangled, mixed-up emotions.

Waiting for him to stop me.

But he doesn't.

I throw the door open and run away from Griffin—but this time I'm not coming back.

37

GRIFFIN

"I LOVE YOU TOO." I WHISPER THE WORDS, LOW AND quiet, into the empty room.

Poppy's gone. And after that epic blowout, I'm pretty sure she's never coming back.

She probably hates my fucking guts—and I don't blame her for one second.

I hate my guts.

How could I have let her walk away like that?

She's wrong about one thing, though, for sure—I am an asshole.

I crash down on my bed, a stack of T-shirts tumbling onto the floor. I've never felt more alone in my life, a deep chasm cracking wide open in my chest. My body hurts, like I just played fourteen innings in the freezing rain. All I want to do is lie down and go to sleep, but I have a lot more packing to do.

Because I don't want to come back here again, despite Aunt Jess's advice about keeping the rental. This place has too many memories of Poppy—we've made love everywhere. The couch, the kitchen counter, the pool, the floor, the shower, the bedroom. Everywhere I look, every single surface, all I can see is *her*.

Her ocean-blue eyes. The dark fringe of lashes as she stares up at me like I'm the most amazing person in the world. Gorgeous tanned legs wrapped around me as I drive into her. Again and again, begging for more. Her tiny, soft hands caressing my chest, tracing the curved lines of my tattoos, asking about each mark. Wanting to know the story behind every symbol inking my skin.

The memory of Poppy is so vivid, so strong, it's downright painful.

Worse than shredding my ACL, and that hurt like a bitch.

I have to get out of here.

I did the right thing, but it still fucking hurts. Each breath sends a stabbing pain through my chest. Then a bout of nausea rolls over me, my gut clenching and spasming.

She's better off without you.

Although I hate it, I know it's the truth. And I'm just going to have to deal with it.

But that doesn't mean I don't have a Poppy-shaped hole in my heart right now.

With a shuddery breath, I bend down and scoop a T-shirt off the floor. A bright red crab smiles up at me, claws in the air, happily declaring "I got crabs at Jimmy's!" I bring the blue cotton to my face, nuzzling the material and inhaling. Coconut and deep floral scents punch me in the nostrils, then jab me right in that Poppy-shaped hole.

I can't believe I let her go.

"Fuck!" I slam the T-shirt into my suitcase, along with the rest of the pile from the floor.

The sooner I get my shit packed up, the better. I need to get out of Seaglass Beach as quickly as possible—and it's going to be a long time before I'm ready to come back here.

38

POPPY

"You really haven't heard from him?" Liv swirls the wine in her glass, eyebrows raised.

"Nope." I raise my hand, ordering another vodka soda from the bartender. I'm glad I decided to walk over to Manta Ray's, the dive bar closest to the inn, because I'm going to need more than two vodka sodas to forget about Griffin Carter.

It's been a little over two weeks since he left, and he hasn't so much as texted me.

Asshole.

"It's over, Liv. Griffin made that pretty freaking clear. I told him I *loved* him! And you know what he said?"

Liv shakes her head, her dark hair swishing over her shoulders.

"Nothing! Absolutely fucking nothing," I hiss, sliding my fresh drink closer to me. I squeeze lime into the clear liquid and suck the sour juice from my fingers. The taste matches my mood lately.

I, Poppy Montgomery, am officially in a funk.

Lifting my glass, I take a long slurp, letting the cold beverage wash down my throat. But I still don't feel better.

"What did I do wrong, Liv?" I gaze at my friend, the one who always has the answers.

She reaches out, touching my forearm. "I don't know, babe. Probably nothing. I think it's more about him and baseball than you."

I frown, my brows scrunching together. "Well, that sucks. I'm okay losing out to another woman, but to baseball? A stupid game? C'mon."

"It's a little bit more than a stupid game, Pops. It's his job. You of all people should respect that. Look how much time you spend at the inn. You live there! Baseball's Griffin's passion. The timing just wasn't right for you two."

My heart sinks, knowing she's probably right. "But he didn't even want to try the long-distance thing. He gave up on us, like I meant nothing to him."

Tears prick at my eyes, and I can't believe I'm still crying over Griffin fucking Carter, weeks later.

Gawd, this is annoying.

"Yeah, that's surprising. I feel like you two should have at least given that a go." She leans in close to my ear, whispering, "I hear sexting can be pretty hot."

"Right?! I could totally have done that. And I love to travel. I could watch some of his games, at least. Atlanta's not that far."

"He probably wants to focus on baseball. I'll bet that's it." Liv sits back and sips her wine, like she's a freaking therapist. Which, to be fair, she kind of has been for the last two weeks.

I can't stop thinking about Griffin. His handsome face, that sexy scar above his eye. Those corded forearms, veins popping as he scooped ice cream. How I could always get a chuckle out of him, the throaty rumble of his laugh.

I want to cry.

"Well, hello, ladies. It's my lucky night." Jagger slithers onto the stool next to me, and the vodka soda curdles in my stomach.

"You just made it unlucky for us." I scoot closer to Liv, the tiny hairs on my arms standing on end as Jagger's cloying musk cologne hits my nose, winding around me.

"Always such a charmer, Poppy." He slings his arm across the back of my stool, and I bump him off.

"Leave me alone, Jagger. Can't you see we're trying to have a girls' night? And you don't qualify."

"Why do you always have to be such a bitch, Poppy? What have I ever done to you, sunshine?" He leers at me, and I have to resist the urge to smack him across the face.

"You're a dickhead. Go away." I turn my back on him, and he grabs my arm.

"Did Rome tell you we filed a land dispute against y'all? We're talking to a law firm."

I press my lips together, my heart hammering. "I'm sure it's nothing. And don't touch me."

I shrug his arm off, but he doesn't let up.

"It's not nothing, sunshine. By the end of this, we're going to own you. And your little hotel."

"Fuck off, Jagger." Inside, I'm seething, my pulse jack-hammering away. But I try to act calm.

"You're going to need to do more than file a dispute, Jagger. The Montgomerys have owned that land for gener-ations." Liv's matter of fact, thrumming her fingers on the bar.

"*Owned* is the important word there. Should be *stole*. And that's what we're going to prove in court."

"Whatever, Jagger. C'mon, Liv, let's dance." I pull Liv off the barstool, then grab my drink and drag her to the dance floor. Only a few other people are dancing, but I can't stand being that close to Jagger for one more second.

"I didn't really want to dance, Poppy." Liv sways to a Metallica song, trying to find the rhythm.

"Me neither. But I really didn't want to keep talking to that weasel. So here we are."

Once Liv and I start dancing, a few more people make their way out onto the dance floor, and I actually start to enjoy myself a little. Two cute guys sidle over, inching in with every beat until they're practically grinding on us. Liv flashes her huge diamond, so her suitor backs off. But mine doesn't get the hint, moving in even closer.

He's good looking enough, but he's no Griffin. Shorter, not as built, and the man cannot dance. I step back and he steps forward, like some kind of cat-and-mouse tango I don't want to be dancing.

Mercifully, the song ends, and I yawn, wide and loud. "Thanks for the dance. But we've gotta go."

Grabbing Liv's elbow, I jerk her off the dance floor so hard she spills some of her wine.

"Hey! I like this song," she complains, dabbing at her hand with a napkin.

"I'm over it. Can we get out of here?"

She nods, setting her wineglass down on a high-top as we head toward the exit. We crisscross the floor, passing by the pool tables. Cash steps out from the shadows, blocking our exit with his pool cue.

"Where you ladies headed? It's so early—we could still

have some fun." He leers at me, his eyes swooping down my body, homing in on my breasts.

A cold shiver shoots down my spine. "Hard pass, Cash."

I try to move around the pool cue, but then Damon shows up, effectively shoving us back toward the pool table and blocking us in.

"Well, well, well. If it isn't the dynamic duo, out to party. And no men in sight." Cash glances around the bar, presumably double-checking his statement.

Unfortunately he is correct. Not that I have a man to protect me, anyway, besides my brothers.

"Fuck off, Cash. Go practice getting something in a hole, why don't you? Pool's probably more action than you usually see." I tip my head at the pool table, and he puffs out his chest.

"I'd be more than happy to show you what I can do," Cash says, stepping in closer to me. Vodka soda round two climbs up my esophagus, threatening to spill out onto the floor.

"Hard pass. Thanks, though." I sidestep, but Cash squares his body, and I don't advance more than an inch.

"Where's your batboy, Poppy? Surprised he's not here with you," Damon sneers.

"None of your business, Damon. Now move out of our way before I make a scene and get the two of you arrested for harassment." I grit my teeth, tipping my chin high. I'm a teeny bit intimidated by these two, but I sure the hell am not going to let them see that.

"Aww, you're such a spitfire, Poppy. I love that about you." Cash trails a finger down my arm, and I recoil with a cold shiver of fear.

"Get the fuck away from my sister." Rome's deep voice

rumbles behind me, and relief instantly floods through me, my knees going weak.

"Oh, hey. It's Mr. Marine, here to save the little girls." Damon's lips curl into a sneer, taunting Rome. Rome's dark blue eyes flash, his jaw clenching.

Not a smart move on Damon's part; my brother fights people for a living.

"Move out of our way, Damon. Now." Rome doesn't mince words, flexing and cracking his knuckles.

"Or else what, Roman? You're going to take all three of us?" Jagger steps in, crossing his meaty arms over his chest, a united front.

"If I have to, Jagger, I will. Now move out of the fucking way."

Jagger's dark eyes narrow; then he steps back slightly, just enough for us to get through the wall of Capelli brothers.

"Have a nice night, Mr. Marine." Jagger salutes Rome, and Rome rolls his eyes. I squeeze between Cash and Damon, my heart thudding as hard as the bass line of the music. Liv follows right behind me, then Rome.

We spill out onto the sidewalk, and I take a deep gulp of the cool night air. "Rome! Thank goodness you showed up. Cash is such a creep. He's the quiet one, but when he does speak . . ." A full-body tremble races through me, and I'm suddenly chilly.

"I'm glad I was there. Try to stay away from the Capellis, will you?" Rome cuts his eyes at me, his dark brows pinching together.

"What?" I throw my hands out. "I didn't start it, Rome. I swear. We were sitting at the bar, minding our own business and chatting, when stupid Jagger slithered up and started talking shit about the inn and how he's going to take it over."

Rome scrubs a hand over the back of his neck, then across his jaw. "Yeah, we need to talk about that."

"Ohmygawd! He's serious?" My voice tips up at least two octaves, shattering the quiet of the night as it echoes off the pavement.

"It's probably nothing, but let's meet up and chat. Coastal Coffee tomorrow morning?"

"Fine."

"C'mon, I'll walk y'all home."

Rome chaperones us back to the Seaglass Inn, dropping Liv at the tiki bar and me at my empty apartment. Even though I still have my brothers and Liv, I've never felt quite so alone before.

I brush my teeth, then rifle through my drawers, pulling out Griffin's team shirt, which I borrowed and never gave back. I shed my own clothes and pull the comically large gray cotton tee over my head, inhaling deeply. I didn't wash it, so the faint scent of Griffin still clings to the fabric, cedarwood and masculinity. A dull ache spreads through my chest, pulsating through my veins with every beat of my broken heart.

Climbing into bed, I curl up and imagine him there with me—wrapping me in his strong arms, the heat of his body as he presses up behind me, his soft breathing on my skin.

I pick up my cell, tap on his contact photo, a miniature Griffin smiling up at me.

Poppy: I miss you

My finger hovers over the blue arrow as I stare at the words.

I shouldn't send the message. He hasn't reached out to me, not even one time. He never said sorry.

He never even really said goodbye.

I shouldn't hit that arrow. I know I shouldn't.

I delete the letters one by one, then slam my phone into the drawer of the nightstand. I need to forget about Griffin Carter once and for all.

39

GRIFFIN

I THOUGHT EVERYTHING WOULD BE BETTER ONCE I GOT back to Atlanta.

I was wrong.

Sure, I don't have memories of Poppy in every room of my apartment, like I did back in Seaglass Beach. But somehow she's still here, haunting me.

When I close my eyes at night, I swear I feel her warm breath on my bare chest, the slightest caress on my skin.

I'm in the frozen foods aisle at the grocery store, and a woman brushes past me, her shampoo the same one Poppy uses. Deep notes of jasmine hit my nostrils, a sharp sucker punch to the gut, and I almost double over in pain.

Driving to the gym, I turn on the radio, and "Walking on Sunshine" blares out of my speakers. And there's Poppy, holding a silver ice-cream scoop, belting out the song at the top of her lungs in Scoops. Her ocean-blue eyes shiny and full of joy and love.

I miss her so much my body hurts. Not just my knee, but every joint, every muscle, aches for her.

I can't sleep.

I can't eat.

I can barely manage the workouts.

"Griffin, good news." Dr. Wofford claps me on the back, all smiles. "Your scan looks good. As long as you keep up with the strength workouts and the PT, you should be good to go by spring training."

Scrawling his illegible signature on my paperwork, he effectively gives me the green light to play ball. "That's terrific, son. The best outcome we could have hoped for. You're officially released back to the team."

He hands me the stack of papers, and I know I should be happy. Relieved. Ecstatic, even.

But all I feel is empty.

I had it wrong all this time.

Poppy doesn't just dance in the sun—she *is* the sun.

She was my sun for a while and life was amazing. Golden bright and shiny, warm and happy.

Now all I have is baseball.

I thought it would be enough.

But it isn't.

I need Poppy like I need air to breathe. She's the first thing I think of in the morning and the last thing I think about at night.

I've never been as miserable as I have these past few weeks, except for when my mom died.

Not when my dad remarried, not when we moved out of our house and he started over with family 2.0, not when I tore my ACL.

This is a new level of misery, and it sucks.

I don't want to feel like this anymore.

"Griffin, you okay?" Dr. Wofford's eyes crinkle with

concern. "I don't think you'll have any trouble with your knee, if that's what you're worried about."

I huff out a shuddery breath.

"I'm fine, Doc. How many years of ball do you think I have left in me? Realistically?"

He chuckles, a deep, hearty laugh. "Wish I could tell you that, son. But I left my crystal ball at home today. The right knee's bionic now, so you don't need to worry about that. Depends on future injuries. A lot of guys play ball for years. You never really know."

I sigh. "Yeah, that's what I thought."

"Griffin, life's a gamble. You gotta get out there and take chances. Big risks, big rewards."

He pats my back again, then hands me my chart. "Good luck, son. Have a great season. Hope I see you at the games, not back on my table."

He walks out, leaving me alone in the exam room, and I know what I need to do.

I need to try to win Poppy back—I only hope I'm not too late.

40

—————

POPPY

AFTER THE SCENE AT MANTA RAY'S, I BARELY MANAGED to get any sleep. So I'm early to meet Rome, which pretty much never happens.

I order an iced mocha for myself and an extra-dry cappuccino for Rome, then snag the table closest to the window. Main Street's not yet awake, except for me, the Coastal Coffee barista, and a flock of seagulls winging in from the beach.

Rome strides through the door, and I wave him over, despite the fact we're the only people in the coffee shop. I signal at the cappuccino sitting on the table, and he nods his thanks, sinking into the chair across from me. A light peppering of dark stubble shadows his jaw, and his frown lines seem deeper this morning. He adjusts his shirtsleeves down over his strong forearms, still uncomfortable in the dress clothes he has to wear for this private security gig.

"Good morning, Roman." I do my best to sound cheerful, but worry still creeps into my voice.

"Hey, Poppy. Here's the deal—" Roman blows on his

cappuccino, sending foam skating across the surface of the mug. "I've been digging around over at Town Hall, asking questions. Seems like Jagger's not entirely full of shit."

Exhaling a heavy breath, I sag back against the metal chair. "Seriously, Rome? He might actually have a claim against us?"

"I said 'not entirely.' Stay calm." He leans back, takes a sip of coffee, seemingly unfazed.

The door chime tinkles, and a tall brunette wearing a black pencil skirt, emerald-green satin blouse, and shiny stilettos walks in. She glances over at us, her eyes lingering on my brother. Rome's eyes flick to her, and a pink flush colors her cheeks. She shoots him a quick wave and he nods; then she teeters to the counter.

"You know her?" I tip my head toward the woman.

Rome shrugs. "Her name's Skye. She works at the courthouse. I've seen her around."

"Hmm." I gnaw my lip, contemplating. She's definitely interested in my brother, even if he's oblivious to it. But now's not the time to delve into Rome's love life and play matchmaker.

"Rome, how can I possibly stay calm? The Seaglass Inn is my life. It's our legacy! Now the Capellis are going to steal it away?" I hiss, not wanting the woman—Skye—to overhear us in the small space. My stomach clenches tight, anger coursing through me.

"From what I'm hearing—and this is all hearsay and courthouse gossip—nothing's been officially filed yet. It looks like they're claiming a portion of the land the inn's built on may have belonged to someone in their family."

"Ohmygawd." My hand flies up to my mouth, bile rising up my throat. "So he's not kidding."

"Notice I used the words *claim* and *portion* and *may*. They have to have evidence, proof. They'll need documents, and then the case could be put before a judge."

"Rome—" I whisper, my voice shaky.

"That's worst case, Poppy. I don't think anything will come of this, but I wanted to get a jump on the situation."

"So now it's a situation?" Hot and shaky, I grip the table. I know I'm getting louder, and Skye's probably overhearing the whole thing, but I don't care. This is even worse than I thought.

"Look—that's all I know at the moment. Jagger could be full of shit, and he may not have evidence at all. His word's not going to be enough for any judge. Plus, the Capellis don't exactly have the best reputation around town; historically, it's not like they've been on the right side of the law."

I focus on breathing in and out, trying to stay calm using my best yoga breathing. Or at least what I can remember from the two classes I've been to with Liv.

"Is there anything we can do? Like, now? I can't lose the inn, Rome."

I've already lost Griffin. I can't lose the inn too.

"I think we have to play defense here, unfortunately. I'll keep my ears open, but until the Capellis fire the first shot, there's not much we can do." He shrugs, sitting back in his chair, calmly sipping his cappuccino.

Meanwhile, I'm jumpy as an anxiety-ridden dog on the Fourth of July during the nighttime fireworks. Waiting for the next pop to sound, the next flash of light in the dark sky. I should probably switch to decaf.

I really don't need Capelli drama right now, not while I'm still reeling from the great Griffin exodus.

"Pops—it'll be okay. Promise." Rome's eyes find mine, and I feel a teensy bit better knowing my big brother has my back.

"Okay, Rome. I trust you. But as soon as you hear anything, I want to be the first one to know. Even before King. Deal?"

Rome swallows hard, his Adam's apple bobbing in his throat. "Can I tell y'all at the same time?"

I lick my bottom lip. "I suppose." I gnaw at the corner of my mouth, contemplating. "But only if you tell me what's up with him and Juliet Capelli."

Rome's shoulders stiffen, his face blank.

"Nothing."

Rome's a freaking vault, I swear.

"Really? I don't believe you." I sip my iced coffee, keeping my eyes on Rome's face. I watch for any telltale signs of lying.

But my brother was a Marine. And once a Marine, always a Marine. Pretty sure he did counterterrorism training or something, because he has the ability to stay 100 percent neutral and not give anything away.

Rome holds up his hands, palms raised. "I've got nothing, Pops. Sorry."

Dammit. I can't even crack the vault this morning.

Skye swish-swishes by us, carrying her iced coffee, and she waves at Roman. "Bye."

Rome gives her a small wave and a tip of his head, and she pushes out the door, a light floral scent trailing behind her.

"She's pretty," I say, watching her cross the street, her hips swaying side to side. For Rome's benefit, no doubt.

"She's all right."

But his gaze follows her all the way down the sidewalk, taking in her perfect proportions.

Even Rome can't control the dilation of his pupils.

"Uh-huh. Sure."

"I need to get to work. I'll keep you posted." He shoves away from the table and stands, then runs his hands down his slacks. "Hey—where's Griffin been? I haven't seen him around in a while."

I shake my head, the pit in my stomach rock hard. "He left."

"Oh. When's he coming back?"

"He's not," I whisper, tears pricking the back of my eyes.

"Oh." Rome reaches out and squeezes my shoulder. "I'm sorry, Pops. I really thought that would work out for you. Griffin seemed cool."

I shrug. "He had to go back to baseball. It's for the best." I jut my chin out, pretending I don't care, that him leaving was a mutual decision between the two of us.

The last thing I need is a pity party from my brother.

Rome doesn't ask me any more questions. He gives my shoulder another squeeze and walks out of the coffee shop.

I rest my head in my hands and wonder when exactly my life went from sunshine and rainbows to thunderstorms and huge, golf-ball-size hail.

The day Griffin left, that's when.

I only hope I can somehow dance my way back into the light.

41

GRIFFIN

I can't believe I blew it with Poppy.

I held the sun in my hands and I let her go.

Not only did you let her go, you idiot. But you hurt her when you did it.

Just thinking about the fight we had before I left town makes me sick to my stomach. She said she loved me, and I said nothing.

Nothing!

She probably hates you.

I shove that uplifting thought away and press down harder on the accelerator. The GPS says I'm still two hours away.

Two more hours to sit and ruminate on all the stupid-ass things I said—and did.

Should I call her and tell her I'm coming? That I want to see her?

And what am I going to do if she says no?

Which she very well may. I would if I were her.

I was an asshole. Why should she give me a second chance?

No, it's better to just show up. At least then I can see her beautiful face, even for only a second. Maybe plead my case.

I cross the state line into Florida, leaving Georgia in my rearview. Every passing mile bringing me closer to Poppy.

I hope I'm not too late.

BY THE TIME I ROLL INTO SEAGLASS BEACH, IT'S CLOSE to midnight and the town's pretty much asleep. I slide my windows down, the salt air a balm to my frayed nerves. I didn't realize how much I missed the fresh air—hell, this whole damn town. Being back here, I'm instantly more relaxed, happier even.

Not if Poppy doesn't forgive you.

I push that thought away and hope for the best as I turn toward the Seaglass Inn, drive past the villas, and park in front of her apartment. The outdoor lamps shine, giving off a soft golden glow, but I don't see any lights on inside her apartment. Maybe I should come back tomorrow . . .

No. I need to see her now. Hopefully she'll answer the door.

With a deep breath, I walk up and knock. Then I wait, the ocean waves a dull, rhythmic roar in the distance.

She doesn't answer. I knock again, louder this time, and wait some more. I'm wired, my stomach a giant twisted pretzel. I'm regretting the gas station coffee right now, the bitter sludge roiling around in my gut.

After a few more minutes of agonized waiting, I turn to go; she's probably sleeping. Maybe I should have called.

"Griffin?" Poppy's voice stops me, and I spin around, my heart hammering hard against my rib cage.

"Hey." My muscles twitch and I'm lightheaded, seeing her after all this time. She's wearing my team T-shirt, and it's so big on her small frame it hits her at her knees. Her honey hair's loose, spilling over her shoulders, and she's so damn beautiful my heart aches.

I'm such an idiot.

"Uh, sorry. Did I wake you?"

"I was asleep, yeah." She rubs her eyes. "What time is it?"

"A little after midnight. You want me to come back tomorrow?"

"No. It's fine."

I had six hours to figure out what to say. I practiced my speech and everything. And now that I'm standing here, face-to-face with Poppy, everything I planned flies straight out of my head.

I clear my dry throat. "I'm an asshole, Poppy."

"Yeah, we covered that off last time we talked." She tosses her hair over her shoulder, jutting out her chin.

I grimace. "I know. What I'm trying to say is, I'm a jerk. My Aunt Jess was right—I ran away when things got complicated, and I shouldn't have."

"Oh-kay." She pops a hand on her hip, biting down on her lip. I want to kiss her, taste her sweetness, but I have no right.

I have to win her back.

"I should have stayed. I know that now."

"You hurt me, Griffin." Her voice is so soft, so quiet,

yet those words hit me hard and solid right in the gut. I hate that she shed even one tear over me.

"I didn't mean to."

"But you did. I told you I loved you, and you said nothing. Not a damn thing. You know how stupid that made me feel?"

I scrub my hand over the back of my neck, sickening regret bubbling inside me.

She doesn't know how I feel. She doesn't know because I never had the courage to tell her. I let her think I didn't care so it would be easier when I left, but instead I hurt her even more. Cut her even deeper.

"I'm sorry." I let the words fall from my lips, my voice low. "I was stupid. But I was trying to protect you."

She bristles, standing up taller, straighter. Fully awake now.

"I don't need protection, Griffin. I'm perfectly capable of making decisions for myself." She folds her arms over her chest, the golden glow from the outdoor light gleaming in her aqua eyes.

"I know, and I'm sorry. I thought I was doing the right thing. The best thing."

"Maybe for you. But not for me. I thought we had something real, something worth fighting for, and you threw it all away. Callously, like I was nothing to you. Like I'm replaceable."

Tears shimmer in her eyes, and I've never felt like more of a dick than I do right now.

How could I have hurt her like this? She's right—I was stupid and heartless and short sighted, and I still don't deserve her.

But I can't live without her.

"Poppy, I'm really, really sorry. And I know that might

not be enough. And you're right—I was callous. I thought I was protecting you—I tried to protect you. But I know now I was also trying to protect myself. I love you."

The words fall from my lips, and a tiny gasp sounds low in her throat.

"What?"

"I love you, Poppy. I didn't want to hurt you, but if I'm being honest here, I didn't want to get hurt. I was scared. I thought the best thing to do for both of us would be to walk away. Because I can't leave baseball. And it's going to be hard and complicated. But you're worth it. We're worth it."

Tears spill onto her cheeks, and I take a chance, stepping forward and gently brushing them away.

"I'm sorry. I was an asshole, and I realize I have no right to expect anything from you. But I'm going to ask anyway. Because I don't want to spend one more second without you in my life."

She takes a shuddery breath and I trace my thumb over her soft, smooth cheek, wiping away the hot tears.

"Will you please forgive me? Give us a second chance?" Then I hold my breath, hoping and praying Poppy's goodness, her light, will shine on me again.

She bites down on her lip, staring out into the darkness for what feels like forever before she raises her eyes and meets my gaze.

Shaking her blonde head, she rests her face in my palm. "I really shouldn't, Griffin. You hurt me. A lot. You never called, or even texted. How can I believe in you?"

My heart squeezes, pain radiating through my chest. But she doesn't pull away, doesn't slam the door in my face.

So I keep talking.

"I know, and I'm sorry. I wanted to talk to you, wanted to hear your voice, your laugh. I picked up the phone to call so many times, but then didn't. I thought I was doing the right thing. That talking to you would only make things harder. It's a dumb excuse, but it's the truth."

A heavy sigh shakes her body. "You have to let me make my own decisions, Griffin. If I'm willing to take a risk, let me. And you have to believe in me—in us—enough to take that risk too."

I swallow hard over the lump in my throat. She's right. I told her I was fearless, but that's not 100 percent accurate.

Turns out I am afraid of one thing: losing her.

With a deep, shaky breath, I take the risk.

"I love you, Poppy Montgomery. More than anything in the world. And you're right—I was afraid to risk getting hurt. So I bailed. I should have manned up and faced my fear. I was a coward, and I don't deserve your love. Or your forgiveness. But I'm standing here now, asking for both anyway. Does that make me selfish? Yes. Am I an asshole? Yes. Do I love you more than I ever thought possible? Also yes."

More tears roll down her cheeks, but she's smiling, and a thousand-pound weight lifts off my chest.

"Please forgive me, Poppy. Let's make this work."

"As long as you let me make my own life choices and stop being an overprotective asshole, I'll forgive you."

"Done."

I bend down and kiss her, touching my lips lightly to hers, and she moans softly into my mouth. Wrapping her arms around my waist, she pulls me into her apartment, deepening the kiss. I kick the door shut behind us, and her hands flutter to my neck. She twines her fingers in my hair, red-hot electricity crackling between us.

I'm never letting her go.

"You deserve so much better than me, Poppy," I murmur into her open mouth.

"Stop talking, Griffin. I love you. You're exactly what I want." She lifts my shirt over my head, unbuttons my jeans, and lowers the zipper. "Now get naked right now and fuck me. Then make love to me and tell me what an idiot you are for ever leaving me. Then let's do it all over again tomorrow. And the next day and the day after that, until you have to go play baseball again." She lifts up on tiptoe, crushing her lips to mine, claiming me.

"And I'll go to as many games as I can to cheer you on. And the games I can't go to—I want you to call me and tell me you won, just for me. And then when you're done playing baseball, let's have lots of babies and raise them right here at the beach." She trails a hand over my chest, my nerves thrumming just beneath her touch.

"I gotta be honest—I love that plan, Poppy." I slide my hand over her satin panties, squeeze the firm globe of her ass. She presses up against me, my erection hard against the soft cotton of her shirt.

I jerk her panties down her thighs, a hot gasp escaping her lips as she kicks them off. Wasting no time, she sheds her T-shirt, and now we're both naked in her foyer.

Gripping her by the hips, I smash my mouth on hers, and she slides her tongue in, tangling with mine. Taking what she wants, possessive. I massage her ass with one hand, while the other glides down lower, finds her clit. She's hot and wet, as ready for me as always.

"I missed you," I murmur, sliding my fingers into her wet heat. She groans, her muscles contracting around me.

"I missed you too." She grinds down on my hand as I thumb her clit, giving her pleasure. Her body's already trembling, and I'm rock hard for her.

She rubs my cock, squeezing, and my balls tighten.

"I need you. Right now," I say, my voice deep and raspy.

She nods, and I spread her legs wider, lifting her up. Wrapping her legs around me, I take a few steps until we back up against the wall. Then I press into her, filling her.

"Griffin . . ."

I thrust into her, again and again, her bare tits bouncing against my chest. The air between us is charged, humming with our need for each other, the feeling so intense I can barely breathe.

I pound into her, her back thumping against the wall as she squeezes and massages my cock. I'm close to exploding inside her.

"Come for me, baby." I rasp the words into her neck, chill bumps rising on the delicate, heated skin. I drive into her, pushing her close to the shimmery edge.

"Griffin!" She cries out my name as she shatters around me, her entire body quivering. I thrust again, chasing my release, finally exploding.

Holding her body tightly to mine, I absorb her shudders, rubbing her back as she comes down.

"I love you," she whispers into my shoulder, nuzzling my hot skin.

"I love you too." I kiss her, soft and slow, cupping her face, trying to make her understand how I feel.

"What's this?" She grabs my wrist, trailing her finger

over the ridges of my fresh ink. It still stings, raw and red, as she traces the outline of the four-leaf clover.

"It's new. I got it to remind me how lucky I was. Even if only for a while."

A grin spreads over her face as she traces over the swirly cursive *P* inside the clover. "And what's the *P* stand for?"

I lock my eyes on hers. "I think you know her."

"Griff." She takes my face in her hands, running her thumb over the stubble on my jaw. "That's the sweetest thing ever."

"You're the sweetest thing ever. And I'm going to spend a lifetime telling you that. Now let's get to the second part of the deal, the part where I lay you down and make love to you and tell you what an idiot I was for ever leaving. Because I kinda need to rest my knee."

She giggles. "Okay, I could go for that."

Sliding down, she laces her fingers through mine. "Let's go to bed."

And for the first time in weeks, I know I'm going to sleep well because I'll finally have Poppy in my arms again. Right where she belongs.

EPILOGUE

Griffin

Now that I'm back in Seaglass Beach, the days fly by, and somehow it's Thanksgiving already.

"You ready, Griff?" Poppy steps out of her bedroom, fastening a sparkly earring. "Because we still have to pick up your aunt, and I promised King we wouldn't be late."

"You look beautiful." I cross the room, wrapping her in my arms. She smiles up at me, her eyes glowing with happiness, a soft blush creeping into her cheeks.

"Stop!" She bats at my chest, but I know she loves the compliments.

It's going to be hard when I go back to Atlanta, and neither of us is looking forward to it. But we have a calendar and a plan, plus Poppy hired a new front-desk manager so she can be away for a week at a time. She's going to come to all the home games and also a bunch of the games on the East Coast. I wish we could be together every single day and night, but having her some of the time is better than not having her at all.

"You know I'm never going to stop, no matter how much you protest." I wink at her, and she bats at my chest again, running her hands over my pecs.

"Well, thank you. And you look damn good yourself. I'd like to see you out of the dress shirt, but we do need to get going."

"Fine." I tip my head down, pressing my lips to hers. "But I'm going to show you just how thankful I am later tonight."

"Oh, I like the sound of that."

We lock up and head over to Aunt Jess's house to pick her up; then I drive us all out to the ranch. Poppy and Aunt Jess chatter about Scoops and all the latest beach gossip, and I listen to the radio, content to sit back and just be.

Recalling the first time I went out to the ranch, I smile to myself. I remember kissing Poppy there in the bathroom, leaving her flustered.

I brush my hand across her knee, beyond thankful to have her in my life. I can't believe how far we've come in such a short amount of time. But it feels like we were meant for each other, and I've never been happier.

Bumping down the gravel drive, I park behind the line of cars.

"Looks like we're the last ones here." Poppy climbs out of the Rover, carrying the corn soufflé.

"We're still on time, though," I point out, taking her by the hand.

The three of us climb the stairs to the wraparound porch, and Poppy squeezes my hand, smiling at me.

I'm super grateful to the Montgomerys for taking me in and accepting me as one of their own.

Still, I'm nervous. Big family dinners have never been my thing; I'm way out of my element. And I need to talk to King, get his blessing.

"Happy Thanksgiving!" Poppy singsongs as we enter, heading straight to the kitchen. Parker, Liv, and Roman all stand at the island, talking and drinking.

"Hey!" Liv runs over to us, hugging Poppy and Aunt Jess.

Pleasantries are exchanged, drinks are poured, and we make ourselves at home. Poppy, Liv, and Aunt Jess sit on the couch, sipping wine and talking about Liv and Parker's wedding. I hang at the counter with Parker and Rome, talking SEC football.

King strolls in, wiping his hands on his jeans. "Hey, y'all. Happy Thanksgiving. The bird should be done in about thirty minutes." He tips back his beer bottle, takes a long slug.

I shift from foot to foot, debating on the best timing. My stomach churns, and I'm not sure I'll be able to eat any of that turkey if I don't get this over with right now.

Swallowing hard, I sidle up to King. "Can I talk to you for a minute? Alone?"

His brow rises, but he nods. "Sure. C'mon."

I follow behind him down the hall, then out to the wide front porch. He leans back against the wooden railing, eyeing me, one leg crossed over the other. "What's up? Everything okay between you and my sister?"

Nodding, I take a sip of my beer. "Yes. That's what I want to talk to you about, actually."

"She driving you nuts yet?"

I shake my head. "No, not yet. Actually—and I know this is kind of old-fashioned, but I wanted to speak with you, since you're the head of the family. I'm planning on asking her to marry me, and I'm hoping for your blessing."

King rubs his thumbs together, gripping the bottle. "You sure you know what you're getting into? Poppy's a wild one. Like an aggressive hummingbird."

I chuckle, my nerves loosening a touch, my breath regulating. "I'm aware. I think I can handle it, though."

King levels his gaze on mine. "Lesser men have failed. But if you're sure that's what you want, you have my blessing. And the rest of the family's, too, I'm certain."

I heave out a huge sigh, relieved. "Thanks."

"Griffin?"

"Yeah?" My eyes slide up to meet his serious navy gaze.

"I know I don't have to tell you this, but I'm going to anyway. Poppy pretends to be tough. And don't get me wrong, she is. But she loves with her whole heart. She'll go to the ends of the earth for you. Don't take that lightly."

I press my lips together and nod. "I understand. And I won't. I'll treat her right. She deserves better than me, but I plan on giving her all that I have, all that I am."

"That's all you can do." He stands tall and pats me on the shoulder. "Good luck. She's a spitfire. But she loves hard and she loves deep. She has a good heart. Take care of it."

"I will." I resist the urge to call him *sir*, even though his presence commands it. He's quite clearly the eldest Montgomery.

He starts to walk back into the house. "King?"

"Yeah?" His head swivels, and he peers over his shoulder at me.

"Thanks. I don't have a ring yet. I wanted to talk to you first."

"I appreciate that. And I won't say anything. It stays between us."

I nod. "Thank you."

Then he goes back inside, leaving me standing alone on the porch.

Dinner's amazing, and I eat way more than I should. Turkey, green bean casserole, corn soufflé, rolls, stuffing, sweet potatoes. The wine flows and so does the conversation, everything from Super Bowl predictions to the latest gossip flying around the beach community.

"Speaking of new developments—" Rome tips his glass back and takes a long sip of his drink. "I know this isn't the greatest timing, seeing as how we're celebrating today. But the whole family's here. So now's as good a time as any." He glances around the table, taking us all in: King, Parker and Liv, me and Poppy, Smitty and his girlfriend, Elyse.

Poppy's hand tenses in mine, and I instinctively know this isn't good news.

"Just tell us, Rome. It's the Capellis, right?" Poppy asks, her voice high pitched, laced with fear.

Rome nods, his jaw tense. "It is. Paperwork was filed yesterday. Right before the long weekend."

Poppy gasps, her face paling.

"They filed an official land dispute. I'll get more details on Monday. All I know right now is they're trying to claim a small plot of land, at the right corner of the inn, belongs to them."

"What are we going to do about it?" Poppy looks at each of her brothers in turn. "We can fight this, right? There's no way the Capellis own any part of our land. Right?"

The room's silent, no one quite sure what to say. Finally, King sets his glass down, producing a soft thud on the wooden table.

"It's bullshit. Our family stole nothing from the Capellis. And they need to prove it."

Poppy sags back in her seat, her lips pressed together in a tight line. "We can prove the land belongs to us."

"We're Montgomerys, Poppy. We're in this together. And they will. Not. Win." King's countenance matches Poppy's, his tone and face serious.

I wonder if the Capellis know they just started a war.

And I'm damn glad to be on this side.

Liv clears her throat. "This might not be the best time to discuss it, but Parker and I decided to move up the wedding."

"What?" Poppy shrieks, her head spinning around to stare at her best friend. "When?"

"We know you want Griffin to be here. And so do we. So we're bumping it up to the second week of December."

"That's two weeks from now!" Poppy cries.

"I know."

"But how?"

"Pops, I plan events for a living. I've got this. And Parker checked the schedule at the inn, and everything fell into place."

"Well, that's the best news!" Aunt Jess raises her wineglass. "To the happy couple!"

Everyone picks up their glasses, clinking and saying cheers and congratulations. Liv and Poppy hug, and Parker grins like he won the damn lottery. Which he kind of did, because Liv is amazing. Almost as fantastic as Poppy.

Dessert's served, and we all eat pumpkin, apple, and cherry pie, talk about the wedding and holiday plans, my team's chances at winning the World Series next year. Everyone avoids mentioning the Capellis.

Finally, we clean up the table and then the kitchen. With so many people, it takes hardly any time at all. King lights a fire in the fireplace, and we sit around, sipping our drinks, full and happy.

It's the best Thanksgiving I've had since my mom died almost two decades ago.

I lean in close to Poppy, my lips at her ear. "I love you."

She smiles over at me, her cheeks flushing the prettiest shade of pink. "I love you too. I'm glad Liv and Parker moved up the wedding. It'll be great having you there with me."

"I am too, babe." I run my thumb across her cheek and tuck her hair behind her ear.

I can't wait to ask Poppy to marry me, for her to be my wife. But right now it's Parker and Liv's time.

For now, I'm content. Grateful. Happy to dance in Poppy's light.

Eventually, it will be our turn to shine. And shine we will, because together we are a force.

Together we are unstoppable.

Want to see what Griffin does next? Keep reading for the bonus scene!

BONUS SCENE

Bonus Epilogue: Poppy

Ten Months Later...

"These seats are great! I can't believe how close we are..."

Liv and Parker settle into the blue plastic chairs over-looking third base while I scan the dugout searching for Griffin. I catch sight of him and wave, giddy excitement bubbling up inside me. I can't help it—the man's sexy as hell on a regular basis. Add in a baseball uniform and he's smoking hot. Plus, it's been a week and a half since I've seen him in real life; as great as technology is these days, Facetime just isn't the same.

But we're almost through baseball season and I cannot wait for him to be back in Seaglass Beach with me. Less than two months to go...

Griffin's tanned face creases into a wide smile as he waves at us, tipping his chin in salute.

I love that man. Even all his grumpiness, even with all

the travel and the long-distance thing. If this is what it takes for us to be together, this is what we're going to do. I know we can make it work, even if it kind of sucks being apart for such long stretches at a time.

The team stands along the dugout rail as the first notes of the National Anthem trill from the loudspeakers. We spring up out of our seats, a huge American flag waving overhead, but I can't take my eyes off of Griffin. His broad chest fills out the white baseball uniform and my hands tingle, the urge to dance across his taut muscles and feel his warm skin powerful.

It's gonna be a long game. At least I have Liv and Parker to keep me company.

"Play ball!" The announcer shouts and both teams take the field. Griffin runs out to third base and my heart races, part anxiety, part excitement at seeing him in his tight white pants.

"This is so exciting, Poppy!" Liv squeezes my shoulder, beaming.

"It's fun watching him play. A little nerve wracking, though, I've gotta admit. Fingers crossed they win..."

"They will, Pops." Parker scoops a huge handful of popcorn into his mouth, despite the fact we ate dinner only half an hour ago. "They're having a great season."

"That's because Griffin's back." I beam down at him as he takes his place next to third base. He shoots me our secret signal, a covert heart, then turns his focus on the game.

The first inning passes with neither team scoring. Same with the second. In the third inning, we shut them down at second and third base, and then Griffin's up at bat. He hits a line drive and runs to first. Next up at bat is his friend,

Danny. He hits a long drive out to right field and Griffin rounds second, making it all the way to third. Balzar's up next and he hits a homerun, knocking the ball out of the park. Liv, Parker, and I jump out of our seats, cheering as Griffin scores the first run of the game.

"Way to go, babe!" I scream, pride blooming in my chest.

Parker and Liv high-five and I blow Griffin a kiss. He winks up at me and lightness fills my chest, heat unfurling low in my belly. Right now, I can't wait for this game to be over because all I want to do is rush down to the dugout and throw my arms around Griffin's neck.

"Poppy? You want anything?" Parker's voice jolts me out of my daydream.

"I'll take a water if you're going to get something. Thanks."

Parker shuffles out of the stands, leaving Liv and me behind to watch the game.

"This is super fun, Pops. Thanks for inviting us." Liv clutches my hand, her diamond rings sparkling under the bright lights of the stadium.

"It's way more fun with you here. I'm glad Griffin suggested this weekend getaway. It's exactly what I needed."

Plus, I desperately miss Griffin, so any chance I get to see him, I take. Having my best friend and my brother tag along is the icing on the cake for me.

"Here you go. Two waters, and a hot dog for me. What'd I miss?" Parker folds his tall frame into the seat, staring out at the field.

Liv and I both shrug. "I dunno. We weren't really paying too much attention."

Parker chuckles. "You're only a Griffin fan, I see. Okay. It's bottom of the fourth and the score's one-zero, us."

"Cool. Thanks for catching us up." I take a sip of water, my gaze trained on Griffin and his strong jaw, that intense stare. He's in the zone now, focusing only on the field and the game.

"I'm going to run to the restroom. Liv, you want to come?"

"No, I'm okay."

I stand and stretch, then hustle out of the stands so as not to block anyone's view. It's a great night for baseball, that brief shoulder season in the South between the scorching summer and the cold autumn nights. The air's cool and dry, with a slight breeze, the sky clear enough to see a few twinkling stars even with the bright lights of the city.

The stadium's packed tonight, people milling about buying burgers and pizza, beer and peanuts. I duck into the restroom, joining a long line of ladies. I'm glad I didn't wait until it was an emergency because we're not moving too quickly.

Thirty minutes later, I'm finally out of the restroom, headed back to the stands. The crowd's roaring, and I know something good happened. I pick up my pace, racing back to my seat.

"What happened? Are we still winning?" I slide down into my chair, glance up at the scoreboard. Now it's four-two, us.

"Yes, we're still winning. It's bottom of the seventh. You didn't miss Griffin—I think he's coming up again soon," Parker says, his eyes glued to the field.

My brothers have all turned into huge baseball fans,

now that they know a real-life pro. I don't think any of us have missed a game. In fact, every bar and restaurant in Seaglass Beach tunes in when there's live coverage. The whole town's rooting for Griffin now and I love it.

"Oh, here he comes." Liv leans forward, clapping.

My heart pounds as Griffin steps up to bat, digging his feet into the clay.

"Strike one!"

"Crap," I mutter, wiping my sweaty palms on my jeans. I take a deep breath, willing him to connect with the ball.

"Strike two!"

"Oh no." Liv's teetering on the edge of her seat and I almost can't bear to watch.

Crack.

The ball flies out to left field and Griffin runs toward first base. The outfielder rockets the ball to second base, but the runner's safe.

"Woo-hoo!" I scream, relief flooding through me. Griffin grins up at us and I wave. Parker shoots him a thumbs-up and Liv claps maniacally.

The next batter hits a pop fly, and the one after that manages a long drive to the outfield. Griffin tags the rest of the bases and scores another run, his entire team high-fiving him as he returns to the dugout.

At the top of the ninth inning, I get a text.

> Griffin: Come down to the field. I'm going to give you all a tour of the locker room after the game

> Poppy: Cool. I'm sure they'll love that. When?

Griffin: Now. Otherwise you'll get swept up in the crowd

Poppy: On our way! Can't wait to see you!

Griffin glances up from his cell, locking eyes with me.

Griffin: I can see you now

Poppy: You know what I mean. Kiss you. Better?

Griffin: Yes. That definitely sounds better

I tap Parker and Liv on the shoulder. "Hey—Griffin texted for us all to go down to the field."

"Okay." Parker and Liv both hop up without asking any questions, but I'm so excited to see Griffin I don't even bother explaining anything.

We hurry out of our seats as fast as we can, then wind our way through the crowds, making our way down to field level. I pull my cell out, ready to text Griffin, but the team security guard comes over.

"Poppy Montgomery?" the security guard asks, his brows raising.

I nod. "Yes, that's me."

"Come with me."

He ushers the three of us down towards the field right as the game ends.

"The final score's seven to three. We win!" Parker whoops and the guard grins, clearly happy the home team won.

"Here we are." The guard stops at the edge of the field, which is huge up close.

"Oh. I thought we were going to tour the locker room," I say, twirling my hair in my fingers.

"I think you have one stop before that." The guard points at Griffin, who's standing next to home plate and waving me over.

"Go on..." Parker nudges my shoulder and now my heart's racing, every muscle twitchy as I walk toward Griffin. I glance up at the crowd, taking in the enormity of the stadium, celebratory music pumping from the speakers.

"Hey." Griffin grins at me, his voice sending a delicious shiver straight through me.

"Hey. I missed you." I want to throw my arms around him, but I'm not sure I should do that here on the field, with so many people watching. "Great game."

"Thanks. I played better with you here."

This man. Cue the heart melt. "You would have won without me here."

"I'm not sure about that. And that's kind of why I asked you to come down to the field."

Griffin reaches for my hands, gripping them. "Poppy, I never in a million years thought this day would come, but here we are."

His blue gaze darkens, his square jaw tense. "I'm gonna be honest with you—I never thought we'd work. And I definitely didn't think we'd make it this far. But after the last year, spending time with you, I know. You're perfect for me. And I know it's a lot to ask, because we don't know what the future holds, but I do know one thing for certain—I want to be with you. For a very long time. Forever."

Griffin locks his eyes on mine, dropping down to one knee in the red clay, and my stomach flip-flops.

"Ohmygawd, Griff..." I whisper, my hand flying to my mouth.

"Poppy Montgomery, will you marry me?"

Tears fill my eyes, blurring Griffin's earnest face, and I can barely breathe.

I nod my head, smiling, as he pops open the robin's-egg blue box, a stunning square-cut diamond ring twinkling up at me.

"Yes, Griffin, yes!"

He slides the ring onto my finger and it's a perfect fit. Then he stands, his hands at my waist, and pulls me into him. He's sweaty and smells like leather, bubblegum, and his crisp cologne as he drops his lips onto mine. My body melts into his and a huge cheer erupts from the crowd, followed by the boom of fireworks.

"I love you, Poppy," he murmurs into my mouth and I've never been happier in my entire life.

"I love you, Griffin. I can't wait to be your wife."

Holding hands, we watch the red and white fireworks explode in the dark night sky, Parker and Liv grinning at us from the dugout.

"Were we really on the KissCam?" I ask, glancing up at the Jumbotron flashing 'Congratulations!' in white curly script.

"One-hundred percent. We're probably going to be on the local news," Griffin says, brushing my knuckles with his lips.

"That's one way to spread the word."

"A pretty smart woman once told me—and I quote—go big or go home. So I went big."

"I like it. Love it, actually. It's going to be a hard one to beat."

"I'm up for the challenge." He grins over at me and I can't believe this is my life. Never in a million years did I expect to fall hard for Griffin, but here we are.

I squeeze his hand and he squeezes back. I know this is right, I feel it deep in my soul.

Together, we really are unstoppable.

Want more in the Seaglass Beach series? Stay tuned for a sneak peek at Roman and Skye's book, UNRIVALED!

SNEAK PEEK

ROMAN & SKYE'S STORY

USA TODAY BESTSELLING AUTHOR
KARA KENDRICK

SEAGLASS BEACH SERIES

It all started with a bang.

Literally.

Hooking up in the alley behind the local dive bar isn't my usual style, but after one martini too many, I gave into my impulses. I banged Roman Montgomery, former Marine and current hot AF bodyguard to the mayor of Seaglass Beach.

So I was shocked when I walked into court the next day and caught the eye of the defendant in my new land title case. The case I was strong-armed into taking—pro bono, no less—to pay the gambling debt my deadbeat dad owes the Capelli brothers.

Now I'm suing my one-night stand and his family on a dubious land claim. Even an embarrassing disclosure to the judge about my sexy conflict of interest doesn't get me dismissed from the case.

I've lived my entire life following the rules, coloring in the lines. And I give my all to every case, every time.

But this time, my heart's on the line—and I'm not sure I want to win.

Even to save my own father.

UNRIVALED releases November 8, 2023!

POPPY'S HOMERUN ICE CREAM SUNDAE

Ingredients:

1 scoop vanilla ice cream

1 scoop chocolate ice cream

1 scoop peanut butter ice cream

Swirl of chocolate & caramel sauce

Crushed peanuts, pretzels, and/or popcorn

Whipped cream (obvs)

Cherry (or two)

To Make:

1. Scoop generous servings of each ice cream flavor into a bowl.

2. Add the chocolate and caramel sauce.

3. Crush the peanuts, pretzels, and popcorn, then sprinkle over the ice cream.

4. Add two dollops of whipped cream.

5. Garnish with a cherry or two.

Enjoy!

ALSO BY KARA KENDRICK

SEAGLASS BEACH SERIES

Unmistakable

Unstoppable

Unrivaled

PEACHTREE GROVE SERIES

Rushing Into Love

Turning Up the Heat

Chasing After Forever

MAN OF THE MONTH CLUB: STARLIGHT BAY

New Year's Renovations

Love in Bloom

Stars & Sparks Forever

MAN OF THE MONTH CLUB: SYCAMORE MT.

Snowbody But You

MAN OF THE MONTH CLUB: CANDY CANE KEY

Reeling Him In

Lights, Camera, Christmas

HOLIDAY NOVELLAS

Christmas in Cayman

Mr. Right Under the Mistletoe

My Charming Holidate

BILLIONAIRE SERIES

Charming the CEO

Flirt Like a (Fake) Groom

HEART OF A WOUNDED HERO SERIES

Soldier On: Heart of a Wounded Hero

Find them all at www.karakendrick.com

ACKNOWLEDGMENTS

Deepest gratitude to all the people involved in helping me put this book out into the world:

My alpha readers, my sisters and mom; Linda Russell and the entire Foreword PR team; James Gallagher at Evident Ink; Shari J. Ryan at Madhat Studios; Stacy Powell at SP Photography; my PA, Tricia Crouch; my cheering squad, the Love Scribblers; and my ARC team and all the bookstagrammers and bloggers who took a chance on me.

Last, but never least, thank you to my home team—Lance, Luke, and Kinsey. I love you all and am so grateful for the opportunity to pursue my passion. Xoxo.

ABOUT THE AUTHOR

Kara Kendrick writes fun and flirty small-town romance destined to give you all the feels. A reformed English major, she also has a master's in counseling and was an elementary school counselor in her pre-mom life.

She loves the beach, wine, and rock-hard abs, not necessarily in that order. When she's not dreaming up Happily Ever After's, you can find her chasing after her boy-girl twins, working out semi-hardish, or walking her adorable Shiba pups with her husband, who's not too bad himself.

Let's be friends! You can be the first to hear about upcoming releases, promos, and giveaways.
Find her at www.karakendrick.com

www.ingramcontent.com/pod-product-compliance
Lightning Source LLC
Chambersburg PA
CBHW030150310726
48970CB00005B/1674